Liberty's pulse echoed the thunder of hooves. This looked like something out of a cineround production, colorful and barbaric . . . only the blood and death were real. Invading riders charged into the defending soldiers, using their lances on some, trampling others under their mount's heavy triple-toed hooves . . .

In the lines of soldiers, arrows flew and swords flashed with a terrible effectiveness. Shields came into use offensively as well as defensively when used to smash in the nasal bulge of an opponent.

And each time a soldier fell, the victor stamped the pommel of her sword down on an exposed piece of the loser's skin. . . .

D1047586

LEE KILLOUGH lives in Manhattan, Kansas, where she is the chief radiographer in the radiology department in the veterinary division of Kansas State University. She is the author of *A Voice Out of Ramah*, *The Doppelganger Gambit*, *The Monitor, the Miners and the Shree*, *Deadly Silents*, and *Aventine*.

Liberty's World is her first novel under the DAW imprint.

LIBERTY'S WORLD

Lee Killough

DAW BOOKS, INC.
DONALD A. WOLLHEIM, PUBLISHER

1633 Broadway, New York, NY 10019

Copyright ©, 1985, by Lee Killough.

All Rights Reserved.

Cover art by Segrelles.

DAW Collectors' Book No. 620

DEDICATION

For PAT, chief critic and
cheerleader, and RICK, who
designed the geography and
made me a gift of it.

First Printing, March 1985

1 2 3 4 5 6 7 8 9

PRINTED IN U.S.A.

Prologue

Text of a voice-only recording found in a Lockheed Ares-15 tachyon courier capsule, recovered at the Vladikov Space Platform July 26, 2078, at 2:53 PM, Greenwich time. Recording is that of a tired-sounding male voice.

"This is Jaes Laurent of the Laheli Colonial Company's ramjet *Invictus*. We launched from the Glenn Space Platform on July 8, 2068. Our destination was the planet Future. At the time of this recording, we have been in flight four months, ship's time. Over the past two weeks, we have experienced repeated breakdowns and failures in the life-support systems of our sleeper sections. The onboard computer has diagnosed system overloading but is unable to give us the cause of the overloading and has been able to instruct us how to make only temporary repairs. We have now lost four hundred of our sleepers and face the possibility of losing more. All ten crewmembers are awake and working to repair the failures as they occur, but we don't know how well we'll succeed. We realize there's no possibility of you on Earth being able to help us. This message is not a distress call. We just want someone to know what happened to us, and perhaps bring a problem to attention so as to save the lives of future colonists."

End of message.

5

Chapter One

They lived not in an expanding universe, but a collapsing one. Since the nightmare began, it had shrunk from infinity to the bulkheads of the *Invictus*—no longer the master of its fate—a nutshell bounded by panels of flashing overload lights, the piercing bleat of electronic alarms, and sleepers dying rack by rack. And for Liberty Siempre Ibarra, it had shrunk still further, to the portside number Fifteen rack, where the acrid scent of hot metal and plastic greeted her as she crawled out across the horizontal rack, ducking her head to clear Port Fourteen close above it. Her reflection spread blurrily across the plastic curve of each pod she passed: a girl looking younger than her twenty-five years, small and wiry with sooty eyes and dark hair bestowed by the hispanics and amerinds among her mixed ancestry. She hissed in disgust as she shined her work light at the nearer of the two open-faced mechanics conduits.

"Damn. You almost managed to sixty-one yourself this time, didn't you?"

The nutrient booster pump had overheated, but rather than simply seize up, it had melted holes in its plastic casing, including around the male connector to the incoming nutrient line. The tube lay in the bottom of the conduit in a puddle of nutrient. The piston, still functioning, pushed air up the out-line.

Hurriedly, she deactivated the pump and clamped the tubing, then swung the work light toward the nearest pod, and swore again. Air filled the nutrient reservoir. A membrane was supposed to prevent anything but the nutrients from diffusing down into the sleeper's bloodstream, but the way this ship had been functioning, Liberty did not trust any of the "supposeds." What confidence could anyone place in a ship that was nothing more than a collection of colonial building materials temporarily assembled into a ship?

Unfortunately, she reflected, the crew was just as jury-rigged, products of Boeing's quickly ship-maintainence course and coming out of mostly non-spacing mechanics backgrounds like hers, keeping Harry Gorman's horse van running from bush track to bush track. Nothing had prepared them to deal with a massive failure like this one. She sighed. Maybe the scraping, low-profile existence forced on a free, Undocumented person on Earth had been a small price to pay for continued life.

Then she grimaced. She was not on Earth any longer and since she happened to be stuck here, at least she could prevent the ship from killing them without a fight!

Using tubing on her tool belt, she by-passed the booster to bleed all air out of the lines and reservoirs and refill each individually, then she went to work with tools and prosthoplastik on the pump itself.

"No mindless pile of plastic and metal is just going to walk away with your lives with me around," she promised the unhearing sleepers.

"Do you often talk to them?"

Liberty stiffened and jerked around. Beyond the work light's bright pool, Noel Hedinger's square face and rusty beard looked back at her from the ladder at the end of the rack. Was he ridiculing her, like so many Documented did Undocumenteds? "It's a habit left over from grooming horses."

"Grooming?" His brows skipped. "I thought you drove the van."

Which showed how little Documenteds, wrapped in their suffocating cocoon of government protection, classified, analyzed, and filed, knew about how free people survived. "I helped groom and exercise the horses, too, and even rode in some races."

Noel grinned. "What did you do in your spare time?"

Now he *was* making fun of her. What would he say if she told him she had shilled for Harry's private card and dice games? . . . both unlicensed gambling, of course, illegal, the winnings—real money, not traceable bank transfers—undeclared and untaxed. She had done almost anything to earn money toward a colonial company share, toward the freedom of a new world. Though without Summer Citadel's unexpected class she might never have made it. Three quick stakes races at dark horse odds had earned her a tidy sum in illegal side bets.

"Actually, I used to talk to my choppers, too," Noel said.

She sighed. "Is there something you need, Noel?"

"Nope. What was the problem here?" His jaw dropped as she told him. "You bled the lines and refilled the reservoirs for half a rack by *yourself*? Good god, girl! One yell would have brought help."

Call for help? He understood nothing at all about Undocumenteds. "I was too busy."

He eyed her a moment, then shook his head. "Well, when you're finished, Jaes wants everyone up in the wardroom. We have a decision to make."

Her stomach knotted. Decision. How to die? She reached down to pat a pod, though whether to reassure herself or the sleeper inside, she did not know.

Climbing up through the hatch from the hold minutes later, Liberty almost recoiled from the tension. Even crowded into space intended for only five people at a time and

sharing a common peril, she usually felt apart from her
fellow crewmembers, especially since Dalyn McIntyre's
wife and daughters died and the others had drawn closer
together in a mutual fear for their own families. This sense
of dread sucked her in, too, plucking at her nerves and
sinking icy claws into her spine. When Dalyn, a whipcord
man with eyes amber as a wolf's, moved over to make
room for her at the table, she sat beside him. In the face of
imminent death, it hardly mattered that he had been a law
enforcement officer, raiding illegal schools and otherwise
harassing Undocumenteds as all leos did.

"I think we can start," Jaes Laurent said. He did not
look quite as tall or young as the shuttle pilot the company
elected captain, but even gaunt with weariness and wearing two weeks' growth of sandy beard, he retained his
calm assurance. "In case the exact figures have escaped
anyone, we've now buried four hundred and twenty sleepers in space. Does anyone want the computer's latest
estimate of when we'll lose the rest?"

"That damned computer!" The curse came from the
bottom of Noel's barrel chest, compounded of disgust and
despair. "Why can't it tell us something useful?"

Jaes smiled faintly. "As a matter of fact, it can. We
don't have many choices right now, but I refuse to lie
down and die. Since reaching Future is out of the question,
I suggest we find a closer planet and get the hell out of this
crate before it completely falls apart."

Liberty sat bolt upright. Had he called the meeting to
talk about *living*, not dying? She hardly dared hope. "Can
we find a closer planet?"

"I don't see how," Cara Lindemuth said. "The Seeker
probes covered thousands of light-years to find the three
hundred odd worlds they finally reported. We can't just
head for the nearest star and expect to find a habitable
planet."

Jaes smiled wryly. "We can shorten the odds by choosing a cool F or warm G star. It'd still be a big gamble, of course, but what do we have to lose? We can't be worse off than we are now."

And it would be action of their own choice, Liberty reflected. Win or lose, they would have acted, not been acted upon . . . masters of their own future.

Dalyn said, "Possible survival versus sure death? Those are good enough odds for me."

Alex Lindemuth covered his wife's hand with his. "Me, too."

"But how do we find the right star?" Frank Riggs asked. The ex-rancher's forehead creased where the weathered lower half met the upper portion, white from years of being covered by his hat. "This isn't an exploring ship and the navigation is programmed in."

"Our computer fundi will explain."

Indra Paris pushed long, pale hair back from her face. "The program has to distinguish star color as part of route-finding. We can ask for a readout that will locate certain classes of stars and compute the distance to them, then I can override the navigation program to alter course."

Liberty pursed her lips. Indra knew about this. Jaes must have been thinking of it for a while and talked it over with her.

"I've already had her locate some stars," Jaes said. "The closest is a G3 two days away. I'm captain but like all our major decisions, I think this should have a vote. How many want to change course?"

As Dalyn had said: possible life versus sure death? Nine hands went up.

Two days stretched out like an eternity. When not working feverishly in the sleeper hold or trying to sleep in the crew dormitory, Liberty watched the viewscreen and the yellow star growing steadily brighter in the center. There had to be a planet. She willed it by the hour, and as they began slowing, losing gravity, so that the crew scrambled to secure furniture and tools, she willed it in every breath.

"It's enough to make a person take up religion, isn't it?" Dalyn said.

Why did comments from leos always sound like accusations? Liberty shrugged and pushed off to float around to the far side of Matt Hoeffler's husky bulk.

"Coming into the system, Jaes," Indra said.

They passed a barren ball of rock, then a larger planet, sheathed in ice. Far off their path to starboard lay a ringed gas giant.

The silence of a vacuum filled the wardroom. Liberty's heart drummed in her ears. The G3 had a planetary system that followed the Dole model, which meant there should be small inner worlds. But would any of them lie within the continuous ecosphere?

The sun swelled, filling the screen with a blazing golden light. Indra's hands played over the computer keyboard, damping the star's image, bringing into view an inner world near it. Even without the notation of distance on the screen, though, Liberty could see that the planet orbited too close to be habitable. The ship swung around the star. Liberty jammed clenched fists into the pockets of her jumpsuit. A planet . . . please.

"I'm beginning to pick up something on the far side," Indra said. "It should come into view any—Jaes!"

Liberty felt like shouting, too. A planet swam onto the viewscreen . . . shining the blue-and-white of atmosphere and water.

"Distance?" Alex breathed.

Jaes leaned across Indra's shoulder to read instruments. "It's .891 angstrom units." Excitement rang under the calm tone.

Within the ecosphere. The sudden loosening of Liberty's chest brought almost physical pain. The others whooped and began hugging each other. She hugged herself and stared at the screen, drinking in the planet. Its color looked incandescent against the background blackness and beside a moon three times the size of Earth's. A new world. A new moon, too. Instead of craters and seas, a network of lines marked its surface, making it look like a great cracked egg.

Dimly, she noticed that Jaes took over the command chair and started talking. "Since we don't have the capability of analyzing the atmosphere, I'm going to coast around the planet and look it over with the camera."

Their camera closely copied those in the unmanned Seeker probes. They grouped in front of the screen, watching intently as the planet swelled to fill and overflow it.

"Big world," Matt said.

"Computer estimates a mean radius of 18000 klicks," Jaes said. "That gives us—ouch . . . one point four g's."

Who worried about a little gravity? Liberty thought. It was a planet.

The camera, focusing farther and farther down into the atmosphere, took them through successive cloud decks to the surface, where sunlight shattered into rainbows and diamond shards on a cobalt sea.

"The planet has life," Dalyn said, pointing at swimming forms.

Noel grimaced. "Yeah, sea serpents."

The creatures did look like the mythical beasts: triangular heads with triple rows of teeth topping sinuous, iridescent-scaled bodies. A scale on the screen measures them at fifty to a hundred meters.

"This is no ocean for surfing," Noel said.

The serpents circled a dark, kilometer-long island. Black coral? Liberty wondered. Then: island? Her heart lurched. The end of the "island" split, opening sideways. The sea churned. A serpent nearby flailed with flippered legs but the vortex caught it and dragged it into the huge maw.

"My god," Vona Riggs whispered.

This is no ocean for *any* kind of ship.

Continuing east around the planet, the searching camera found more ocean life . . . serpents; "island," some as large as three kilometers; innumerable other smaller life forms, but no land. Liberty's stomach knotted. No land at all.

"Jaes, are you focusing too close and missing islands or something?" Cara asked.

Jaes looked around at her. "No, I'm afraid not."

A leaden silence filled the wardroom. They continued to watch the screen, but grimly. Liberty tasted the thickening despair and clenched her fists. Close . . . so close . . . She swore, silently and bitterly.

Below, the water darkened as they entered the night side. Phosphorescence limed the waves, but otherwise, the viewscreen remained without detail. Unlike the Seeker cameras, theirs, intended only to find a landing site in daylight, did not come equipped with infrared. Any benefit they might have had from the moon disappeared, too, as the clouds of a weather system thickened to heavy overcast, blocking the camera's view of the surface. Around her, Liberty heard curses echoing her own. If there *were* real islands, they might never see them.

Then Jaes whooped. The view on the screen blurred in the dizzying swing of the camera. When it snapped back into focus, however, Liberty wanted to cheer, too. Ahead below them, faintly visible in the moonlight, a range of mountains thrust up through the clouds, and the needle-sharp peaks ran a long way east and west. They had to indicate not just an island but a continent!

"Thank god," someone sighed.

Through gaps in the cloud cover, the camera picked out a shoreline of towering cliffs, which the computer gestalted into an outline and spit out as numbers. The roughly 8-shaped continent lay across the equator, divided by that four thousand kilometer belt of mountains. The northern half stretched eight thousand kilometers east to west and forty-eight hundred into the temperate zone. The southern part measured eight thousand by fifty-four thousand kilometers.

"Plenty of room for growing," Vona said happily.

"All we have to do is get down." Noel looked around at the wardroom. "It's supposed to survive a landing, but it was supposed to get us to Future, too."

"Think positively, Noel," Jaes said. "Strap down, though. I'm sure it'll be the roughest landing I've made in years. I think I'll head for that clear area in the western third of the southern continent. The camera has a smooth-looking river valley spotted there."

The nine of them shared the crew dormitory's five bunks. Liberty wedged into one with Indra and pulled the safety webbing over both of them.

"Cross your fingers," Indra said.

Now *this* was a time to take up religion. Or would even that help? Liberty wondered as the bulkhead became the deck and the ship wallowed and lurched and jolted down through the atmosphere on retrorockets that had been fueled and balanced for Future's 1.1 gravity. The ship groaned around them, straining against the planet's pull. Liberty bit her lower lip until it bled. It sounded as if they were coming apart at the seams!

The landing ended in a savage impact that bounced her from bunk to the bulkhead-become-deck with concussive force. Indra slammed against her, driving all the air out of Liberty's lungs. Somewhere between fighting to restart her diaphragm and counting the impressions the safety web had made in her skin, however, she noted the most important fact: the ship had landed. They were safe at last!

Noel groaned as he kicked loose from the safety web. "Thank god this thing only lands once. I couldn't take it again."

Vona laughed, shrilly, near hysteria at first, until the others joined, then joy. Crawling weakly on hands and knees on the deck after the half gravity of flight, they pounded and hugged each other. Liberty watched with a smile, privately relieved. One more gamble won.

Then she heard the alarms bleating in the wardroom. *The sleepers!* With the gravity hauling at her, she staggered to her feet and to the hatch which had gone from a doorway to a hole in the deck. No ladder had been moved in place yet. She had to drop through to the deck below. It slammed into her, bruising, and she barely scrambled off between the jumble of wardroom furniture in time to miss being landed on by the others. The continued scream of the alarms wiped away all thought of bruises, however. Followed by the others, she jogged for the sleeper hold doorway.

The shift in orientation changed the racks to vertical. They towered above the crew, alarm lights flashing on the ends of almost every one. A quick check showed that many of the patched systems had not survived the landing. Pumps hung loose and split tubing poured nutrient down the conduits to the deck. Wiring dangled.

"This ship is a real bitch," Matt snarled. "We find a planet and make it down, and she still tries to kill us off."

Liberty lost track of how long they worked. Tending to the alarms came first, but even with obvious problems solved, doubt nagged her . . . and the others. They began a pod by pod check of the sleeper hold. The drag of gravity made the task doubly exhausting, and frightening, turning what would have been a tedious but routine crawl in flight into a harrowing climb up to higher tiers. Liberty pushed aside both fear and weariness. A refrain from some forgotten poem her mother once read her echoed over and over in her head, buoying her: *This is the last. This is the last.* As soon as they checked the area outside for carnivores or other obvious hazards, they could open the racks and start bringing up sleepers.

She patted the pods. "Soon," she promised.

At long last the hold appeared secured. Liberty hurried back to the wardroom to look eagerly at the screen. They faced the nearing sunrise. Few details showed yet in the gray light, but a pewter ribbon of river ran to starboard and the outline of bluffs rose on both sides out of misty bottomland.

"There's something on the riverbank," Frank said.

The shadowy shape walked four-legged, larger than a dog, broad-headed, hump-shouldered. Liberty breathed slowly. The planet *must* be habitable. When would Jaes open the air lock?

He faced them. "One more choice. Do we proceed cautiously, as in I put on an EVA suit and take a walk, or do we go for broke?"

"Christ, what's the point of being cautious?" Noel asked. "If we can't breath the air, we've had it."

Around the wardroom, everyone nodded in agreement.

Jaes looked past them at Indra. "Take the com and be ready to shut down all the racks if necessary."

Despite her eagerness, Liberty swallowed as the inner door slid sideways, and held her breath when Jaes stepped into the lock to press the controls of the outer door. It took an eternity to cycle. Finally, however, it split down the center and, with a hiss, both halves disappeared sideways.

An animal cry reached her first, a high, maniacal whoop. Then moving air touched her face, warm and humid. In a rush, she let out her breath and sucked in a new lungful. Nothing happened. It smelled of damp earth and other scents she could not identify, fresh and sweet. She breathed again, and again, swiftly and deeply, until her head spun. Breathing had never felt so good.

New air on a new world, where she could live visibly and still be as free as the mountain men, vaqueros, and Wichita and Potawatomie tribesmen whose blood she carried. Her heart pounded.

"What do you see, Jaes?" Cara asked.

He leaned out of the lock, looking down. "The retrojet skirt is collapsed, of course. Amazingly enough, the drive bay and ramscoop funnel absorbed the worst of the shock, just the way they were supposed to. I can't see the river from this side, of course, but the bottomland looks broad and level. It ought to make good cropland. There are rows of . . ."

Liberty never heard his voice trail away, only the one word, echoing in her head. *Rows.* She snapped around toward the viewscreen.

Her stomach closed in a cold knot. Distinct rows did not show on the screen yet, but in the growing light, she saw squared sections of vegetation separated by narrow paths, a patchwork pattern spreading along the bottomland on both sides of the water until it faded in the haze.

Jaes came back into the wardroom and sagged against the bulkhead. "We've landed square in the middle of someone's cornfield."

Alex swore. Cara said, "Now what do we do?"

Jaes sighed. "I'd say that's something we're going to have to wait and ask the locals when they find us."

Chapter Two

Vona stared out the open hatch. "Inhabited. I don't understand. We came over the continent at night and didn't see any lights."

"We wouldn't if they don't have large cities of electricity," Jaes said.

"I'd say they have to be non-industrial." Frank frowned at the screen and the crazy-quilt of various plants and greens in yellower or bluer shades than Earth had, now clearly visible with the sun peeping over the horizon. "These fields are too small to be worked with tractors."

Vona came back to sit at the table with her husband. "Agrarians. This is terrible! We could culture shock them into destruction."

"Oh, I don't know." Noel scratched at his beard. "Maybe selling them technology is a way to buy ourselves a welcome."

"Noel!" Indra cried, aghast.

He leaned toward her chair to pat her arm. "Hey, defuse. I'm only skinning you."

Jaes arched a brow. "I hope so. For once in our history, let's not destroy the locals. Will everyone agree to a policy of non-interference? We don't show them technology; we don't talk technology with them. Okay?" He glanced around with a square line to his jaw that belied the easy tone.

Everyone nodded.

So did Liberty, but with a feeling of suffocation. The policy was right, and moral. Still . . . spend the rest of her life testing every word and action to be certain she gave nothing away? That made a worse prison than Earth.

Movement on the viewscreen caught her eye. Looking up, she sucked in her breath. "Jaes, we've been found."

Every eye in the wardroom snapped to the screen. Figures stood on the bluffs on both sides of the river. The shape looked humanoid but distance prevented seeing any detail.

"Camera," Jaes said.

Indra jumped for the command console. As the camera zoomed in on the group on their side of the river, Liberty felt her pulse race. Aliens . . . a new, totally different species, man's first proof that he really did have company in the universe.

Her first glimpse brought vague disappointment, however. They scarcely looked alien . . . thick and squatty as might be expected in this gravity, of course, but their skin tones ranged in a very ordinary brown-red-yellow spectrum and they wore unexotic loincloths with bolero-type vests, sandals, and straw hats with low crowns and wide, fringed brims.

Then one of the taller individuals—160 centimeters the screen scale said—removed his hat and Liberty caught her breath. Lemon yellow eyes sat widely spaced on either side of a nose that seemed to be no more than a convex bulge ending in spiral nostrils. The wide mouth looked lipless and the ears grew so long that the tops drooped like the ears of Jaes's Labrador retrievers sleeping in a pod near his wife and children. The bright lines of paint or a tattoo swirled across the bald scalp.

The whole group stared at the ship with square jaws slack. Some pointed in a gesture that used three fingers with the thumb and little finger tucked into the palm. The motion opened the vests, revealing four nipples. Liberty stared at the tools they carried, poles ending in square blades or tines curved like talons. Something about the way they gripped seemed odd.

"Focus on a hand, will you, Indra?" she asked.

The camera zoomed closer yet and Liberty sat up with a start. Three digits came around the pole in one direction. Two more counter-gripped to the outside . . . a thumb on each side of the hand!

"Now there are people who are really all thumbs," Noel murmured. "Hey, Matt, how would you have liked students like that around when you were putting together your high school wrestling teams?"

Matt grinned.

The focus retreated to include more of the group, then zoomed in again. One of the group had stopped staring and was charging down the bluff through the brush and trees, ears flapping, mouth moving in soundless shouts. A hand waved one of the talon-ended tools and as the hat flew off and hung bouncing by a chinstring, thick furrows showed in the ochre scalp.

"That one is fused," Dalyn said.

Frank grimaced. "It's probably her crops we've ruined."

Liberty decided Frank had awarded the farmer the female gender because the screen scale indicated she was smaller and slighter than the sumo types, just about Liberty's own 145 centimeters and only twice as broad.

Reaching the bottom of the bluff, the farmer pounded toward the ship down the paths between the fields. Jaes sighed. "I wish I knew how to apologize to her. Go down and smile, I guess." He started for the lock.

Dalyn caught at his arm. "I wouldn't go down just yet. Talk to her from the lock."

Jaes glanced back at the screen at the waving talons of the farmer's tool. "From the lock."

Once the farmer came close, the ship blocked her from the camera's view. Liberty could only hear the angry jibbering, a high-pitched, chanting cadence, and watch Jaes's back while he called down, "We're sorry. We didn't know there were fields here."

The tirade continued unabated.

"Smile, Jaes," Alex said.

Jaes half-turned to show them he was, then turned back. "We want to be friends."

The screaming rose in pitch, accompanied by the screech of metal on metal. Liberty pictured the farmer beating at the ship with her rake.

Dalyn tugged an ear. "I wonder if we ought to break out a few rifles, just to be safe."

Indra's head snapped around, eyes hard. "Those are for hunting food, McIntyre."

Indra, Liberty remembered, had lost her husband to a sniper in the street one gentle spring day.

"I want to be friends with them," Jaes snapped back over his shoulder. He held out his hands. "Friends. You, me. Let's talk."

The rake screeched on the ship again. Liberty sucked in her lower lip. She hated losing sight of the farmer, particularly when she could see on the screen that other farmers were working their way down toward the riverbottom. If they came very close, or went around aft, no one in the ship would know what they were doing.

No one in the ship.

Lips pursed in thought, she slid through the group to the aft wall and climbed the ladder set there, up to the dormitory. An emergency hatch had been built into one corner of the ceiling. Climbing on a bunk to reach it, Liberty stripped the seal away and undogged the hatch.

It opened with difficulty in the planet's gravity, but gave way at last and swung up, letting a pillar of sunlight slant into the cabin. Liberty pulled up through the opening out onto the ship.

The flattened-cylinder hull stretched before her in a

metal plain the size of two soccer fields. Space junk had scored the surface, dulling the gleam she remembered from the Glenn Platform above Earth. The heat of the air and that gathering in the metal promised a searing day as she jogged across the surface to the stern. To her relief, none of the other farmers had approached closer than the edge of the fields. Good.

She moved forward again to where the hull curved downward above the lock. Behind her, the river murmured, accompanying birds trilling in trees on the bluffs.

Below, the farmer still flailed at the hull, though as Liberty peered over the edge of the ship, the handle snapped. The farmer stared at the fragment in her hand for one furious minute, then howling, hurled it up at the lock.

Liberty heard Jaes sigh. "Anyone have any suggestions?"

Abruptly, the farmer went silent, but only for a moment. She quickly resumed, but directed the shrill harangue up at Liberty, not at Jaes.

"Who's up there?"

Liberty glared at the farmer. "Bitch." Louder, reluctantly, she said, "Me. I wanted to be sure no one was sneaking up from the rear." What had made the farmer change her focus? "I'll move back out of her sight."

"Wait," he called up. "This may be a matriarchal society and because you're short like she is, she thinks you're the boss here. You smile and talk to her. Maybe you'll have better luck calming her down."

"Me?" Stand here being deliberately visible? It went against the entire pattern of her life.

"Try."

She gave the farmer a broad grin. "Peace, sister."

Shrieking, the farmer jerked a scorched plant up by the roots and hurled it at Liberty. When it fell short, she reached for another. Before she could uproot it, however, two taller beings, sons perhaps, raced into the fields. They picked up the little farmer bodily, one on each side, and carried her away from the ship.

Liberty blinked. One of the sons had erect, pointed ears. What did they do, crop the tops the way humans did the ears of dogs?

The farmer resisted, struggling and yelling, but her sons did not set her down until they reached the edge of the fields. Once on her feet, she whirled back, extending a spread hand toward the ship and closing it abruptly into a fist. Threat or obscenity, Liberty wondered.

Out of sight below her, Jaes sighed. "So much for friendly first contacts. Maybe the second will be better. Look up there, Liberty."

More movement stirred on the bluffs . . . riders, this time, half a dozen of them. Where had they come from? Had one of the farmers slipped away to bring them? Would they be easier to talk to?

Somehow she doubted it. Even from here she could see that the riders winding their way down the bluff carried oval shields and wore bows slung across their backs. Swords curved like scimitars hung down over their loose trousers. Those mounts did not look like saddle horses, either: organic tanks, like some hornless cousin of the rhino, apparently near two meters at the shoulder with hides that looked thick as armor plating.

"Maybe you'd better come back inside," Jaes said.

She glanced at the hatch with a grimace. Go back inside . . . to blindness and the imprisonment of fear? She squatted down, hugging her knees.

The riders rode through the group of farmers, who parted for them, crossing their arms over their chests . . . all but the little farmer, who raced up to one rider wearing trousers and an embroidered vest of rich scarlet material and spoke with much waving and pointing. The scarlet rider listened impassively through the recitation, head bowed toward the farmer. Liberty sucked in her lip. The scarlet rider, who looked no larger than the farmer, obviously had authority. A noble, perhaps? Though armed, the riders did not quite strike her as soldiers.

As the farmer finished, the scarlet rider motioned to a taller rider in green. The rider slapped the neck of his mount. It lunged into a ponderous gallop and began a wide swing around the ship. The other riders hung their shields on their saddles and slipped off their bows.

"Liberty!" Jaes snapped. "Get in here!"

Not while anyone could approach the ship from the rear. She remained stubbornly where she was.

The mounts of the waiting riders shook their massive heads and pawed, crying in keening voices. Their riders held them in place, however, and watched the green rider.

Something scraped behind Liberty. She snapped her head around to see Dalyn climb out of the hatch. Her lip curled. "Did they send you up to drag me to safety?"

He shrugged. "Oh, there's some concern about you, but I explained that UDP's are free people and I wouldn't dream of forcing safety on you against your will. Mind if I keep you company for a while?"

Keep her company? Who was he trying to skin? "Is that lump in your thigh pocket a gun?"

He squatted down a few meters away. "An old habit, like UDP's playing invisible. I never go anywhere without it."

It struck her suddenly that as much as she despised his profession, a leo's contact with various sub-cultures probably gave him a better understanding of her than most people had, certainly more than her shipmates had. A leo. It might be better not to be understood by anyone.

Below them, the green rider finished his circuit and when he reported back to the scarlet rider, she pointed at a burly rider in blue. The blue rider crossed his arms over his chest and slapped his mount's neck. The animal jogged down the nearest path toward the ship. Liberty braced to throw herself flat if necessary and from the corner of her eye she saw Dalyn shift position to kneel on one knee, hand near his pocket. The blue rider never raised his bow, however. Instead, he halted below them and picking up his shield, swung a leg over the front of the saddle and climbed down loops on the girth. On the ground, he laid down his bow and sword and walked away from them. The shield stayed with him, held in front of his body with a grip on each side.

"Interesting," Dalyn said.

Liberty smiled thinly. "Wise, I'd say. 'We come in peace but not as fools enough to make ourselves targets.' "

"Liberty, as long as you're still up there, respond," Jaes called.

She held out her hands to show they were empty. "Welcome."

Oval pupils of lime-green eyes dilated. Without moving one from its focus on her, the blue rider splayed the other sideways to glance back at the scarlet rider.

Liberty stared. "That's wierd." It hurt her eyes to watch.

After a moment the blue rider focused both eyes on her again and pointed at his sword, saying a word. His voice had a higher pitch than Liberty would have expected, judging by his size, almost as high as the farmer's. Tapping his shield, he said another word, then a third as he pointed at his mount. Finally, he extended his arm up to Liberty, palm up, and bent the arm back on itself.

Liberty blinked. "Jaes, I think he wants me to come down for a language lesson."

Dalyn frowned. "I could be a trap."

"We need the contact, but it's your choice," Jaes called up.

She sucked in her lower lip. To go or not. It could be a trap, of course. Still, the blue rider was laying down his shield, too, and the humans had to deal with the locals sooner or later. "I'll go," she said.

Her shipmates surrounded her on her way back through the ship. "Be careful."

She nodded, but once out of the lock and descending the ladder, apprehension became a growing excitement. She stepped off the last rung with her pulse racing. Her boots trod alien soil! No human had ever walked it before, or touched the waxy yellow-green leaves at her knees. She faced the rider almost eagerly.

He crossed his arms over his chest and said what sounded like, "Shoe it in."

Up close, he looked even broader than he had from the ship. So did his mount. Both smelled faintly like licorice. She guessed she smelled a little less sweet. The blue rider's nostrils pinched.

"Sorry," she sighed. "We didn't have bath water. Just stay upwind."

After a moment's hesitation, the rider repeated his . . . greeting? then spoke another word, tapping his chest where the cream-colored skin showed bare between the edges of his vest, or perhaps *hide* would be more accurate. This close it looked leathery thick and covered with short, stiff bristles.

The word, though . . . name or noun? She tried to copy the sounds. "Say-*bay*."

The alien pulled in his chin. "Tsebe."

Liberty tried again, still stumbling over the initial consonants.

The blue rider seemed satisfied, however. He pointed at her.

Name or noun? She took a chance. "Liberty."

The rider's scalp furrowed. "Ib-ih-tee."

Liberty grinned. "Well, we're even. I can't say your name and you can't say m—"

She broke off with a gasp as the rider's pupils dilated

and his hand jerked out toward the sword just beyond his reach. "Hey, loosen! What did I do?" She gave him a reassuring smile. "You stay easy, too, Dal," she called up.

A lime-green eye jerked toward the sword again.

Understanding came in a rush. The smile did *not* reassure; it upset these people. Baring the teeth must be a hostile gesture to them. She straightened her face carefully.

After a few moments, the rider—Tsebe—relaxed. He squatted down in the immaculately weedless soil between the plant rows and used his middle finger to draw outlines of two broad humanoid figures, one markedly smaller than the other.

Good, Liberty reflected. Start with the basics: man, woman, people.

"*Thees, xees,*" Tsebe said, pointing to the smaller figurer, then the larger. The opening consonant of the second word came from his throat like the German *ch*. "*Hees,*" he went on, indicating both figures, and for good measure himself, the other riders, and the group farmers. "*Hees.*"

Liberty repeated the words and started to give him back English equivalents, then stopped. Tsebe, apparently not satisfied, was embellishing his sketches. He added a short line down from the crotch of the smaller figure and after widening the abdomen of the larger, put in a tiny form. "*Ba-ma.*"

A baby in the *larger*? Liberty stared. Did he mean the males carried the babies, like male sea horses, or were the brawnier of his people *females*? But that would mean the little farmer was male, not female, and the scarlet rider. Tsebe, then—

She pointed at the baby-bearing figure, and from it to Tsebe. "*Xees?* Tsebe?"

Tsebe's broad chin lifted. "Tsebe *xees.*"

Judas. Liberty's head spun. The hees had women built

like sumo wrestlers and they smiled in hostility. So . . .
this promised to be an interesting world at the very least.

Once they had named all the parts of their bodies and
clothing and all the tack on Tsebe's mount, an *u-tse*, they
toured the fields learning nature names. Liberty strained to
pronounce and remember each one. Learning Potawatomie,
which she had done out of pride, had been simple by
comparison. At least it had sounds reproducible by the
human throat.

The morning stretched into eternity. Between the growing heat, the drag of gravity, and the effort of learning,
Liberty began longing for wraparound trousers and a vest
like Tsebe's. Not even unzipping her jumpsuit to the waist
stopped the sweat filming her forehead and trickling down
her chest and sides.

At the sun's zenith, peasants across the river stopped
work to sit along the riverbank staring at her and the ship
while they unrolled cloths and ate the food wrapped in
them. The peasants on her side squatted down at the edge
of the fields where they had remained all morning and ate,
too. Liberty eyed them, her stomach growling. She did not
remember her last meal.

Tsebe said the word that Liberty had decided meant
come and picking up her u-tse's reins, started out of the
fields toward the peasants and dismounted riders. Liberty
trudged behind. Reaching the group, she found herself
surrounded by licorice-smelling hees who crossed their
arms over their chests and stared at her hair, hands, and
ears and murmured to each other, nostrils fluttering behind
their hands.

"Kxa-Thi," Tsebe said, pointing at the scarlet rider.

Name, title, or noun? Name, perhaps. Going around the
circle of riders, Tsebe started the designation of each with
Kxa.

A peasant handed them both heart-shaped lavender fruit

and a patty of something cooked crisp. The former tasted sweetly acid, the latter like sesame.

"Ha-pim-ba," Tsebe said, pointing at the fruit, then held up the bread patty. "Ka-i-heema-na."

And the language lesson went on.

Until someone shouted her name.

From time to time through the morning, she had looked back toward the ship. Dalyn always sat on top, watching her. Now he stood, shouting and pointing at the bluff. Liberty twisted to follow the arm's direction . . . and went cold.

More hees came over the bluff, but not farmers this time, nor elegant nobles. These marched on foot, wearing helmets and scale cuirasses over trousers tucked into knee-high, wrap-topped boots. They carried shields, bows, swords, and lances.

Soldiers! Liberty forgot hunger, weariness, and heat. Jumping to her feet, she bolted for the ship. And cannoned squarely into a female rider. It was like hitting a wall. Thick arms closed around her.

Instinct took over, the same that had seen her out of childhood attacks by Documented kids in Topeka's Oakland area, who thought that no matter how poor *they* were, an Undocumented was even lower and therefore fair game. Liberty exploded into a cursing, clawing, kicking dervish . . . gouging eyes, ripping at ears, kicking knees . . . going for blood. She might as well have been a mosquito assaulting an elephant. The rider never flinched.

Liberty sank her teeth into one of her captor's arms . . . and instantly let go, howling, her mouth smarting from bristle punctures.

This accomplished nothing. Liberty surrendered for the moment to gingerly tongue her wounds and pity any predator that tried to make dinner of a hees.

Feeling the end of resistance, her captor released her.

It was then that she looked around and discovered that

the soldiers had only surrounded the ship, not attacked it.
Some rode u-tse and others chunky, pony-sized, cream-
colored animals with black stripes on their neck and legs—
four horns made the beasts look vaguely antelopish, two
growing from the pole, two from the middle of the nose
below the eyes. Most of the soldiers, however, pushed
wheelbarrows fitted with a square sail. Liberty blinked.
Sailbarrows?

"Come." Tsebe pulled her toward the soldiers. *"Dshi."*

What? Was the heest female really just going to go on
with the language lesson, pretending that nothing had
happened, that they had not taken Liberty and the others in
the ship prisoner? "You're a toad, you know that, Tsebe?"

But she followed the hees through the troop, mostly
female, and carefully repeated every word Tsebe gave her,
naming armor, equipment, tents, weapons, and animals.
The horned ones were called *dxee.* And around them,
splaying eyes to stare at Liberty while she grimaced at her
visibility, the soldiers unloaded their wheelbarrows and
chopped down a wide circle of plants before setting up
square, flat-topped, brown-and-orange striped tents.

In spite of her discomfort, and anger at being taken
prisoner, Liberty became fascinated. The officer in charge,
a Lieutenant? Captain? Ath'—*th* as in *then*—a mustard-
brown male with a bright blue collar and lapiz collar studs
under his armor, carried a metal sword, but that was about
the only metal outside of knife blades that she saw. Their
helmets and scale cuirass were both of leather, and the
skirt of vertical strips around the bottom of the cuirass.
Their swords had been made of a hard black wood with
obsidian chips set in the outer edge of the curved blade.

"Liberty!"

She looked around to see Jaes waving at her from the air
lock. "Are you all right?"

I'm a prisoner! she wanted to shout. *How can that be
all right?* "I'm learning the language," she said.

"If things go ugly, don't hesitate to yell," he called. "We're watching you all the time and we'll—" He broke off, turning his head toward someone behind, then suddenly stiffened and snapped back around to face her. "Run for the ship!"

A whistle overrode his shout, a short blast followed by two longs and another short. Tsebe gasped. The soldiers instantly dropped mallets and tent ropes to snatch at shields and weapons and whirl toward the river. Following their line of sight, Liberty swore.

Down the river came a flotilla of raft-like barges propelled by paddlers on both sides. Soldiers filled them, only these wore black and scarlet armor. The sun shone on polished helmets and cuirasses, shields and lance points. U-tse aboard several of the barges keened in shrill voices.

The short-long-long-short whistle sounded three more times. Tsebe picked Liberty up bodily and raced toward the peasants and other riders.

Moments later the barges ground against the shore. Soldiers leaped from them on foot and u-tse.

They met a hail of arrows and hastily-formed lines of brown-armored soldiers and a few arrows found targets. Black soldiers dropped into the river and on the bank. Most missed, however, and moments later, defending and invading lines collided.

Kxa-Thi and the other riders except Tsebe scrambled up the girth loops into the saddles of their u-tse. Slapping the beasts into a gallop and drawing swords, they charged across the bottomland into the fight.

Liberty's pulse echoed the thunder of hooves. She bit her lower lip. This looked like something out of a cineround production, colorful and barbaric . . . only the blood and death were real. U-tse shook the ground with their strides. Invading riders charged into the defending soldiers, using their lances on some, trampling others under their mounts' heavy triple-toed hooves. The u-tse, many black but others brown or piebald, appeared to relish the madness. Their keening rose above all the shouting and clash of swords and shields. In the lines of soldiers, arrows flew and swords flashed with a terrible effectiveness. One invader collapsed with neck crooked sideways at an impossible angle, flesh half sawn through; blood spurted from the leg of a defender. Shields came into use offensively as well as defensively when used to smash into the nasal bulge of an opponent.

And each time a soldier fell, the victor stamped the pommel of her sword down on an exposed piece of the loser's skin.

The browns fought hard, but the black line pushed even harder and the browns retreated before them until the line stumbled into the tents. Amid cracking poles, the tents collapsed. Squealing dxee leaped out of rope pens to bolt up the bottomland. The fighting even washed against the bottom of the ship, with a mounted invader charging a defender beneath the air lock. The defender parried the invader's lance with his shield and thrust his spear at the belly of the passing u-tse.

It sank deep. The u-tse's keening cry changed to a scream of pain. It spun, twisting to snap at the impaled spear. When the shaft proved beyond reach of its mouth, the u-tse threw itself onto the ground and pawed at the spear with its hind feet. The rider barely had time to cry out as the huge body crushed her beneath it.

Now the u-tse's hooves reached the spear, but the frantic pawing ripped the weapon through the belly. Flesh gave way, spilling torn, bloody entrails onto the ground.

In the main area of fighting, the lines had become a circle, with browns in the center, surrounded by blacks. Tsebe thrust Liberty backward into the peasants and dashed out across the fields toward the fight.

What if the browns lost? Liberty suddenly wondered. The peasants seemed unconcerned, yelling and making a

shrill trilling sound with all the boisterous spirit of spectators at a soccer game, but a cold ripple of foreboding
worked its way along under Liberty's skin and into her
gut. She bit hard on her lip.

Tsebe picked up the lance of the dead rider by the ship.
Beyond her, the invaders pounded away at the wall of
shields the remaining defenders had built for themselves.
They never noticed Tsebe, who lunged, ramming the lance
through the black leather scales of one cuirass into the
back of an invader.

His scream attracted attention, though. Three soldiers
whirled on Tsebe. She wrenched the shield off the arm of
a dead soldier and picked up a loose sword.

Liberty clenched her fists. Tsebe could not fight all of
them. "*Dalyn*! I want your gun!" Ducking away from the
peasants, she ran for the ship.

The gunshot cracked before she was halfway there.
Looking up, she saw everyone but Jaes and Indra on top of
the ship, sprawled on bellies and elbows with rifles at their
shoulders.

One of the soldiers facing Tsebe froze in the act of
swinging her sword. She stood like a statue for what
seemed an eternity, blood spurting from her cuirass, then
with dreamlike slowness, she collapsed, folding one joint
at a time.

Tsebe froze, too, but her remaining attackers did not.
Both closed in, swords swinging. Dalyn and Frank fired
together and both soldiers kicked around and dropped in
mid-stride. While Tsebe gaped around her, Liberty yipped
a Potawatomie war whoop and leaped for the ladder of the
ship.

Jaes tossed her a rifle. "Make your shots count."

She crouched behind the dead u-tse, ignoring its stench
of blood and intestinal contents, and aimed past Tsebe for
the black-armored soldiers.

Nine invaders went down in the volley of fire from the

ship, then nine more. Liberty gave thanks for Dalyn's insistence that every member of the company become a crack marksman. *"Our first year, before the crops come in, hunting can make the difference between life and starvation."* It might still mean life or death. She worked the bolt to push a new shell into the breech, sighted down the barrel at the back of an ochre-hided invader, and fired again.

Confusion boiled through the lines of fighters. Invaders stared at their fallen comrades and on around, eyes splaying wildly in search of the killer agent. They held their shields tight. Liberty deliberately fired through one.

As that soldier collapsed, the rest spotted Liberty behind the carcass of the u-tse. A rider wheeled her own mount and charged with lance poised.

The fiery cold of fear washed through Liberty, but at the same time, great calm flowed in. Except for the tremble of the earth beneath her, the universe slowed to a standstill. The great brown u-tse and its rider hung suspended while she stood, measured the beast's vulnerability, and leisurely fired three shots at its nearest eye.

One of them must have bored through into the brain. The massive head flung up, then plunged earthward. The rest of the body hurtled on, cartwheeling past an open-mouthed, still-paralyzed Tsebe to land on its back and rider with an earth-jarring crash.

Panic erupted among the invaders. They wheeled, clutching their shields and swords, trying in vain to protect themselves from both the brown-armored defenders on one side and this unseen weapon on the other. Tsebe broke free of her stupefied astonishment. Whooping, she joined the defenders in a renewed offensive.

Minutes later, the battle ended. An invader officer called out and his soldiers dropped their weapons to stand with arms crossed over their chests.

Liberty fought an urge to dance yelping and waving her

rifle on the carcass of the u-tse she had killed. The sight of
Tsebe coming toward her with Kxa-Thi and Captain Ath'
cooled her excitement like a dousing of ice water. Which
she would not have minded right now, she reflected, jumping for the ladder and scrambling high enough to hand Jaes
the rifle.

"Better take this."

Above her, his forehead creased in concern. "What
about you?"

She hesitated. She could go back to the ship, yes, but
why? Hiding in it made it just another kind of prison. To
be with her own people, then? But she felt as alien from
them as from the hees. And who would learn the language,
if she came back? "I'll stay here."

Without her rifle, she fortunately became less interesting
to Ath' and Kxa-Thi. Tsebe beckoned to her but the two
males turned away, back to the surrender.

After all the screaming and clash of weapons and thunder of hooves, this quiet sounded unnatural, as though
Liberty had gone deaf. It looked even stranger. Instead of
making the invaders prisoners, the defenders were letting
them leave, even helping move invader wounded to the
barges. The invaders took corpses, too, but to Liberty's
bewilderment, not their own. They picked up only defender dead. A few dead defenders and all the invader
corpses remained on this side of the river, divided into
piles by surviving defenders and helpful peasants. Liberty
wished she had the words to ask what they were doing.

A short time later, she had no need to ask. She saw for
herself, and wished she had not. Stripping the dead she
accepted, keeping the armor and weapons of an opponent
one killed, but . . . skinning them, too? At least now she
understood the reason for hitting each fallen soldier with
the sword pommel. A sharp, raised pattern carved on a
seal-like stone there marked the corpse for claiming later.

The invaders skinned out the bodies they took back, she saw.

She also saw, with dismay, that stakes, ropes, and black-and-scarlet tent material were being unloaded from the barges. The invaders obviously intended to camp for a while, which must mean that today's fray had been only an opening skirmish. Cold fear climbed Liberty's spine. What the hell had they landed in the middle of?

Chapter Three

Under other circumstances, Liberty would have enjoyed herself. For three summers as a child, she had gone camping on the Potawatomie reservation with third and fourth cousins and her great-grandfather. Camping with the hees evoked those days . . . going barefoot, turning her jumpsuit into a romper by tearing off the legs and sleeves, sleeping in a tent on a grass-filled pallet, eating new food with unfamiliar utensils, swimming in the river—a welcome relief from the heat and relentless gravity—learning to ride the spring-loaded dxee, struggling with an alien language. Like them, she turned browner by the day, until she had become darker than many hees. In the evening these people, too, made their own entertainment, telling stories, dancing, and juggling. Even in the similarities, however, lay reminders of grim differences. The hees forbade her to ride cross-country, and the hides they stretched and dried for tanning were "men," not rabbits killed to teach a new generation old skills. No soldiers had camped across those rivers, nor had she been an object of curiosity, the unwilling center of attention as the troops surrounding the ship grew into an army. New arrivals trickled in each day, putting up additional tents and swelling the perpetual Fivedice games. In her childhood there had also been no ashes from cremated soldiers, no lingering odor of burned meat.

Reinforcements did not join the invaders, Liberty noticed, and their apparent lack of concern disturbed her. If only she had the vocabulary to question Tsebe about it.

The situation obviously disturbed those in the ship, too. Liberty saw Noel and Dalyn on top the day after the battle, watching both camps narrow-eyed, and that evening Jaes called to her from the lock. "As soon as you can, find out what's going on, and set up a meeting with someone in authority."

An urgent note in his voice made her ask: "Is there trouble inside?"

"We have to start bringing up sleepers."

In *this* situation? She stared at him in disbelief.

He grimaced. "I don't like it, but I won't give up more lives. If a rack goes critical, I'm opening it. That's why I need a meeting, to reach some kind of agreement before we turn into sardines in here."

He needed a meeting. "Ah, Jaes." She told him about the hees sexes and not setting them straight on hers. "I thought they ought to think they had a valuable hostage. Shall I tell them the truth?"

"No, that's fine, but when you arrange a meeting, ask for me to be there, too."

That had been two weeks ago, or almost three, figured in five-day heest weeks, but though Thi and other members of the Kxa household visited daily, they avoided her. Liberty could do nothing except watch new humans appear on the ship each day, where they took turns at watch, fresh air, and staring back in stunned bewilderment at the camps, peasants working the fields beyond the camps, and at passing boats and barges. How many had been brought up in there now?

Fortunately, she had discovered that Fivedice bore striking similarities to Five-Card-Draw. Joining the incessant

games with a small stake from Tsebe not only enabled her
to accumulate a long string of pierced round and square
coins, which she wound around her waist under her romper,
but to increase her vocabulary and ask casual questions
that brought her new information. Like the opinion ex-
pressed by one young female who wore her ears cropped
in a style common among the soldiers, chopped straight
across the top to make short, plain points. "I'd rather be
readying for the war against Shapeen, but this one might
still let me put my mark on enough A-thin-wet hides to
earn me the breeding right and give me some money to
take my future husbands and sisters."

All the soldiers looked forward to profiting from the
war; none knew or cared why they were fighting. Liberty
decided to be direct. One morning while she and Tsebe
stood watching soldiers groom u-tse by rubbing licorice-
smelling oil into the thick hides, she waved a hand at the
camp around them and asked, "What is this for?"

An u-tse lowered its head, snuffling, its ears wiggling
and long, pointed upper lip working as it begged for treats.
Tsebe held out a handful of shuka grain and looked toward
the far shore of the river, where a soldier drawing water
had paused to give them the hand-closing-into-fist sign.
"It is a curse." She made it sound like "cuss," *l*'s and *r*'s
still eluding her pronounciation. "The Five abandon you.
Old curse. No danger. Only peasants worship the Five
now. Enlightened people know God is One, all people, all
animals, all gods good and bad."

Granted that even after being immersed in the language
twenty-eight hours a day—which the hees divided into
twenty periods—for fourteen days, Liberty's vocabulary
and pronounciation lacked perfection, but she doubted they
were bad enough for Tsebe to mistake the question as a
request for religious instruction. Was it the only way the
girl knew to avoid answering?

Bhada-wu-tsebe of the house of Btha-u-tse-Kxa, professional breeders of the black u-tse, was, after all, just an adolescent girl. She told Liberty that her grandfather had made her Liberty's tutor because of a gift for languages, but Tsebe admitted to little experience with foreigners. Which apparently also included no practice in diplomatic lying.

Liberty persisted. "Why—" She broke off, heart leaping, as the ground shuddered under her. "My god!"

Tsebe tipped her head one way then back. "It is only a groundshiver. Very common. What were you asking?"

They had landed in earthquake country, too? Shit. "Why are all these soldiers here?"

Tsebe's gracefully pointed ears twitched. "You are guests. We wish to protect your nights from ha-gho-wu, wild axa, and bandits, who take hides if they can't find anything else of value."

Axa Liberty knew, the soldiers used domesticated ones as guard animals, striped beasts that looked canid and sounded feline, and ha-gho-wu were the hunch-shouldered animals who made the maniacal whoops she heard along the river every night. They might present a danger. So might bandits. Still. . . .

"Why so *many* soldiers?"

Tsebe frowned. "You ask questions but never answer them."

"I'll answer questions for your leaders," Liberty replied. "Why won't they meet me?"

"They will soon. They wait at our compound for word we have learned to speak." A lime-green eye glanced toward her. "I told my grandfather yesterday that it is time."

Liberty's heart lurched. So it would be *very* soon. "I'll want another of my people with me at the meeting."

"Of course." Tsebe gave the u-tse a pat and pushed

away the great head. "We are not barbarians to refuse attendance by advisors and house."

Liberty headed for the invisible line marking the closest point to the ship the hees permitted her. As always, the restriction galled but she swallowed irritation in the interest of necessity. "Jaes! We have Poo Bahs coming!"

A boy on watch in the lock vanished. Moments later Jaes appeared. He was clean-shaven again these days and looked bathed, too, thanks to the water Captain Ath' had the soldiers bring up daily from the river in empty sleeper pods. "Who, and when?"

"I don't know. Maybe—"

Three short blasts of a sentry whistle interrupted her. She whirled, looking for the arrival that signal heralded. "It's now, Jaes."

A line of dxee picked their way down the face of the bluff. As they came onto the bottomland, Liberty recognized Kxa-Thi and other males Tsebe had identified as her fathers and grandfathers. The other riders were all strangers, but she had no doubt of their identity. Their clothing screamed Important Persons . . . fabrics with a sheen or shimmer, richly embroidered and styled in flaring sleeves, shelf-like shoulders, and collars rising like walls around fancy-cropped ears gleaming with gems on gold or silver wire. Bells hung from the tack on their immaculate dxee and soldiers in highly polished armor rode before and behind them.

Boots rang on the ladder, then Jaes's voice spoke behind her shoulder. "They're real dinked up glads, aren't they?"

Liberty glanced down at her own jumpsuit-become-romper and thought with regret of her clean clothes somewhere in the cargo hold. She owned nothing to match the opulence of the Poo Bahs' dress, of course, but almost anything might be better than trying to treat with them while she looked like a peasant.

The party dismounted at the camp perimeter, where Captain Ath' met them with much crossing of arms over chests and long greetings.

"Come," Tsebe called to Liberty. The heest girl led the way to a tent soldiers were hurriedly turning into a pavilion by tossing all four side flaps up on the top and covering the floor with sleeping pallets folded into cushions.

The Poo Bahs finished their round of greetings and marched toward the pavilion in the flat-footed stride of hees. Liberty stiffened her spine and lifted her chin, pulse racing. If she could not *look* important, she would have to act it.

Tsebe's grandfather led the group. Stopping before Liberty and Jaes, he spoke to Tsebe in a language Liberty understood little of, though she recognized it as the regional dialect, quite different from Akansh, the imperial/trade language Tsebe was teaching her. Tsebe crossed her arms over her chest and replied briefly.

Kxa-Thi turned to Liberty, arms across his chest, and switched to Akansh. "*Shui-xin*, God's good to you, honored visitor. My granddaughter Tsebe tells me you have learned enough Akansh that we may speak directly to you."

Liberty understood about half the sentence. The rest she filled in from context. In reply, she copied the hees, crossing her arms. "God's good to you, honored landholder. Your granddaughter is a fine teacher." Should she apologize for her lack of Deferential and Polite speech forms? No. There had been no time to learn them, which the visitors should realize, and, having seen heest Authority, Liberty found secret satisfaction knowing they would be forced to address her as an equal to make themselves understood.

"Then, honorable Ib-ih-tee of the house of Iba-ha," Thi said, "I would present you to His Eminence Lord Dshu-

imi-ka of the house of Bhin-igha-Ibda, honored envoy of His
Royal Highness King Po-xan of the kingdom of Gthe-ge,
and to His Imperial Lordship E-do-ishda, son of the Imperial House of Th'da-sha-Thim and brother and honored
envoy of His Imperial Highness the Emperor Xa-hneem of
the Thricefive-and-one Kingdoms.'' He pronounced the
name of the imperial house with the first *th* as in *then* and
the second as in *thin*.

While she crossed her arms over her chest and acknowledged the introductions, Liberty studied both men. Lord
Dshu characterized easily . . . politician. The keen yellow
eyes studied her in return. Lord Ishda puzzled her, however.
Except for the soldier-cropped ears, he looked like all the
other courtiers, down to the same elaborate clothing and
scalp paint Dshu wore, but his eyes, pale as pond water
and blind-seeming in their colorlessness, neve looked at
her. Instead, he gazed beyond the pavilion at something
near the river, remote . . . as though with the other hees
but not of them. Surely an Emperor's envoy should command respect, but Liberty read disapproval and even contempt
in the pinch of Dshu's nostrils as he slid an eye toward
Ishda. Now why would the Emperor send someone like
this to be an envoy, even if he were a brother?

She puzzled over the question while Thi introduced the
rest of the party: the provincial governor, head men from
several local villages, and their entourages. With further
uneasiness, Liberty noted that except for the head men,
who had come alone, Lord Ishda had the smallest retinue,
just two . . . the brawniest females Liberty had seen yet,
with soldier-cropped ears.

With the interminable introductions finally over, they
took their seats on the cushions, Liberty flanked by Tsebe
and Jaes, facing Lords Dshu and Ishda. Everyone else,
including the governor, ranged somewhere behind or stood
outside the pavilion. The licorice scent of oiled heest hides
filled the air, cloying in the humid heat.

"Do you want me to tell them who you are?" Liberty whispered to Jaes.

He shook his head. "I'd like to keep a few surprises handy in case we have to throw them off-balance sometime."

She glanced toward Lord Ishda. "You don't trust them, either?"

He smiled thinly. "It isn't distrust exactly, but—we're so afraid of disturbing their society with culture shock, and just now it's occurred to me that we're a handful, facing an entire population who evolved here. If there's any pushing around, do you really think we'll be doing it?"

Ishda looked down the valley, oblivious of her, but Dshu's eyes measured the two humans with cold calculation. Liberty sucked in her lower lip.

Dshu began the inquisition, with polite formality, of course. "His Most Wise Highness King Po-xan wishes me to extend to you his warmest greetings and welcome you to Gthe-ge. I hope I do not give offense by stating that you pose a most interesting puzzle. Both His Majesty and I have traveled extensively through the world as royal officers and of course during our imperial conscription as youths, but neither of us has met any of your kind before, or seen arts which can build a metal house overnight. His Majesty wishes me to inquire, therefore, which kingdom is your home?"

Liberty's brows rose. Build a house overnight? Yes, it must seem that way to them. Now how should she reply? Before Tsebe learned enough English to understand Jaes's shouted conversations, he had instructed Liberty to keep as close to the truth as possible without giving anything away. "We come from a distant land far beyond the water." She pointed west, the direction they had come in landing.

Ishda cast an eye lazily in her direction. Dshu, however,

straightened on his cushion. "Beyond the sea! How did you avoid the sea monsters?"

She sighed. So they knew about those. She could not claim to have sailed, then. "The metal house flew us here."

Now both of Ishda's colorless eyes focused on her, though without losing their remoteness.

"Flew?" Dshu asked. "Like a bird?" His scalp furrowed. "I beg your pardon if I seem to doubt you, but how can a metal house fly?" His nostrils flared like those of a horse smelling water.

Jaes jogged her arm. "Don't forget I'm here. What's going on?"

She told him quickly, then switching back to Akansh, said, "The great magician Boeing moved it with magic." Which was true enough by one definition: science advanced beyond their understanding.

The furrows smoothed abruptly. "Magic moved this house? That is fascinating. Here, I'm afraid, magic is mere superstition and myth. Will you show us how it flies?"

Damn Jaes for making her deal with these people! Liberty crossed her arms over her chest. "I regret that is impossible. The magic works only once."

Lord Ishda spoke for the first time. "Then you came knowing you could not leave again. It was your intention to, what, settle here?"

So he had been listening after all. She gave him the answer she had prepared. "We had to come. Our land Atlantis was sinking into the ocean. The magician Boeing had a vision of safe land here, but an uninhabited land. It was never our intention to trespass and ruin crops."

She watched for his reaction, but oddly enough, he did not appear to listen to the answer. He glanced away again toward the river, apparently focusing on a line of peasants paddling their reed boats upstream. She frowned inwardly. Had the Emperor sent a fool after all?

Dshu, however, fairly purred. "How fortunate your magic brought you to Gthe-ge, then. His Majesty Po-xan has instructed me to extend you the aid and hospitality of his kingdom and house. You are therefore invited to the royal palace in Ba-si-ne, where on hearing of your tribulation, my lord will surely make you his retainers, and of course, pay Kxa-Thi and the sharecroppers the damages you owe for the crops your house and the military camp have destroyed."

Tsebe whispered excitedly, "God smiles on you. Perhaps you'll even be given noble rank."

But Liberty, translating for Jaes, felt shock reverberating through her. They owed damages? She fought a giggle that rose at the image of aliens being dragged into court, laughter that died as she suddenly pictured the ship being confiscated. "Lord, the King honors us, but we are too many to impose on His Majesty's hospitality and too humble, only simple farmers with few needs. All we want is land on which to live and raise our families. Can you direct us to wilderness?"

"Wilderness?" Dshu asked.

"You know, an uninhabited region, like a desert."

Thi said, "The Thim emperors turned the deserts to farmland generations ago. The Empire looks like this from the Cliffs of Dawn to the Cliffs of Sunset and from the Southern Sea to the Wall of the World." He gestured at the bottomland.

Liberty swore silently, then in the midst of translating the bad news to Jaes, hope stopped the plunge of her stomach. "Wall of the World? You mean the mountains to the north? What about the land beyond?"

Dshu frowned. "There is no land beyond the Wall."

"Unless you believe in myth," Ishda said. The blind-looking eyes went out of focus. "When men stopped believing in the creatures of legend, the A-ta-ku and Tse-shada, the We-hesu and De-muth', they fled beyond the Wall. There, 'A-ta-ku, cloud white, still dance on on sunfire hooves—' "

"In reality," Dshu interrupted, nostrils pinched tight in disapproval, "the Wall is the end of the world, or rather, the end of the land."

If they thought so, far be it from her to disillusion them, Liberty reflected. "There's land, Jaes," she muttered, "but it'll be a little difficult to reach," and she explained why.

The King's envoy held out both hands, palms up, fingers and medial and lateral thumbs spread wide. "So, please accept His Majesty Po-xan's hospitality. Even if there were land, he would consider himself ill-mannered to allow survivors of tragedy to continue their hardship by living like peasants."

Ishda's attention drifted back to the river. "King Po-xan is a very generous King. As a scholar, he is interested in all subjects. No doubt he looks forward to learning about your vanished homeland."

Liberty eyed him in surprise. There might be something to Lord Ishda after all. For all its praise of Po-xan, that speech sounded like a warning about the price of the King's hospitality. "Does the Emperor have no interest in tales of faraway places?"

His gaze never wavered from the river. "Regrettably, he is much too busy governing the Empire. All my brother could provide would be land, giving or leasing you one of his larger estates."

Oh, yes. Lord Ishda thought about more than rivers and poetry indeed. But, how much more? What, exactly, was he? Liberty regarded him warily.

Dshu said, "Po-xan can give you an estate, too, and on the rich Kuge-ke plains, not the rocky hills of the central kingdoms."

Liberty glanced back toward Ishda. Would he have a second bid?

He spoke almost absently. "With the main body of Po-xan's army massing on the eastern border for the war with Shapeen, who will protect these visitors from bandits that are sure to raid for their metal? With all respect due your rank, my lord Dshu, the smallness of the force assembled here to face Nui-kopa's army is a sad example of your King's strength."

"And may I respectfully admonish Lord Ishda for using an invalid argument?" Dshu countered in an equally polite voice. "Bandits travel in small bands, not armies, and are easily repelled by good walls and a few well-trained archers."

The bidding appeared to have become a sparring match, which the hees obviously relished. They leaned forward with eyes bright and nostrils flaring, but Liberty stiffened, a terrible, cold suspicion seeping into her.

"Who is Nui-kopa?"

Her interruption brought eyes staring toward her. Ishda replied, "The King of A-thin-we." He pointed across the river.

She sucked in her breath. "He sent those soldiers."

"His governor of Zhen-th'u province did, anticipating how much the King would want to meet you after hearing of your metal house and miraculous overnight appearance. Since you spurned the governor's overture, however, he's sending three of his generals and their entourage to extend a more forceful invitation." Ishda paused. "Nui-kopa is a man of poor manners and no subtlety. He won his throne from the battlefield, leading his army against the King he was supposed to be supporting. You would not enjoy his company."

Jaes hissed something in her ear, but she barely heard him. "Is it a very large army?"

Dshu said, "No matter what the size, there can be no conflict if you are gone when it arrives. We could start for Ba-si-ne this afternoon . . . or has Lord Ishda come with the imperial army at his back to remove you to Ku-wen?" He rayed an eye toward Ishda.

The colorless eyes blinked. "My lord, I am here to extend an invitation, not take prisoners."

He avoided actually answering Dshu's question, Liberty noticed. "Do you have another suggestion than fleeing, Lord Ishda?"

"On the contrary. I concur with the honorable royal envoy. In choosing this dishonorable action, Nui-kopa is lost unless he can strike quickly and decisively and withdraw to his own borders again, where he can use the courts to fight the complaints of undeclared hostilities and destruction of civilian property that will be brought against him. His army cannot afford the time to foray in-kingdom after you."

"Liberty, talk to me!" Jaes hissed.

"Not here." Standing, she left the pavilion and pulled him after her, until they were too far away for Tsebe to overhear. Then she gave him the bad news.

He swore.

"How fast can we move out?" Liberty asked.

"In a hurry if we're talking just people. The last four racks can be cleared by tomorrow evening. But"—he ran a hand through his hair—"there's the cargo, too . . . supplies, machines, including the chopper and computer, and there's the metal in the ship itself. We can't abandon all that."

She glanced around at the river and far bluffs. Would the army come by water or overland? And how soon? "Can't we ship the children and pets and whoever else isn't necessary someplace away from the river and then the rest of us stay to guard the ship?"

He rubbed his chin. ''We can try. Maybe there would be time to move some of the cargo, too. The computer can go as soon as the last rack is cleared. I'll talk to the others. You tell those envoys—'' He hesitated a moment. ''Tell them we'll decide whose hospitality to accept after this Nui-kopa is disposed of. Maybe by that time we'll have a way to reach the other side of the mountains.''

Chapter Four

Time was their real enemy, Liberty decided. Nui-kopa could be a pirate and graceless host; his army might consist of bloodthirsty legions; still, they remained mortal. They could be met and fought. Nothing held back time. The humans used it at such an alarming rate, too . . . waking sleepers; moving them, still groggy, into carts Kxa-Thi had ordered brought for transport to the Kxa compound for safety; going through the cargo hold choosing which crates should leave, too. Time chewed steadily through even the long hours of this planet's day.

Helping load bed rolls into a cart with a group of children, Liberty glanced across the river, then up it, half-fearing to see soldier-filled barges. "Why can't we move faster?" The first group of evacuees had not even left yet. "Come *on*; bring those packs down!" she called up to the ship. For once, she wanted to be very visible. "Hurry!"

"Watch out," Tsebe said.

Liberty had already caught the movement from the corner of her eye. With reflexes developed by grooming temperamental race horses, she side-stepped a kick delivered by the beast pulling the cart, a jug-headed, pony-sized cousin of the u-tse with the temper of a wasp. "Why do you use these brutes?"

"They're very strong," Tsebe said.

"And handy for discouraging lovers," added the soldier drafted to drive the cart.

Liberty blinked. "What?"

"It is a joke, Ib-ih-tee," Tsebe said, and took a bundle from a woman until the woman settled herself and two children in the cart.

The soldiers still felt like joking? Her gaze strayed across the river. A-thin-wet soldiers milled along the bank there, teeth bared. Liberty tossed them a one-fingered human gesture.

"What is that curse, stranger visitor?"

She looked around to find Lord Ishda beyond the line of carts, blind-pale eyes focused on her. "It's more in the line of an instruction. Do you know how far away that army is?"

Ishda dodged through the cart line to join her. "I can only guess. Assuming the governor sent word of you to Nui-kopa by a courier riding relay mounts and that the King dispatched orders to the army by courier bird—he is not half-souled enough to make the same mistake his predecessor did and keep the main army near his capital— and that the generals are force marching their troops, they could arrive any time in the next few days.

Liberty eyed the camp across the river again. She swore. "Why aren't our soldiers more concerned? They're telling jokes and not even trying to put up—" She searched for a word meaning fortifications. "Not trying to put up defensive barriers."

The colorless eyes stared at her for a long minute, unreadable. Liberty frowned. What could he be thinking?

Finally he said, "The object of war is to engage one's opponents. That is how hides and spoils are taken."

Anger sparked in her. "In this case isn't the object to protect us?"

He regarded her steadily. "These soldiers have no commitment to you. Indeed, since warfare is supposed to be between matched forces, so that both have an equal opportunity to win, they have the right to refuse to fight if Nui-kopa's army obviously outnumbers them.''

The air stuck in the middle of Liberty's chest. For a moment the sunlight, humid heat, noise, and scents of licorice and acid human sweat swirled dizzingly around her. She fought to breathe. ''You mean they'd just leave us undefended?''

Before he could reply, Tsebe's voice broke in. ''Please forgive my intrusion into your private conversation, my lord Ishda and visitor Ib-ih-tee, but may I beg to correct you, my lord? Our soldiers will not refuse to pick up their arms. A host must protect his guests.''

''But they are not King Po-xan's guests yet,'' Ishda said.

The spark blazed higher. In other words, in order to be defended, they would have to give themselves into Poxan's custody, or someone's. Making her voice silky, Liberty asked, ''If we accept the Emperor's 'hospitality,' could *he* protect us? *Do* you have an army here?''

Not a muscle in his face and scalp moved. The late afternoon sunlight glinted in eyes opaque as a cat's. ''I would go to the generals when they arrive and inform them you are under imperial protection. Not even Nui-kopa dares risk reprisal from the Emperor.''

How much could she believe? Liberty turned away to look for Jaes.

Tsebe followed her. ''Please, visitor Ib-ih-tee, the Emperor is a great and powerful man, but my house has dealt with King Nui-kopa, selling him u-tse, and my fathers and grandfathers say he is a tanner, a ruthless fighter. You would be wise to ask protection of a host with an army present.''

Liberty frowned. How much *could* she believe? Did the heest girl speak truthfully, or was she shilling for Dshu? Damn. On Earth at least she had known the rules of the

game and who was playing. "And what if the army outnumbers yours? Do you want us to condemn you to die
fighting for a lost cause?"

Tsebe tucked in her chin. "You condemn no one. God
chooses who becomes One, as my father was chosen in the
last battle. It would be an honorable death. Our houses
would put our name cups in the family shrine and ever
after, pray to us in God for advice and guidance and God's
good."

Did hees really look at death that calmly? Perhaps.
Tsebe had shown little grief at losing that one father the
day the ship landed.

A whistle sounded across the river. Liberty turned. An
armored rider plunged down the face of the distant bluffs
and pounded across the fields into the A-thin-wet camp.
Around Liberty, a murmur ran through the local soldiers.

Her heart lurched. "Is the army coming?"

Tsebe's pupils dilated. "The forerider means it's here."

Now Liberty did run for Jaes.

She found him with Noel, tucking his family and two
dogs into a cart beside Noel's sister and her children.
Quickly, but keeping her voice low, she told him about the
approaching army and the possibility of being left to face it
on their own.

Noel swore. Jaes used his voice to yell: "Forget about
off-loading cargo! All children, newly wakened sleepers,
and anyone else who can't walk climb into the carts!
Able-bodied people hike! Liberty, tell the drivers and Kxa-
Thi that I want these people out of here as fast as possible.
Get these carts moving! God, I wish waking went faster.
There are still two racks—"

Another whistle carried across the river, a high, trilling
piping. Every head in the Gthe-get camp turned . . . and
froze.

Nui-kopa's army came over the bluffs . . . outriders on
dxee, platoons of u-tse, black-armored foot soldiers march-

ing in what looked like endless ranks, each pushing a sailbarrow. Liberty sucked in her breath. The scarlet sails gave the appearance of a wave of blood pouring down the bluffs, and out across the bottomland to engulf the cheering soldiers in the A-thin-wet camp. Scarlet flooded the fields.

"God's evil," a soldier driver muttered.

Liberty's stomach plunged. Nui-kopa must really want them. Even with rifles and all the Gthe-get soldiers fighting, they could not hope to overcome the sheer size of that army.

"Move those carts *now*!" Jaes barked. He ran for the ship, shouting above the crack of whips and creak of wheels and protesting squeals of tseki. "Noel, issue rifles to everyone who's staying!"

Damn, damn! Liberty clenched her fists. One way or another, fate seemed determined to destroy the Laheli Company.

Then she blinked and stared at the invaders. They were not drawing weapons as she expected them to. Instead, riders vaulted off their mounts. Foot soldiers furled the sails and began unloading their barrows.

"They're setting up camp!"

She did not realize she had spoken in Akansh until Ishda's voice replied from behind her, "Of course. After the pace they must have maintained, they need a night's rest before going into battle. It is almost sunset in any case, too late to begin fighting."

"Then we have at least until morning?"

She sprinted after Jaes, dodging the wheels of a cart and a passing tseki's teeth. Maybe something could be done yet.

The group of men and women around Jaes at the foot of the ship's ladder frowned, however, as she repeated what Ishda had told her. "What difference does one night make, except that it gives us time to wake and evacuate the rest of the sleepers?'' one woman asked.

"It might give us time to even the odds,'' Liberty said. "What if we put up fortifications?''

Above Dalyn's grin, the glint in his amber eyes made him look more wolfish than ever. "And traps.''

With a glance at him, Jaes nodded. "Bring Ath' and those envoys here, will you, Liberty?''

When she had done so, Jaes looked around the group. "Ask them if the soldiers will fight if we can promise them an even fight.''

She asked. Dshu replied, "Of course, but how can you promise that?''

"By thinning out their numbers before they reach us,'' Liberty said. Translating for the humans, she passed on suggestions for fortifications.

But the hees's eyes dilated and nostrils pinched as they listened to descriptions of trenches with pointed stakes, earthworks faced in pottery shards, and thrown burning lamp oil.

Tsebe spread her hand in the middle of her chest. "We cannot dig up crop land! It's evil enough to fight on it during the growing season.''

"The methods sound like something Tu-Nan-see the Usurper would have used back before the Second Darkness,'' Ath' said. "An army should meet hand to hand, with skill, strategy, resolve, and God's will determining the outcome. This manufactures an advantage, like an ambush. Only bandits fight from ambush.''

Righteous bastard, Liberty thought. "How much do you want to win?''

Ath' drew himself up stiffly. "There is no victory without honor. I will fight to the death if King Po-xan is your host and protector, but I refuse to be a party to barbarism.'' Crossing his arms over his chest, he turned and marched away.

One of Dshu's eyes followed the captain. "Honored visitors, while I have no doubt that your suggestions would bring the effect you promise, I must agree with the commander. We cannot dishonor ourselves and His Majesty Po-xan in fighting even an unprincipled bandit like Nui-kopa this way."

Watching the envoy's ears twitch and the furrows shift in his scalp, Liberty suspected that Dshu would really have liked to have surrendered his principles long enough to use the weapons offered him. What about Ishda, though? He stood looking west, watching the sun slipping behind the horizon, seemingly oblivious to all else.

"Honorable imperial envoy, have you no thoughts?" she asked. She had no doubt he had heard every word.

Ishda turned from the flaming sky, straightening his vest and shaking the lapped edges on the front of his trousers to improve the drape. "Such actions are indeed dishonorable. Therefore, if the visitor Ib-ih-tee will agree to accompany me, I would like to call on the generals."

That caught Dshu completely by surprise. "God's evil!" While Liberty translated for the humans, he went on, struggling to cover his anger with politeness. "In all respect, my lord, have you become half-souled? You would expose the human leader to the very persons seeking to capture him?"

Ishda pulled in his chin. "With pardons to the humans and meaning no personal offense, they are grotesquely spindly in appearance, like the bird greatlegs, and they wear peasant-plain clothing. The generals are wise men. One close look will demonstrate to them that the humans cannot possibly possess anything worth capturing."

Dshu's scalp furrowed and his nostrils pinched tight. "Convince *Nui-kopa's* generals? You *have* become half-souled, my lord."

Dalyn whispered in Liberty's ear, "It looks like our

defense is all up to us. If you'll scout the camp, we can make a commando raid tonight.''

She nodded. ''Lord Dshu, I think Lord Ishda has a good idea. I want to go.''

''As you wish,'' Ishda murmured.

They located his two attendants and poled across the river through the warm twilight on one of the raft-like reed peasant boats the soldiers used for ferrying supplies from villages up and downstream. A sentry met them on the southern bank with a drawn bow, challenging them in a language full of grinding consonants. Ishda flung back a reply in the same language. The sentry stared past him to Liberty and after a moment, lowered the bow, nostrils flaring. Ishda led Liberty and the women up the bank and between the rows of tents.

A medley of familiar sounds and scents that had come to mean ''military camp'' met Liberty: the scent of licorice and cooking, the smell of lamp oil, grunts and squeals of u-tse and dxee, the grumbling roar of simultaneous voices. She even caught the click of dice somewhere hear. Conversation died around them, however, as the soldiers stopped polishing armor and checking weapons by the light of lamps outside the door of their tents to watch the newcomers pass.

Where were the good old days of comfortable invisibility? Liberty grimaced, then tried to ignore the feeling that every eye followed her as she looked around and studied the camp. Rope pens at the rear held dxee and u-tse, she noticed, and most of the tents, square and flat-topped like those across the river, had their side flaps tossed on the roof, opening them to the evening breeze and revealing four sleeping pallets in each.

Ishda stopped before a large tent in the center of the camp. Its occupants must have seen the boat land, because the entire group stood waiting, ranged in a curve around three men whose camp shirts had purple collars embroidered in copper wire. They crossed their arms over their chests.

Liberty sighed inwardly. If only heest greetings were not so interminable. Then the thought broke off in surprise. The hide at the back of Ishda's neck was twitching. She eyed the three in purple collars curiously. They must be the generals, but why did they disturb Ishda? Or was it just the one with an umber hide and lemon-yellow eyes? Ishda seemed to be concentrating on that officer.

"General Hoth-Tasat," he said, "on behalf of the Emperor, may I congratulate you on your recall from the southern provinces? Of course, it was inevitable that a man of your ability be restored to favor."

"I'm honored the Emperor concerns himself," Tasat replied.

But Liberty heard a wry edge that belied the words.

"Have we met before, my lord? You seem—ah, I know. It's your eyes. They remind me of those of an aide I had at the time of my disgrace. He disappeared mysteriously afterward. Curious, isn't it?"

Liberty sucked in her lower lip. Curious indeed, and . . . enlightening? Could Ishda have been that mysterious aide? She could see where one ruler might benefit from the disgrace of an influential military officer in another court, and if Ishda had engineered that fall, however it happened, it might explain a good deal about what he was.

She watched him closely to see how he would react to Tasat's statement.

He did not, except to furrow his forehead and say, "Very interesting. It would seem my eye color is not as unique as I've been led to believe. And speaking of leading, may I ask which of you is commanding the troops tomorrow?"

The general with a chestnut-red hide crossed his arms said, "I have that honor, my lord."

Liberty thought that was not the answer Ishda wanted.

"General Xuo, let me appeal to you, then. As a soldier of ability and integrity, surely you cannot agree with this undeclared invasion of Gthe-get territory."

The general's scalp rippled, but he replied, "I am a soldier, my lord. I follow my orders, and those are to attack."

Soldiers. Liberty snorted inwardly. They thought alike the universe over, it seemed.

"Attack to what end, honorable general?" Ishda asked. "Look at this creature." He gestured toward Liberty. "It is a thing of no rank, poor manners, and little intelligence. It believes *magic* put that metal house where it stands, and it has been able to learn only a few words of Akansh. This is the human leader, too. Of what value can it possibly to to His Majesty?"

"It built the metal house," Tasat said.

Ishda's nostrils flared. "Another built and moved the house, a person who did not come with the others. This is merely a peasant. The Emperor my brother has extended it his hospitality purely out of pity."

All three generals and their staff glared. Tasat's eyes gleamed. "So the Emperor is their host? Then he should prepare to exercise his duty to defend them. God's good to you tomorrow, my lord."

Liberty sucked in a deep breath. So much for peaceful solutions. Now everything depended on the men tonight.

Back across the river, Tsebe, Dshu, and Captain Ath' met them anxiously. "What happened?"

Ishda replied cautiously, "I regret that the generals still intend to attack."

He did not sound very dismayed about it, Liberty noticed, though that appeared to escape the other hees.

"Then the humans are forfeit," Ath' said.

"They continue to refuse all offers of protection." Dshu

focused both eyes on Liberty. "You are their leader. Why do you permit them to destroy themselves?"

"They are free people. I won't force safety on them against their will. Now I'd better tell them the mission failed."

She started to turn away but Ishda's hand closed around her wrist, halting her. "Don't tell your people just yet. It will only distress them."

In the fury boiling up at the restraint, Liberty barely noticed the hees staring at Ishda. She snapped her wrist against his thumbs, but that maneuver, which never failed to break a human grip, failed this time. She could only stand twisting her wrist and hissing at him. "They're entitled to know."

"Surely so, my lord," Tsebe said.

The last daylight had faded, but lamplight from the camp glittered in the colorless eyes. "I will pray to my ancestors for aid. I know God is always for and against both sides, but the Thims in God have always proven very influential. So, may I suggest we have lastmeal and watch the dancing which I see being organized?" He started toward the soldiers' mess, still gripping Liberty's wrist.

Anger blazed in her, but with the choice of either following or being dragged, she chose to stay on her feet. Eventually he would have to let go, and then she would sneak away at the first opportunity.

"Ah, captain," Ishda said, "are the extra guards in place around the humans' house?"

Liberty groaned. "Extra guards!"

Ishda glanced an eye toward her. "Before we left I suggested to Lord Dshu that he might want to make certain your people could not attempt to implement their own suggestions and perhaps place themselves in a position where they might be captured by Nui-kopa's troops."

"You son of a bitch." She felt more dismay than anger. *Damn* him, and double damn. How could he have guessed—

She sighed. That hardly mattered. What mattered was how to counteract what he had done, and that *did* knot her gut. If Dalyn and the other men could not raid the enemy camp, it became her responsibility. With a deep breath, she shoved her anger deep, where it would not interfere.

Dshu and his retinue left for the Kxa compound, but Ishda remained, sitting on the ground to eat with the soldiers, finery and all. He appeared to be ignoring Liberty, but she did not try to test that . . . yet. Sitting silent beside him, she worked her scoopspear from bowl to mouth and used the time to search her memory for all the stories her great-grandfather had told about the horse stealing raids of his great-grandfathers. After dinner, while the soldiers flung themselves into first an exhibition of dancing and then tumbling and juggling, she planned her strategy. Not even the astonishing skill of the young soldier spinning swords and knives into the air slowed down her racing thoughts.

She was still planning when she and Tsebe went to their tent.

Lying on her sleeping pallet listening to the camp settle into silence around her, she had no idea how much time passed. The internal clock that always served her well on Earth had not readjusted to this planet's time yet. But she monitored Tsebe's breathing and when the heest girl seemed deeply asleep, Liberty glanced once toward the entrance to make sure the guard outside was not looking in, then rolled soundlessly off the back of her pallet and wiggled under the side flap of the tent. She grinned. They had staked it down, but their conception of *down* still left room enough for a thin human to use.

Outside, the camp lay quiet except for the occasional grunt of a dxee or u-tse or the *oow*? of a watch axa accompanying the padding of sentries' feet on the perimeter. In the west the cracked-egg moon, now almost half full, blazed even brighter than a full moon on Earth. Liberty felt spotlighted as she slipped down the tent row, diving from shadow to shadow.

At each tent she paused, and finally found what she needed, a tent with the side flaps up. Belly-crawling inside, she searched the nearest pile of clothing and armor until her fingers closed around the knife she needed. She backed out with it clamped in her teeth and continued down the tent row.

At the end she hesitated, huddling in an inky pool of shadow. The next problem was crossing that open space the sentries patrolled. Her one advantage, though, ought to be the reason for the patrols; they would be watching for wild animals, bandits, and other intruders, not someone going AWOL.

The sentry padded past, luckily without an axa. Liberty gave her a few strides more, just to make sure the peripheral vision of those wide-spaced eyes would not detect motion behind her, then bolted toward the river in a crouch that Liberty fervently hoped imitated the silhouette of a ha-gho-wu. At the bank, she dropped flat, waiting for any sound of pursuit. When none came, she grinned again and turned her attention across the river.

The A-thin-wet camp lay quiet, too. Moonlight and the lamps outside each tent shone on empty space. Only in the command tent did shadows move across the lights. A scent of burning lamp oil curled around her on the night breeze along with the yowl of a wild axa hunting somewhere upriver.

Ignoring the tempting outlines of the soldiers' reed boats hauled up on the shore, Liberty slid down the bank and, keeping low, slipped upstream along the edge of the water until well above both camps. There, she finally waded into the water.

It raced icy cold around her thighs and belly. Gritting her teeth on the knife, she plunged in to her neck and struck out for the opposite bank with skin rippling into gooseflesh. Then the current caught her and Liberty no longer noticed how much colder the river seemed by night than it had during the day. She was too busy fighting to keep from being carried downstream past the camps. The current ran faster than she anticipated, must faster here in the channel than near the bank where she and Tsebe swam. Suddenly all the years of swimming in rivers because Undocumenteds had little access to municipal pools no longer seemed unfair. As she had learned then, she angled across the current, driving with powerful kicks, using her arms to keep her head above water where she could watch for eddies and snags. Still, the southern bank came as a welcome relief and she dragged herself out panting, reflecting that survival skills came from the most unexpected sources.

After her breathing returned to normal, she climbed the rest of the bank and crawled into the nearest row of crops. Crouching to keep below the tops of the leaves, she used them for cover as she circled the camp to the side nearest the bluffs, hoping that would be the direction they least expected to find intrusion. Entering the camp could not be as easy as leaving the Gthe-get camp, of course. Lying flat and peering out between the heema-na's thick stalks, she saw that like her own soldiers, these, too, had removed all vegetation within the perimeter of the camp, creating a broad space to cross before she reached cover. This sentry patrolled with an axa, as well.

Directly opposite her lay the animal pens. Liberty studied them while she counted off the sentry's patrol timing. The u-tse included several breeds, among them ones with the looming obsidian shape she knew from her own camp: Kxa u-tse. Quietly, the knife sawed the maize-like heads from several plants, then Liberty waited for the sentry to pass.

The ground moved. Oh, god, not again! Liberty flattened, hugging the ground and hoping the drumming of her pulse would not attract the guard's attention. The tremor subsided, and so did the icy fire of adrenalin in Liberty's veins. She resumed breathing.

The guard and axa barely paused in their strides. Still, peering through the stalks again, Liberty saw the animal's round ears tilt toward her and heard a questioning sound rise in its throat. The sentry nocked an arrow.

The quake faded from importance. Liberty drew her knees under her, gathering herself and planning her defense. If the sentry freed the axa to flush what it smelled, she would use the knife on the animal and run like hell, taking her chances that she was too small a target for the sentry's arrows.

The axa hissed. Liberty tightened her grip on the knife.

Behind her, the heema-na rustled and some tiny animal chirruped in a high-pitched cry of alarm.

The sentry stared, head cocked, then snorting, slipped her arrow back into the quiver. Muttering at the axa, she dragged it on. Liberty sighed.

The hand closed around her mouth so fast she did not even see the direction it came from.

Reflex sent her knife slashing backward. Her attacker caught her wrist, however, then fell on her, pushing her face-down into the dirt.

"Be still or the sentries will hear you," Ishda's voice hissed in her ear.

Fear and fight died instantly. She went limp. After a minute, his weight lifted off of her. Liberty rolled over to face him, and stared. Without seeing his eyes, milkstones in the moonlight, she would not have known him. Dressed in only a loincloth, he looked like any peasant.

He leaned forward to put his mouth to her ear. "How did you get here? You're risking capture. Return to camp."

She shook her head emphatically before remembering that the gesture would mean nothing to him. Nor did Akansh have a simple *no*. She had to settle for hissing,

"Not as long as these bastards are a threat to my people!" She used English where Akansh lacked the word she needed.

He regarded her for a moment, then tipped his head side to side. "We should move before the sentry returns, then."

She moved . . . easing out of the field and dashing soundlessly across the perimeter to dive under the rope into a Kxa u-tse's pen.

The beast whirled with remarkable agility for an animal so large, but did not charge, merely lowered its massive head, small ears twitching in curiosity. It sniffed the handful of heema-na heads Liberty extended to it, then delicately raked the grain into its mouth with its long upper lip. The sweet licorice scent on its hide filled her nose.

Ishda dived into the pen beside her, also with grain. While the animal took that offering, too, the hees blew into its nostrils and tickled its muzzle, as Liberty had seen Tsebe do. The u-tse sighed happily. Before the sentry passed again, both hees and human were crouched under the massive body, hiding in its shadow.

"How do you intend to remove this threat?" Ishda asked.

"I thought I'd turn their animals loose and set fire to their camp."

"It would be even better to make the catastrophe look accidental."

"Fine. How?"

"Use the Gtso and Susum u-tse. They tend to be even more nervous than dxee." Quickly, he explained exactly what he had in mind.

For someone who considered this dishonorable, Ishda seemed very adept at it, Liberty reflected. One might even suspect that his entire reason for the evening's visit had been not to seek peace but to scout the camp.

She followed him under the rope into a pen with a piebald u-tse. At his signal, she sprang toward the animal with a piercing war whoop.

The u-tse woke explosively. Without even looking for the source of the sound, it squealed and bolted. The charge took the piebald through its rope barrier into the pen of a hump-shouldered u-tse, which woke keening in startled rage. Suddenly every u-tse around them was awake and on fighting edge, even the Kxa among them. Hump-shoulders lunged at the piebald. The two bodies met thunderously, screaming. Every other u-tse echoed them.

A soldier dashed out of her tent next to the pens. U-tse rage focused. Even the combatants forgot personal differences to turn on the object they had been taught to target, the foot soldier. Charging with them went panic-stricken dxee.

The soldier fled, screaming a warning, but for those in the nearest tents, it came too late. The wave of massive bodies flattened the tents. Lamps fell, shattering, scattering oil and flame over people, tents, and animals.

Sparks sent the dxee into new panic. Though they did not have the mass to knock over tent, they blundered through, into poles and guy ropes, upsetting still more lamps.

The hump-shouldered u-tse screamed at every spark, too, and whirled, hunting the cause of its pain, to charge everything that moved. Within minutes the entire camp had become chaos, a good third of it burning and the fire spreading fast.

Liberty bit back the war cry in her throat. This was better than she had hoped for. Gloating, she chased after the stampeding animals with Ishda, as though the two of them were A-thin-wet soldiers. A serious number of soldiers should be injured or killed, forcing the rest to stay up all night restoring order and treating the wounded.

"You!"

She whipped around at the yell to find General Tasat staring, nostrils flared. Snapping back to the front, she doubled her speed.

Tasat yelled something in his own language. A soldier whirled and raced for her. Liberty slashed the reaching hands with her knife. She bowled over a boy who looked no older than Tsebe and dashed past a veteran-looking female.

The female yelled to a group just ahead of Liberty.

Liberty changed direction abruptly, dodging around a blazing tent . . . and found herself face-to-face with a piebald u-tse.

It halted, momentarily startled into immobility. The moment gave Liberty just enough time to duck under its neck before her pursuers rounded the tent.

They reversed direction abruptly, scattering before the u-tse's charge.

Where was Ishda? she suddenly wondered, but did not take the time to look around. The posse would be regrouped any minute. A dxee thundered past with a guy rope draped around its neck. Liberty grabbed at the rope and vaulted onto the animal's back. Whipping with the bight of the rope, she drove the dxee on through the camp toward the river.

Hoofbeats drummed behind her. In her peripheral vision, she saw a rider on the second dxee. Gathering up the end of her rope, she turned to swing it at her pursuer if necessary.

Ishda called, "Are you satisfied?"

As though this had been all her idea with him just along for the ride. But she said, "It will do."

Across the river, Gthe-get soldiers poured out of tents and down toward the river, wakened by the noise. Human shapes showed on top of the ship.

"Don't let anyone see us," Ishda called.

Their own people, he meant? They swung east before reaching the edge of the camp and raced upriver until they were out of the casual line of vision and there, bailed off the dxee. More hoofbeats sounded from the direction of the camp. In one motion, the two of them dived into the river.

This time the current helped, sweeping them toward the north shore, where they crawled out and sat side by side in the moonlight, dripping and panting. Downstream, the A-thin-wet camp blazed to the accompaniment of shouts and animal cries.

Liberty felt like hugging Ishda in glee. "That little bit of fun ought to even the odds."

He glanced an eye toward her. "Do your people really enjoy such banditry?"

Elation and the sense of comaraderie evaporated abruptly. "You seemed willing enough to help," she snapped.

His eyes focused on the burning camp. "It was necessary in the service of my house. I might refuse to be a party next time, however."

Cold seeped through her. "Next time?"

"The world contains many ambitious men, and as long as you lack a powerful protector, you will tempt them." Downstream the invaders formed a bucket line from the river. "My house owns an estate called Swordwood. I spent my childhood there. It has rich land that has never seen a plow. It is also the training ground for the imperial mounted divisions, which guarantees its security. It would provide your people with everything they need."

"Everything except freedom." The anger she had pushed down earlier came leaking back. "What's the difference between the 'hospitality' offered by your brother, Po-xan or Nui-kopa?"

A pale eye shot toward her. "My brother does not want your weapons."

She frowned at him, mind churning. Every fiber of her protested bitterly at any surrender, but he had one point she could not dispute: they needed sanctuary, someplace safe to stay until they could move everyone north of the mountains.

"You can guarantee the transport of all our people and supplies to this estate?"

Both eyes focused downstream. "Two divisions of the imperial army are waiting three hours away at Ka-sapa for my signal to escort you."

The *bastard*! She jumped to her feet, glaring down at him. "You mean you brought an army after all, but you were just going to let them *sit* there when we needed them against Nui-kopa?"

He tucked in his chin. "I would have sent for them if necessary . . . but I could hardly arrive for a diplomatic mission at the head of an army."

Could she believe that? "You never planned to use them in the negotiations, not even if we accepted Po-xan's invitation?"

He lifted his head. The setting moon glittered in the colorless eyes. "I would never use them to force you to come with me."

What *would* he have used them for? Or did she want that question answered? She shivered, suddenly cold despite the warmth of the night. "I'll relay your offer to the others and bring you their answer in the morning."

Chapter Five

Of course those members of the Laheli Company still at the ship voted for Swordwood—at least it might be a roomy prison—and Liberty reported the decision to an Ishda now dressed in the simple camp clothes of a soldier. In the midst of asking him for details about the estate's topography and buildings, a long string of barges appeared out of the dawn mist upriver. Liberty regarded them wryly, noting the blue and white pennants they flew and the sky-blue armor the soldiers wore. This had to be the imperial army, of course. Ishda must have sent for them last night, confident of their acceptance, to have them arrive here this early.

She did wish she could be in the A-thin-wet camp and able to understand their language, however. What must they be saying as they looked up from treating their wounded and picking through the smoldering ashes for still-usable armor and weapons to see this force landing? Then again, perhaps she was content to remain here. General Tasat strode down to the riverband and, after glancing at the barges, turned his gaze toward Ishda and her. Holding one arm up in front of him, he plucked at the hide with the fingers of his other hand, then whirled away, beckoning to an aide.

"I don't think he likes us," she said.

"He promises to take our hides," Ishda replied absently. "Now, you may please tell your leader Ah-ent-Zhes that—"

Surprise jolted Liberty into interrupting. "My leader?" How the hell had Ishda discovered that?

"With all respect, honored visitor, it is obvious that the woman Zhes leads, not you. You speak with almost none of your people but she, and you stand apart not like a house headman who leaves command of the house to the headwoman but like one who is merely *with* his people rather than *of* them . . . a wild axa kenneled by accident with a household pack."

That echo of her observation of him reverberated in her. Like recognizing like? Probably, but it made her feel uncomfortably visible and transparent. She set her jaw. "I'm not wild. My people are merely free, living apart from the rest of human society by their own rules."

"Ah, like the Bethxim of our highlands. But why are you alone? Did your house perish?"

"I have no brothers or sisters and my mother chose not to come. I have no father."

His ears flicked. "You *admit* that?"

So bastards still carried a stigma in this society. "Of course. Now, what is the reason why *you* stand apart from *your* people?"

In the quick intake of his breath, Liberty heard his dislike of being read, too. "Please tell Ah-ent-Zhes that whatever assistance she needs to move your people and property, the soldiers are ordered to provide. She need only ask Kxa-Tsebe to pass on her requests and instructions."

At least he had still not straightened out the sexes, but what was that emphasis on Tsebe? "Won't the soldiers listen to *me*?"

The colorless eyes focused past her on soldiers marching down the gangplanks. "You won't be here. You're coming with me to Ku-wen."

Liberty stiffened. "Oh, I am, am I? Like baggage. You just decided that, without bothering to ask me?"

The hiss in her voice brought both his eyes around toward her. "It is the Emperor my brother's wish to meet one of you."

And that settled the matter? She deliberately bared her teeth at him. "You just tell the Emperor your brother to stick all four thumbs—"

She broke off, cursing herself. What the hell was she doing? Maybe he had violated her autonomy but until the humans found a place for themselves beyond heest hands, none of them could claim autonomy. And to escape they would need enough knowledge of their hosts to outmaneuver them, knowledge which would come easier in heest society than on a country estate.

"I thank your brother the Emperor for his invitation," she went on. "Now, please excuse me while I inform my leader of my departure."

She left him staring after her.

Indra looked up from directing packing of the computer to point Liberty to the sleeper hold, where Liberty found Jaes moving back and forth between the crew opening the last rack and a work gang dismantling the stripped racks. They pulled seals from the pods, so that when washed by the heat of a blow torch, the memory plastic unrolled into flat sheets, ready for storage until needed as windows or for remolding into other objects. Jaes frowned at her news.

"I don't like the idea of your being by yourself among these people. I'll send two men along for protection."

Liberty snorted. "I've been looking after myself since I was fifteen."

"Consider them extra eyes and ears, then," he said, and frowned. "It should be Noel and Dalyn. Except for Noel's sister, they don't have families to be separated from."

Dalyn and Noel. There could be worse choices. She

nodded. "I found out part of what you wanted to know about the estate. I gather it's very large and hilly. The military compound is adjacent to the family compound."

Jaes's frown deepened. "Damn. Well, maybe the hills will be enough to hide projects we don't want the hees to see. Let's find Noel and Dalyn."

Both men were part of a group dismantling the bulkhead of the cargo hold. With a glance at a husband and wife working together, Dalyn readily agreed to accompany Liberty, but Noel hesitated. "We're not going to be gone so long that there's any danger of being left behind, are we?"

Left behind? Liberty started. That possibility had not occurred to her. She snapped around toward Jaes.

He shook his head reassuringly. "Certainly not. It's going to be a while before we go. First we have to find transportation, then send a small exploring party, so we won't be jumping blind again."

What was the problem with transportation? "Use the chopper," Liberty said.

"Sorry," Noel said. "It's a workhorse but it wouldn't last that distance."

Jaes grimaced. "According to the computer, we're facing five to seven thousand klicks. It's too far for any plane we can readily build without a foundry and other facilities that the hees couldn't help noticing."

Plane? Liberty smiled. They were thinking too modern. "Build a blimp."

The three of them turned to stare at her. "I'll be damned," Noel said. "Of course. How did you happen to think of that?"

She shrugged. "I read about them once." No sense bothering to explain that an outclassed claimer named Flug Zeppelin sent her to the library by coming in dead last. *"What a joke,"* an embittered bettor had snarled, *"naming a dog like this after a flying machine."* What flying machine?

she had wanted to know. "We could use the Habitent for the envelope."

The air-supported dome had been intended to provide communal living quarters the first weeks on Future, but they would not need it for that now, and the kevlar fibers in the plastic should make it a strong balloon.

Jaes's eyes went thoughtful. "I don't know that it would make a blimp large enough to move very many of us at a time, but it'd do for exploration. And maybe we could move out in small groups without arousing too much suspicion. We'd have to use hydrogen, of course, and that's a risk. Still . . ." He turned away, muttering to himself, forgetting the rest of them.

Dalyn stared after him for a moment, then turned to Liberty. "Did Ishda say when we're leaving?"

They left less than an hour later, giving Liberty and the men no time to locate their clothes in the hold. "My brother will provide clothing," Ishda said.

Jaes and Tsebe saw them off, wishing them a safe journey and a not-too-distant reunion at Swordwood. Rowers on the bank side of the boat pushed off, using their long-handled paddles as poles, then reached out over the rail to dig the paddle blades deep into the water and put the boat into forward motion. Jaes and Tsebe stayed on the bank waving to them.

"She's very friendly," Liberty remarked.

"Of course," Ishda said. "Interpreting for you will win her the breeding right, and allow her to satisfy Conscription early and more pleasantly than on some road or canal repair crew. Most of all, though, it brings great honor to her house."

She eyed him. "Honor is important to your people, isn't it?"

"House even more so."

Oh, yes. He had made the commando raid for his house,

he claimed. And done what else for it? Arranged Tasat's disgrace? She bit back the question on her tongue: *What are you, your brother's hatchet man?*

The boat moved farther up-river with every dip of the paddles. Liberty continued to look back. Now why did her throat feel so tight? Beyond Tsebe and Jaes's shrinking figures, the striped tents circling the flattened cylinder of the *Invictus* looked almost carnival-like. Across the river, new smoke rose from the ruin of the A-thin-wet camp, a funeral pyre this time. "Will this put Tasat out of favor again?"

"All three generals may spend the rest of their careers commanding village garrisons in obscure provinces. I saw Tasat riding south with two aides shortly after he delivered his threat, presumably to explain his failure to Nui-kopa."

A bend in the river hid both camps, but Liberty felt oddly reluctant to leave the stern.

On her other side, Dalyn cleared his throat. "I never thought I'd be sorry to see the last of that crate."

Suddenly Liberty understood her feelings. Even cursed and hated, the ship was a link to Earth . . . to her mother, her great-grandfather, to Harry and Summer Citadel and the other horses in her care for the past ten years. Now it was gone. Looking over her shoulder at the line of broad, inhuman bodies along each side of the boat, she realized just how very far away, how irretrievable, Earth had become.

Angrily, she wiped her eyes. No, she would *not* be homesick! Instead, she forced herself to study the boat.

Except for a sharper prow, it seemed basically like all the other low, broad, shallow-draft barges she saw hauling freight and passengers. An open cabin occupied most of the deck, leaving only a narrow strip between it and the straw-hatted sailors kneeling at the gunwales with their paddles. The roof of the cabin provided not only shade but storage space and a lookout point for guards.

The sailors interested her more than the boat, though.

That paddling style, stretching far out and down with each stroke, looked exhausting. The sweep of oars in rowing would probably interfere with other river traffic, however. "How long can they paddle like this, Lord Ishda?"

"All day," he replied. "Once we're under way, only half will paddle at a time unless we have a strong current, and if we should pick up a good tail wind, we'll step the mast and use the sail." He pointed at a long shaft lashed to the cabin roof.

Then the river bent again and Liberty forgot even the sailors in her first sight of a heest town.

A long pier followed the riverbank, mooring barges and a myriad smaller reed boats. Hees crowded the quay: peasants in the familiar flat-crowned straw hats, vests, and wraparound trousers; leather-armored soldiers; other hees more richly dressed, presumably merchants. One drove a two-wheeled trap pulled by a team of white, brown-striped dxee. Beyond rose the gray stone walls of the village. They looked no higher than those of a two-story house, but the outer surface had a glassy smoothness. Traffic streamed in and out through a single entrance, beneath inner and outer portcullis-like gates. Liberty could see little of the village itself except what looked like a large open space inside the gates, where she caught a glimpse of stalls as in a market. Beyond another wall farther inside rose the tops of house walls, and thick hedge planted on them. From her distance, the hedge looked similar to the thorny brush growing on the side of the bluffs. Did all that security indicate that bandits were really as big a danger as Tsebe claimed?

While she studied the village, hees—peasants, soldiers, and merchants—stared back open-mouthed. She waved at them.

They passed more villages in the course of the day, all alike, on both sides of the river and, as the hills lowered into gently rolling land, scattered across the crazy quilt of fields. They lay close together, no more than five or ten kilometers apart, but all very small, too, housing no more than a few hundred people each, surely.

The heat of the sun and monotony of the scenery soon drove the humans into the shade of the cabin.

"This promises to be a very boring trip," Noel complained.

"Perhaps Liberty can teach us the language. We won't be much good as eyes and ears unless we understand what we're hearing." Dalyn lifted a brow at her.

He had a point. "You'd do better learning it from a hees, though," Liberty said. "I still can't pronounce the words right. Let me talk to Ishda."

The envoy sat in the bow, chin resting on forearms folded on the gunwale, the remote, opaque gaze directed out across the peasant-dotted fields. Nearer peasants looked up from hoeing to stare back at the Emperor's boat.

"If you're bored, I have a cure," Liberty said.

He sent an eye around toward her. "I'm not bored. I enjoy the peace of travel. There is time to contemplate the beauty of the land and to reflect on the lessons it teaches us through the philosophers and poets."

Liberty raised her brows. A philosophical hatchet man? "What lessons?"

"Humility, for one. Look at them." He gestured at the peasants. "In the words of the Third Dynasty poet Bue-Pe: *'The laboring keepers bent over their hoes amid the greens of life . . . earth-colored, immutable, like growths sprung from the immortal soil.'* These are the true rulers of the Empire, not the nobles. They built canals to create farmland that would end the great famines, but these people husband the land. It belongs to them, not to the holders. Nobles are as transient as this boat passing their field of vision. These stand *'watching splendor pass.'* What conceits the nobles entertain of their own importance."

The nobles, they . . . apart from him. How did Ishda,

raised in a palace, come to stand outside of his own kind?
Liberty sucked on her lower lip.

Abruptly, the colorless eyes turned to focus on her.
"What cure do you propose for boredom?"

She shoved aside her questions. "My companions want
to learn Akansh."

He blinked, a lazy, feline gesture. "Of course . . . if
you teach me your languge in return."

They convened in the shade of the forward part of the
cabin. Ishda and the men attacked the lesson with enthus-
iasm, but Liberty quickly discovered that she had difficulty
concentrating on such elementary vocabulary, especially
when full of lunch. The heat and gravity dragged at her,
too. Perspiration beaded her forehead and neck and trickled down her chest and sides under her romper.

On both sides, heest arms rose and fell in perfect unison,
accompanied by the creak of wood and plash of paddles in
water. The shore slipped steadily past. Clouds of insects
hovered over the glittering water in buzzing swarms. In
counterpoint, a shrill babble of voices reached them from
passing boats and villages. Fivedice dice clicked in the
rear of the cabin. That sound made the belt of money
pieces around Liberty's waist itch, but for the most part,
the hypnotic rhythms wrapped her in a thick cocoon of
lethargy which she made little effort to resist.

Yawning, she wondered if introducing the hees to sies-
tas fell within cultural interference.

As the afternoon waned, the river traffic lightened, until
by sunset, they remained alone on the water. People vanished from the village quays and gates dropped shut. But
with the twilight came a stiffening breeze and the sailors
raced to step the mast and secure it by lines lashed to the
gunwales. The blue and white sail snapped, filling with the
breeze as it rose into place, adding the creak of rigging and

hiss of water slipping past the hull to the sounds around them.

Eating supper of grain cakes, fruit, and vegetables by the light of a flickering lamp, Noel sat back on his cushions with a contented sigh. "Maybe I could become very fond of this trip after all."

"Do we keep going all night?" Liberty asked Ishda.

"Until midnight, when the moon sets. After that—"

A shrill whistle of alarm overhead interrupted him. One look ahead told Liberty the reason for it, and brought her to her feet along with everyone. A broad shape sprawled across the channel just around the next bend, a barge run aground on a sand bar. Loincloth-clad sailors pried and pushed at it.

Imperial sailors were racing for lines even before their captain started shouting orders. The sail dropped to the deck in a rattle of canvas and halyards. Seconds later, sailors snatched up paddles and leaned over the gunwales to plunge them into the water. As they paddled furiously, the helmsman hauled at her tiller. Slowly, the boat changed course, crawling for the far side of the channel . . . but not soon enough.

Without warning, the barge came free of the sand bar, dragging some of its sailors into the river. Others were left on shore to watch helplessly as the current caught the vessel and carried it straight for the imperial boat. The crew still aboard seemed paralyzed by surprise. They stood frozen, staring into the narrowing gap between boat and barge.

Hees could forgo ritual and politeness, Liberty discovered. Nothing remained of either in the accusations of mental incapacity and miserable quality of hides that both soldiers and sailors hurled at the other crew. The sailors paddled even harder, but in vain. Inexorably, the two vessels drifted broadside toward each other.

Liberty joined the verbal abuse. "Those squashbrains! What the hell's the matter with them?"

Finally the trance broke. The other crew bent down for their paddles. No, not paddles! Liberty's breath caught. Even in the fading light she could tell the difference between a paddle and a bow.

"*Ishda!*" she shouted.

But he had seen, too. "Major! Pilgrim tanners! Arms!"

The soldiers dived for weapons and shields just as a hail of arrows arched between barge and boat.

Sailors dropped behind the gunwales and Ishda pushed the humans flat on the deck. Soldiers leaped to build a wall with their shields. Not before arrows struck several sailors, however, including the helmsman. Two soldiers dragged her groaning into the aft part of the cabin while a sailor crawled out to take the tiller. A second flight of arrows almost hit her, too.

"Pilgrim tanners?" Liberty asked from the deck.

Ishda picked up a sword. "Bandits."

"Maybe I don't care for their lazy river cruises, after all," Noel murmured.

A third flight of arrows came in, but this time the soldiers returned fire from behind the shield wall of their sisters. Screams told Liberty that at least a few of the imperial arrows had found targets. How long could they go on shooting arrows, though? Soon boat and barge must collide. Then the battle would become hand-to-hand.

"Dalyn, do you still have your habit?"

Grinning, he reached behind his back to bring out the pistol.

Noel swore. "Have you gone brainbent, bringing that cannon along?"

"It's for medicinal purposes," Dalyn replied calmly. "A .45 lead slug administered intracardially to a hostile entity keeps me healthy."

A wrenching jar shook the boat. Wood ground scream-ing against wood.

"Swords!" the major commanding the soldiers shouted.

Bows and arrows dropped aside. The soldiers, Ishda among them, surged forward to meet the bandits at the gunwale with swinging blades.

Liberty scrambled to her feet, heart pounding, and snatched up a paddle. She hefted it, testing the weight while she braced for the first bandit that might break through the soldiers' line.

Dalyn thumbed off his gun's safety. "Will someone watch what happens to my brass? I want it for reloads."

Liberty had a succinct suggestion regarding his reloads.

She sensed rather than saw or heard the movement behind her. Spinning, Liberty found a dozen bandits slip-ping silently out of the river and over the gunwale. Hoods covered their faces.

Years ago, her great-grandfather had once said: *In fight-ing any enemy, you must convince him you are fearless, even insane, that nothing, not even mortal wounds, can stop you.* She stared at the bandits, then charged howling, swinging her paddle at the nearest form.

The blow caught him across his nasal bulge. Bone crunched audibly. He screamed and dropped his sword to clutch at his face, blood pouring from his nostrils. Without pausing, Liberty turned to drive the end of the paddle into the stomach of a second bandit, then club him over the head as he doubled in pain.

In the edge of her vision, Dalyn dodged a sword and smashed his gun barrel down on a hooded head. Noel swooped in to grab the first bandit's fallen sword and engage yet another boarder. Liberty lost track of him while she blocked a bandit's blade with her paddle, then he moved back into her field of vision, hacking away with more energy and determination than technique.

She and her own opponent had a stalemate . . . at least

as long as her paddle lasted. The bandit used such a limited repertoire of moves, forehand and backhand slashes, principally. Recalling that battle the day they landed, Liberty realized that with the addition of some variations in wrist motion, all hees fought that way, ignoring the lunges that would use the point of the sword.

"Go for his gut, Noel!" she yelled. "Stab him!"

Noel promptly lunged. The blade sank deep into the bandit and withdrew in a spray of blood. The bandit stood swaying and clutching at his abdomen, staring down open-mouthed at the crimson fountain spurting between his fingers.

Liberty never saw him fall. Her paddle splintered under her opponent's sword. Catching the blade end, she threw it into the bandit's face, and when he flung his head to avoid it, drove the jagged remains of the handle under his sword toward his stomach. But she never reached him. Her foot slipped in blood on the deck, sending her sprawling. With visions of the bandit's sword above her prone body, Liberty tried to roll away.

A forest of legs blocked her . . . heest ankles thick as young trees, booted soldiers, barefoot sailors and bandits, and human legs, looking spindly as birds' by comparison. She reached for the latter.

Hands grabbed her by the collar and seat of her romper and lifted upward. A brief hope that she was being helped by a sailor died as she found herself hoisted high into the air above a hooded face. Spitting, she began kicking and clawing, but the bandit swung her as though she weighed nothing and let go at full extension. Liberty sailed out over the heads of hees and humans toward the river. She had just time to cut off her yell of angry surprise before plunging into the icy water. By the time she clawed her way back to the surface, she had been swept half a kilometer downstream.

"My lord, please, may I assist you?" a female heest voice called.

She turned in the water to see a man and woman in peasant dress poling their reed boat across the current toward her. Kneeling, the woman extended a hand. "Give me your hand, my lord."

But Liberty made two observations, that the woman did not stare at her and that even now with the sun down, the man still wore a hat pulled so low that his face existed only as a shadowy blur beneath it. In retrospect she realized that the boarding pirates exhibited no surprise at seeing humans, either. Her mind raced, exploring the disquieting possibilities.

She reached up for the "peasant" woman's hand, but also made sure she had a firm grip on a reed bundle with her other hand and her knees braced against it from the underside. As their fingers locked, Liberty jerked. The woman tumbled into the water with a startled yelp and Liberty swam furiously for the nearest bank.

To no surprise, the bandit male followed. So did the female, but the current had already carried her far enough that she posed no threat. The boat, however, gained steadily, until Liberty felt the reed bundles brush her shoulder and a hand grab her collar.

She made no attempt to repeat her trick with the woman, but let himself be hauled into the boat and forced to her knees, describing the man with the choicest epithets from every language she knew.

"And you are *ugazh*," the bandit said, "you and His Imperial Highness Ishda." He leaned on his pole with one hand, anchoring the boat in place, and held her with an arm across her throat. Bristles bit into her skin, painful as thorns. "If that word has been omitted from your education, in my language it means one so revolting and worthless that even the hide is left to rot with the rest of the carcass."

His voice confirmed all her suspicions. She strained experimentally against his arm, but stopped, grimacing at the pain the bristles brought. "How can I be *ugazh* when delivering me to Nui-kopa will restore your lost favor, General Tasat?"

He did not reply for a minute, but when he spoke, he voice had become thoughtful. "Perhaps you're right, but for different reasons than you think. With you in my possession, why do I need to care about that usurping peasant? You will tell *me* where you find all your metal and how you make the weapons that kill even u-tse, then I can restore nobility to the throne."

Her lip curled. "You mean, you'll become King?"

"Not me. I am a soldier, not a King, but my house will rule. My brother Min would make a good King." His body twisted, as though he turned to look up-river. "Ah, the skirmish seems to have ended, and since neither of your women has appeared, I must assume my fighters could not manage to throw them into the water, too."

Now that he mentioned it, she did notice the absence of yelling and the crack of swords crossing. "God's good to my side."

"To mine. You're all I need." Still holding her, he began to pole one-handed toward shore.

Cautiously, moving her arms as little as possible, Liberty eased open the pressclose flap of her romper at the waist and found the ends of her money belt. Untying them, she slid the string out and wrapped it around her right hand.

Tasat did not hold her throat with a constant pressure now. It loosed and tightened as he worked his pole. She waited, feeling the rhythm of the sequence until she could anticipate it. Then as a looser phase came, she suddenly grabbed his elbow and wrist. Pulling down on the wrist, pushing up on the elbow, and gritting her teeth against the bristles scraping across her face, she slid free of his arm.

Kneeling on the boat restricted movement, but as his arm fell away and before he could react she pivoted her upper body to smash the money-wrapped hand sideways with all her wiry strength, straight into his throat.

"The problem is keeping possession of me, frogface."

He fell backwards, choking. Liberty grabbed the sash of his trousers barely in time to keep him from falling into the river, and the pole just before the boat swept away in the current. Ishda would want to see this prize.

Tasat thrashed, clawing at his throat, gasping and gurgling. Liberty frowned. Could he be seriously hurt? Even as she wondered, he went limp and the terrible rasping faded. Gut knotting, she felt his throat. No pulse moved beneath her fingers.

"Damn," she whispered. She had not intended to hit him that hard, just hurt him a little. He did not deserve to die, surely. His ambition had been for his family, not himself. He might even have been thinking of his kingdom's welfare.

"Liberty!" Noel's voice called from upstream. *"Liberty, is that you down there in the reed boat?"*

She looked up. "Yes!"

"All is forgiven. Please come home."

With a last glance at Tasat, she sighed and began poling upstream.

She found both the barge and imperial boat lodged on another sand bar. Lamps hung on the cabin cast a flickering light on Noel's rusty hair as he reached over the gunwale to help her aboard.

"Are you all right?"

She nodded.

A sailor dragged Tasat's body aboard. Shouldering it, she led the way across to the barge, where she laid it with a row of bandit bodies on the deck. None had bullet holes in them, Liberty noticed. She eyed Dalyn. He must have confined himself to pistol-whipping.

Ishda bent over Tasat's body with nostrils flaring. "This explains everything. In my prayers I must ask my ancestors to congratulate the general on the speed with which he organized this ambush."

"What are they, soldiers?" Liberty asked, gesturing at the bodies.

He fixed an eye on her, scalp furrowing. "A-thin-wet soldiers would not allow themselves to be ordered into such an attack any more than Gthe-get or imperial soldiers. These are all convicts. See the ears." He pointed to notches cut in the lower edges of ears on both dead bandits on the deck and a group of living ones surrounded by soldiers. "Where did the general acquire you?" he asked the group. "You must have known from the beginning that failing at this ambush would extend your sentences to a lifetime. How did Tasat convince you to participate? Threats? Or did he perhaps promise pardons if you succeeded?"

Inside their circle of guards, the bandits stared at the deck in silence.

The sailor captain crossed his arms over his chest. "My lord, may we begin freeing ourselves from the sand bar now?"

Ishda lifted his chin. "Please, but be sure the barge is secured to us so we can tow it to Se-a-dath'." As the captain turned away, he again stared at the bodies.

Tasat's corpse held Liberty, too, the sounds of his death echoing in her head.

Dalyn said softly, "Killing someone with your hands isn't quite the same as shooting them from fifty or a hundred meters away, is it?"

Damn. Had she become transparent to everyone now? But looking up at him, she saw a shadow haunting the amber eyes and she knew his understanding came from some similar personal experience. Irritation faded. "No, it isn't," she agreed.

Ishda drew his sword. Lamplight gleamed on the metal as it chopped down through Tasat's neck.

Liberty winced. "What are you doing?"

He glanced a pale eye toward her. "We still have nearly thricefive days before we reach Ku-wen, at least half of them on the border of A-thin-we. By using the general for one last task, I hope to make those days safer ones."

Chapter Six

Se-a-dath' must be an important village, Liberty decided. Not only did it look twice as large as most she had seen but two gates pierced its walls. One opened onto the river quay as usual. The other faced west toward two broad strips of water coming together at the river from the southwest and southeast. Canals, obviously. Stone facing lined their sides and they lay so still the moonlight turned them to ribbons of polished silver.

"The Stream-Of-Life and Blood-Of-the-Land Canals," Ishda said. Pride echoed in his voice. "Before them and before the Thim Dynasty, all the land south for many marches was once barren desert." During the voyage upriver from the ambush point, he had changed from camp clothes back into his court finery and for the moment looked and sounded very much as Liberty imagined a son of the imperial house should.

Moonlight also reflected off the polished helmets of soldiers watching them from the village walls as the sailors moored the boat and barge in empty spaces on the quay. One called what Liberty presumed must be a challenge, though the Polite or Deferential forms prevented her understanding most of it. Polite, probably, superior-to-inferior until rank was established.

Definitely Polite. The major replied in the same mode

and Liberty understood most of his speech. "His Imperial Highness the Lord E-do-ishda of the house of Th'da-sha-Thim requests the attendance of his boat of the commander of your garrison."

A helmet vanished from the wall. Minutes later the gates creaked upward one at a time, the inner lowering before the outer raised, and a soldier emerged wearing a light blue collar on his shirt. Stepping onto the boat past the guards, he stopped before Ishda with arms crossed over his chest. "God's good to you, my—" He broke off, staring in astonishment at the humans behind Ishda.

"With all respect, lieutenant," Ishda said, "I asked to see your commander. Surely a garrison this size is not commanded by a mere lieutenant."

The lieutenant looked back at Ishda. "Of—of course not, my lord. But I am the duty officer." And eye slid toward Liberty. "If you please, Major Ke-teke is asleep."

"I do not please. Wake him."

The lieutenant stiffened, eyes widening. The words cracked like a rifle shot in Liberty's ears. She could just imagine how shockingly terse they must sound to a hees. They brought results, though.

"At once, my lord."

The lieutenant spun and hurried back across the quay.

Major Ke-teke appeared within minutes, still buttoning the rose quartz studs on the scarlet collar of his dress shirt as he ducked under the outer gate.

"Bring him to the barge," Ishda told the guards, and headed aft to leap across to the barge himself, beckoning to the humans to follow.

When the garrison commander presented himself, Ishda interrupted the formalities to point to the captive and dead bandits. "These persons used this barge to attack my boat three hikes downstream. Do you know any of them?"

The major's coppery eyes snapped wide. *"Attack you!* My lord, I—are you certain?"

Silently, Ishda untied the cuff of one sleeve and pushed the material up to show a bandage on his upper arm. "I do not call this a friendly gesture, major. You know these persons and this barge, then."

The major's scalp twitched. "The barge belongs to the house of Hnu-xo-Shao, but these persons aren't Shaos; they're all convicts."

"I had observed that already, major," Ishda said dryly. Liberty watched in fascination while he one-handedly re-tied the sleeve cuff in a bow knot. "Do you have a work gang in the area?"

The major's stare slid to Tasat's headless body. "It is impossible that these could be any of that group. They are all five hikes down the Blood Canal dredging it and refacing the sides."

"Sergeant." Ishda beckoned to a soldier.

The sergeant unfolded the hide bundle she carried to reveal Tasat's head. The major froze.

"He commanded the bandits," Ishda said. "Now, did General Tasat have custody of the convicts today?"

The major sighed. "He did. He arrived on a post mount in great haste about noon and presented authorization allowing him to take custody of the work gang. But I cannot believe he would use them for banditry, my lord. General Tasat is one of our most capable and honorable—"

"The general has suffered an unfortunate character change, it appears. Don't forget the scandal with General Te's wife. I don't suppose you still have that authorization for the convicts? It's probably forged."

The major blinked. "Ah. That would be why the general insisted on keeping it." He sighed again. "What a tragedy to see such a fine officer become a renegade. How I pity his house their disgrace. I'll call my soldiers to take over your prisoners, and record the identities of those killed before you skin them out."

"The dead convicts you may take, too, major, and the

bodies of my own soldiers, though we will keep their armor. We don't have the time or facilities to deal with hides.''

The major crossed his arms over his chest. "You are most generous. What of—'' He nodded toward Tasat's head.

"I wish you to send that to King Nui-kopa by fast messenger.'' Ishda's eyes caught the lamplight with the chilly glitter of sunlit ice. "Let it be known that it comes from the Emperor's envoy, so that all may see how the Emperor deals with those who molest his guests.''

The major glanced past Ishda at the humans. "His Imperial Highness is a conscientious host. The messenger will leave tonight, my lord.''

Taking the wrapped head from the sergeant, he left the barge.

Liberty moved up, frowning, beside Ishda. "We don't surprise him. Tasat must have told him about us and maybe even what he planned to do with the convicts.''

A pale eye rayed toward her. "I assumed that from the beginning. How else could Tasat have obtained custody of the convicts? Of course there was no authorization for them, forged or otherwise. Even if Nui-kopa had the fore-sight to consider it might be necessary, he would never trust any of his generals with a weapon that might be turned against him.''

"He trusted them to bring my people to him.''

"He trusted three mutually jealous generals to share that duty. Captain Ine,'' he called, "please release the barge and cast off whenever you're ready. Major Dxao, set up a double guard day and night from now until we reach Ku-wen.''

They leaped back to the imperial boat.

Liberty persisted. "Why did you give the major a way to make himself look innocent by suggesting that Tasat had forged an authorization?''

Sailors hurried to step the mast and hoist the sail. Ishda watched them while he sank onto a cushion in the cabin. "I saw nothing to be gained by accusing him of complicity."

Liberty pursed her lips. The reverse might also be the reason, that he gained something by not accusing the major . . . a hold over an A-thin-wet officer that might be useful sometime in the future.

Canvas snapped overhead, filling with the night wind, and the boat slipped away from the quay.

Once in the channel again, everyone except the soldiers and sailors on duty unrolled their sleeping pallets. Most quickly fell asleep. Noel and Dalyn lay whispering for a while, but eventually that stopped, too. Liberty, however, had never felt less like sleeping, despite her exhaustion. Tasat's face swam inside her closed eyelids, not the dead one, but as he had been when alive, talking about using her to depose Nui-kopa. She sat up on her pallet, hugging her knees. Jaes had been right about who would do the pushing on this world, only . . . it seemed more like a tug-of-war.

Her gaze wandered from the soldiers patrolling the deck and sailors tending the rigging and tiller to the brilliant half circle of moon just above the western horizon. Soon darkness would force them to stop for the night. Was mooring safe, or could someone else be out there waiting for that? Surely Ishda would not be sleeping if he considered that a possibility, though.

She turned her head to confirm his sleep . . . and found him sitting up watching her.

"Can you not sleep, stranger guest?" he whispered.

Her fears were none of his business. "I'm just following your suggestion to contemplate nature." Taking a deep breath, as though savoring the air, she discovered that it did smell nice, of green growing things and, more faintly, of licorice. The breeze felt cool, too. "I'm fascinated by the moon."

He rolled to his feet and stepped across Noel and Dalyn to sit on the end of her pallet. "The ancients believed the moon to be an egg laid by the great Uo on the Wall of the World, which the earth goddess Mio built to protect her children from the sea. The fire god Shada snatches it up as the sun passes his house, but it is blown from his hands by Ga-xe-ke, god of the air, and hangs in the sky growing until the mature fledgling eats its way out."

"The Uo must be a big bird."

"Presumably, though no one ever saw one. They were invisible. It was said that on a sunny day, though, the shadows sliding over the ground with nothing above to cast them meant an Uo had passed. They were believed to carry people away, sometimes to eat but other times for exciting adventures. When I was a boy at Swordwood, I wrote a poem about that." His eyes focused past her at the moon. " *'I dream of shadow wings,/Of unseen talons lifting me/Past bird and cloud/And sky-high rise of Mio's Wall/To the lands where Wonder dwells.'* "

Liberty stared. *He* wrote that? A poet, too. "That's nice. Is there more?"

His chin rose. "That's just the beginning. What are your people's moon myths?"

Her mind raced, even as she cursed herself for not expecting the question. The Man-In-the-Moon would not fit this cracked egg. Hastily, she gave him the first lie she thought of. "The magicians say a race of little green men live there mining metal, which they trade to our magicians for food and water. The lines are their roads."

"Miners." His scalp furrowed. "Is that all? Is there no poetry?"

He made that sound like a tragedy. "Of course there's poetry. I've just never had time to learn it." She had better find a way to end this line of conversation before it trapped her. Feigning a jaw-cracking yawn, she said, "My lord, may we continue this another time?"

He eyed her a moment, then lifted his chin. "Of course. I bid you a safe night and kind dreams, stranger guest."

He moved back to his own pallet and Liberty stretched out, but she still lay awake, watching Ishda through the lashes of half-closed eyes. The poetry echoed in her head. *I dream of shadow wings.* A hatchet man, philosopher, and poet. And what else? If all hees were that complex, learning about them might be harder than she thought. She might have to work.

They followed the Winding Water River east, but when it swung south, the boat continued on east on the Three Rivers Canal to the Shada's Blood Canal, where they turned south. All through the long, sultry days, Liberty studied with grim intensity, driving herself to absorb information as she had back on Earth when she snatched at the rare opportunities to sneak into a college lecture or spend a day in a library. If they were to understand the hees, every detail counted. She strained to observe and remember everything around her, from the number of canals to military routines, from common crops to the dress of various heest classes and professions.

Of course she drilled herself every waking minute on language. That was the key to everything else, especially language in its Familiar forms. Knowing those would let her eavesdrop on conversations. Their state of semi-alert had ended the Fivedice games, but she listened as she strolled the deck or swam with the crew after the boat anchored, and even when she sat pretending to wrap herself in solitude as Ishda did.

At first she might as well have been meditating, for all she understood, then one morning she woke from a dream of language lessons and sat hugging her knees in the cool of pre-dawn with excitement bubbling up through her. In the dream, she had found a key that let her understand every mode of Akansh. Now, if only she could remember the dream.

Jumping to her feet, she stepped over sleeping soldiers and sailors to the deck and padded forward along it to the bow. The dream . . . what had it been?

She might have been the only person in the world awake. The landscape had begun rising after they turned south and now hills loomed on either side of the canal slit, mist-wrapped, silent except for a few sleepy bird songs and the lap of water against the anchored hull and the canal's stone facing. Mist crossed the water, too. As the light brightened, the mist collected it into a radiance that made the canal look as though it were afire. For a moment, she forgot trying to remember the dream in a sudden memory of Earth, dew-jeweled dawns exercising Harry's horses, with fog shrouding the backstretch and the rising sun turning the steam of breath and sweat incandescent. She sighed. For all its faults, that life had had its fine moments, and certainly a comfortable, familiar pattern.

Liberty straightened. Pattern! Memory rushed at her. *That* was the dream! She bit back a war whoop. In the dream she had walked through a maze made up of heest vocabulary, only it was not a maze at all but a symmetrical design. For all Akansh's complexity, the prefixes, suffixes, and modifiers that differentiated Formal from Familiar and Deferential from Polite and Equals fell into a clean, predictable pattern!

Footsteps padded up behind her. "It is a memorable dawn, is it not? I'm told this is why the canal is called Shada's Blood. It burns at sunrise."

She smiled without turning around. "A memorable awakening indeed, my lord." Now all she needed was to try out this discovery.

The chance came later that morning when they encountered their first lock. The mechanism looked primitive, a water wheel on the high side that dumped water over the gate into the lock and was operated by a crew of husky women at the bars of a capstan-like post. It took a long time to fill the lock, though the hees accepted the wait without impatience. Clearing the forward part of the cabin, a group started sword practice while everyone else watched . . . all but a handful of soldiers who appeared more interested in the compound of the family maintaining the lock. Those hees nudged each other and pointed out the half dozen hides drying in stretching frames outside the compound walls.

"Ah. A few more bandits have found useful service."

The nostrils of the speaker's companions fluttered. Another soldier said, "They ought to make indestructible boots."

Still another tucked in her chin. "I think a sergeant's hide is tougher."

"If you please," the first soldier said, "you're both wrong. Without a doubt, the very toughest hide has to be from the headwoman of the house you marry into."

The group brayed in laughter.

Liberty grinned, too. The soldiers spoke only Familiar Equals, yet she understood every word.

The group's conversation went on, but Liberty switched her attention to others. She listened to soldiers evaluating the sword technique of various comrades. They admired Ishda, who danced agilely among the larger, slower women.

"That's why men make officers and women don't," one watcher sighed, and as Ishda came out of the group to give his place to another soldier, said, "You should have stayed in the imperial army, my lord. You would have made general even without being the Emperor's brother."

Liberty had been about to compliment his swordwork, too, but did not, stopped by the sudden freezing of his face. An eye watched south. "My brother had other uses for me, corporal."

The incident changed him. While Liberty enjoyed each

new day more because she understood the jokes the soldiers told, and their sly songs about tax collectors, bankers, and civil servants, he became increasingly withdrawn. The language lessons continued, but the poetry and pieces of heest literature disappeared from them and when not working with the humans on English or Akansh, Ishda sat alone, shutting out everyone. As though to match his mood, the weather turned rainy. Around the boat the contour-planted hillsides faded to dripping pastels in the drizzle.

Liberty could think of only one reason for the change, and it sent cold down her spine. They were approaching Ku-wen, and the Emperor. The corporal's remark reminded them of that. But if the Emperor inspired such depression in his own brother, what could he be like? Was he another Nui-kopa?

The boat turned east again on yet another intersecting canal and the sun broke through the clouds, casting double rainbows ahead of them.

"God welcomes the visitors to Ku-wen," someone said.

A few hours later activity rippled through the boat. Soldiers slipped into their armor. Sailors unstepped the mast and resumed paddling. Two cities appeared ahead, one on the north side of the canal, the other across the river that the canal joined. Liberty did not bother asking their names. A single glance at Ishda's shuttered eyes told her one had to be Ku-wen.

Chapter Seven

The imperial city. In the bow of the boat with Noel and Dalyn, Liberty pushed the sticky mass of her hair off her forehead and shaded her eyes against the now glaring sunlight. It did not look threatening from the outside. Both cities seemed very much alike, in fact; rusty-brown walls enclosing two broad hills each but looking more like walled forest because of the hedges atop each house. The river had been widened before both, too, and behind the protective breakwaters of the marinas moored boats of all sizes and shapes made an undulating carpet on the water. The only real difference lay at the top of each. Where the city on this side was crowned on one hill by rusty walls visible above the surrounding yellow-green, across the river the topping walls stretched from one hill through the shallow saddleback to the top of the other and glowed pearly gray in the sunlight. Blue-and-white pennants fluttered above it. The Imperial Palace looked peaceful, even beautiful.

Yet Liberty's gut still knotted. The Emperor waited there for them.

Ishda joined the humans in the bow. She did not see in him the anticipation she had heard in the soldiers and sailors. He still wore soldiers' camp clothes and he did not even look at the city; his eyes focused somewhere beyond it.

But perhaps dressing up would have been a waste, Liberty decided after they crossed the river and moored at the quay. No royal reception greeted them. To her disappointment, an emotion she discovered in herself with profound astonishment, nothing ceremonious happened at all. The soldiers simply gathered their weapons, slung the bag with their sleeping pallet and other belongings across their backs, and disembarked. Ishda picked up a bag of his own and urged the humans after the soldiers. They marched together through the nearest city gate with only the indifferent glances of locals on the quay to note their arrival. Liberty wondered whether anyone even saw her and the men among the soldiers.

Then disappointment evaporated in the satisfaction of finally seeing inside a heest town. No one with a straight-edge had laid out Ku-wen's streets. Liberty could never see more than a dozen meters ahead at any one time. Whether so narrow that someone with outstretched arms could almost touch both sides at once or just wide enough for two carts to pass each other, the streets all wound tortuously up the hill, intersecting with other streets and twisting around and between walls of stone, brick, or plaster. Of course thick, thorny hedge topped every wall.

Through the maze moved more people than she would have dreamed could live in a city this size. Peasants and artisans carried bundles or pushed wheelbarrows. Merchants and nobles rode or drove dxee, often accompanied by leashed axa or Great Dane-sized creatures Liberty had never seen before. Soldiers patrolled. Children followed many people; there seemed to be three or four for every adult.

And everyone, even nobles, pressed aside to let the imperial soldiers pass.

Scents filled the air, shifting as the people changed. She smelled licorice, naturally, but dozens of other odors, too, sweet or sour or spicy, all unknown and all tantalizing because of their mystery.

In her fascination with everything, they were halfway to the summit before she finally noticed that not a single building had windows. Instead, the spaces between the heavy gates had been chiseled into bas-reliefs or painted to make murals, some depicting battle scenes, others showing what looked suspiciously like manufactured products.

She touched the arm of a soldier. "What are the pictures?"

"Each glorifies the history or profession of the house," the soldier replied.

"My god . . . billboards infecting their culture already," Noel said with a grin when she translated for them.

Some of the walls had groupings of vertical and diagonal lines associated with the murals. Writing? Liberty sucked in her lower lip. That was something else she needed to learn.

The streets wound on and up, with gravity dragging at her and humidity bringing sweat rolling down her temples and sides, until, panting, she pitied any invading army that had to fight its way through this city.

Finally they reached the saddleback and the street opened into a plaza, a plain of varigated red and grey paving stones, barren except for a scattering of people and broad enough for six lanes of floatcar traffic. On the far side rose pearly-gray walls polished to glassy smoothness . . . the Imperial Palace.

Noel whistled. "When I was flying air taxi runs for G.R.M., I landed the chopper at some big houses, but none like this. I'm impressed."

So was Liberty. The plaza-belted walls stretching up and away from them to span the twin hilltops could have easily contained half a dozen villages.

Far up the hill to their right hees marched to and from the gateway there with the purposeful stride of people with important business. Those Liberty's group passed on the way to the central gate in the saddleback simply stood staring, however, faces rapt, eyes splayed—to see as much as possible at once?—obviously tourists. She would not have minded stopping for a minute just to look herself. The red and gray stone made a pattern she could not make out while on the move. But the soldiers pressed forward, chattering about baths, Fivedice, and a drink called *koem*. Never mind asking Ishda to stop; his face and eyes had the blankness of someone focused so completely inward that he was oblivious to everything external.

Guards at the open central gate stepped aside to let the group enter. Inside more bare paving spread before them, but smaller and unpatterned. It made a courtyard surrounded by arched doorways and filled with the unmistakable smell of stables. The soldiers peeled away through an arch to the left but Ishda continued straight ahead.

That arch opened into another maze, of courtyards instead of streets, one-story squares and rectangles with rooms opening into the loggia running around the edge of each. Sometimes the centers held millstones or tanning hides. Other courts had wells or tiny gardens with a pool surrounded by flowers, a bench or two, and interestingly shaped rocks and pieces of wood. A city within a city. It had the same density of people as the city outside, endless numbers of them in all manner of dress, from nothing but loincloths or livery-looking blue-and-white trousers and vests to military armor and stiff, lavishly embroidered court clothes. Especially, however, there were children . . . children everywhere in pairs and trios: toddlers tumbling naked in the sunlight or sleeping—three identical babies curled up against an axa among the animal's cubs—older children clumping along in miniature armor, others gathered in groups in the courtyards with adults who might be tutors. The palace seemed awash in children. Both they and the adults stared at the humans.

Dalyn murmured, "Someone needs to tell these people about contraception."

"I would speak with you, E-do-ishda," a voice behind them said in Polite Familiar.

Ishda spun around and crossed his arms over his chest. Liberty turned, too. A woman crossed the court toward them, elderly, judging by her seamed copper hide and limply dangling breasts, but walking with an erect carriage that matched the authority in her voice.

"God's good to you, my mother," Ishda said.

"And to you, my son." Eyes with the brilliance of emeralds studied the humans. An uncropped ear twitched. "You must be the guests my son Xa-hneem asked me to expect. I welcome you to the Imperial Palace. I am He-po-nio, house headwoman." She spoke to them in Polite Formal, but switched back to Polite Familiar as she cast an eye on Ishda. "Why do you bring guests and strangers through the servant and family courts?"

He answered with great deference. "It is the path to the guest courts from the stable gate, my mother."

Her nostrils flared and pinched. "You bring *guests* into the palace through the *stable gate*? God's evil. Xa-hneem was half-souled to ask that we— You dishonor them and shame this house, E-do-ishda."

Anger flared in Liberty. How could the headwoman talk to him that way in front of strangers? Maybe she thought they did not understand the language very well; even so, surely she saw that Ishda must be acting under orders from the Emperor.

Ishda made no attempt to explain or defend himself. To Liberty's annoyance, he virtually cringed. "I beg your forgiveness, my mother. I'll remove them from the family courts immediately."

She stood aside. "I have prepared a room in the Court of Lost Souls."

Beckoning to the humans, he strode past her down the loggia.

Court of Lost Souls? Liberty grimaced. That did not sound auspicious.

A short way farther on, Ishda opened a wooden grille. Beyond it lay a park, a vast expanse of yellow-green lawns surrounding an irregular oval of lake. Water fowl swam on the lake while others with brilliant plumage strolled the grass. One of a group of tall yellow and scarlet birds looking strikingly like ostriches followed them across the park, honking.

"Noisy bird," Liberty said.

Ishda shot one eye back toward the creature. "The greatlegs has never seen people shaped like itself before."

Dalyn must have understood part of the sentence. He nudged Noel. "Did you ever think someone would consider you skinny and knobby?"

Teeth flashed in the rusty beard. "Maybe these people aren't so bad after all."

The maze resumed on the far side of the park. They followed an arcade off of which more courtyards opened. Ishda stopped at one archway. "This will be your quarters, honored guests."

The Court of Lost Souls looked like many of the others. Its garden had a tree with a flat umbrella of silvery leaves that shaded a bench and a pool surrounded by copper-leafed groundcover and tall pieces of wood black as ebony and gnarled like Terran cyprus knees. A broad-shouldered woman with blue-and-white trousers and vest greeted them with arms over her chest, then slid back a door.

"This is the room He-po has ordered prepared, my lord. I am Adee, the servant assigned to attend our honored guests."

Servant? She looked more like the soldier women Ishda had brought to that first meeting.

"May I bring you tea or food, or perhaps you desire a bath?"

"They'll want a bath," Ishda said, "but first will you please show them the room? They are strangers to the Empire and don't know our ways."

The servantwoman crossed her arms over her chest again.

"I'll rejoin you in the bath," Ishda told Liberty.

After reporting to his brother, no doubt, Liberty reflected. She watched him march away down the loggia, then followed the servantwoman into the room.

Hees did not believe in over-decoration. The only furnishings were a covered urn in one corner—the night jar, Adee explained—stylized scroll paintings on the plastered walls, cushions spread on the bare wooden floor around a low table, and a dish with stones and flowers decorating a low chest against one wall. The chest held half a dozen rolled sleeping pallets. Liberty's brows rose. Six. Hees must like togetherness.

The room had no windows. Light came from the courtyard through a group of three floor-to-ceiling slots in the wall next to the door. A screen of woven grass sat where it could be pulled across the slots for darkness or privacy.

In her concentration on the room, she almost missed Adee's instructions for locking the door . . . a thick peg pushed into a hole in the floor behind the closed door.

"And what are those holes?" Dalyn asked, pointing to two in the track of the door.

Adee took them into the loggia and slid the door closed to show them how the holes matched with oblique notches cut in the bottom of the door. "It is traditional, honored guests, so that a house taking in strangers for the night may peg the door from the outside also."

Liberty translated and exchanged dubious glances with the men. So they could be locked in?

"But of course we do not do so in the Imperial Palace," Adee said.

That remained to be seen, of course.

"Shall I show you the bath, now, my lord and ladies?"

Dalyn sent Liberty a quick glance. "In a bath, they might guess we're not the sexes we claim to be."

Liberty smiled. "Who says they have to see us naked? We haven't taken our clothes off yet, not even to swim. Let's claim extreme modesty is a human custom."

Somehow, perhaps because the hees obviously enjoyed their swims during her stay at the Gthe-get camp and on the trip to Ku-wen, Liberty expected the bath to consist of a long, luxurious soak. The bathing room two courtyards away had a vat of hot water, but only for filling buckets. The rest of the bathing equipment consisted of cubelike stools in the center of the duckboard floor—to sit on while being soaped and rinsed—and tall benches around the edge. Liberty peeled off her romper and money belt under the cover of a sheet-sized towel and sat down on a soaping stool with the towel across her lap.

The soaping and rinse proved moderately pleasant, once she convinced Adee and the other attendants that their scrub brushes might be suitable for floors and heest hide but not human skin. Afterward, however, lying face down on a bench, reduced to boneless euphoria by Adee massaging licorice-scented oil into her skin, Liberty decided that the heest bath had much to recommend it.

"This is wonderful, Adee."

The servantwoman's nostrils flared. "Thank you, my lord. I learned from my mother, a talented healer. Daily massage keeps the body vital and healthy."

Far worse medical philosophies existed.

The door opened. Ishda slapped the edge and leaned in. "The Emperor wishes to see you."

Euphoria evaporated abruptly. So soon? She had expected a little more time to prepare. "Get dressed, ladies; we're being paged."

The men were already reaching for their clothes.

"He wishes to see you alone," Ishda said.

The men understood that sentence perfectly. Noel frowned. "Jaes said we're supposed to stay with Liberty wherever sh—"

"Noel!" Dalyn interrupted. "Remember, Liberty is a *man* and can look after himself. Would you like to take my habit along?" he asked in English.

She arched a brow at him as she wrapped in a towel to dress. "Tucked inconspicuously into my romper?" She shook her head. "I'll be fine without it."

Following Ishda down the loggias minutes later, however, she wondered if she really believed that. Where was Ishda taking her? She had expected the meeting to take place in the cold grandeur of a throne room but they were crossing the park into the family courts again. The court where they finally stopped looked nothing like a throne room. It had no grandeur, either, only quiet. Little sound but the buzz of insects disturbed the close, hot silence. The two people in the court, both adolescents, sat unspeaking on a bench in the center, shaded by a tree of such girth it had to be ancient. Perhaps as old as the palace?

Ishda slid back a door and motioned her through.

Even deeper silence enveloped them inside. Liberty felt almost deaf. At first she felt blind, too, but after a minute her eyes began adjusting to the dimness. Then she stared. The room was barren except for shelves, shelves lining the walls of the large room from end to end and floor to ceiling, and all filled with cups. The cups ranged in size and shape from large thimbles and shallow saucers to tulip-shaped vessels, while they appeared to be made of everything from wood and leather to stoneware and eggshell-thin porcelain. Cups. What had she heard about cups?

"Welcome to Ku-wen, stranger guest Ib-ih-tee," a voice said from the far end of the room.

Only then did she notice the figure standing there. The dark copper of his hide and his plain brown vest and trousers blended into the shadows. He crossed the room toward her and to her surprise, she saw the seamed hide of an aging man. His voice had sounded so rich and strong. As he came nearer, she saw that his eyes remained youthful, too, pearly green, focusing keenly on her.

"I am Thim-Xa-hneem, and this is a great honor," he said. "I have been eagerly awaiting this meeting since Kxa-Thi sent word of your arrival. Please, I beg you not to think me discourteous or disrespectful for receiving you here without ceremony."

The warmth of the voice set Liberty smiling in response. "Of course not."

"Actually, I do you honor. Almost no one beyond our house or servants ever enters this room. It is our house shrine." He moved over to the shelves and straightened a leather cup with writing inked on the side. "These are the name cups of my predecessors and other ancestors stretching back to the founding of the house of Th'da-sha-Thim pentaba years ago."

Liberty calculated quickly. If *ba*, their century equivalent, was a hundred-twenty-five years, then five *ba* meant six hundred-twenty-five years. She looked around again in awe. He knew over six hundred years' worth of ancestors? And she thought herself special for knowing her great-grandfather personally, and the names of another century of Potawatomie braves beyond him.

Xa-hneem breathed deeply. "I come here often, not just out of duty, to read my ancestors' names and remind them of their living existence, but to touch history."

Liberty felt it pressing around her, too. "How long has your family ruled?"

"This *house* of my family has ruled since its founding, when Thim-Kuo united the kingdoms." He touched a pink cone of a cup whose translucence gave it a luminous glow even in this light. "The Thim dynasty is the longest in recorded history. I take pride in that, and that our rule has been beneficial as well, not only building the canals and eliminating famine, but maintaining highways and an efficient postal system. Civilians and their property are no longer devastated by war. Those accomplishments require a coordination between kingdoms that would probably not be possible without a higher power than the Kings to oversee them.''

Considering Earth's history, Liberty tended to agree, but what was the point of this? Xa-hneem did not strike her as a man to ramble aimlessly.

The Emperor left the shelves to face her. ''Diplomacy is not a game that often permits total honesty, but my young brother thinks I should speak whole truth to you . . . even though you have not chosen to be honest with us.''

Her skin tightened all the way up her spine. ''What do you mean?''

''You let us assume you were the headman though my brother informs me you are neither. After that I can hardly trust your statements regarding who and what your people are.''

Liberty looked around at Ishda. ''What makes you think I'm not a man?''

Xa-hneem answered for him. ''In a crisis, surely any people saves its young and childbearers first, and of the normal adults, the smallest accompanied the children and ill adults in the evacuation carts. It is astonishing that females so small can bear children, but my young brother says that observation of the children indicates you must have singleton pregnancies.''

Had Ishda been figuring all that out while he stared at the river and quoted poetry? Liberty's gut knotted. How much else had he seen? She turned back to the Emperor. ''Yet you're still speaking to me instead of the men with me?''

His chin lifted. ''Why not, when you are obviously a person of courage and intelligence chosen by your leader to be his representative. Also, you speak our language better than your men do." He paused, then went on: "So, to speak plainly and honestly . . . I meet you here, amid history, so that you will understand why I must place certain restrictions on your people."

Liberty frowned. "I *don't* understand. They've done nothing against you. It's wrong to imprison them, even in protective custody."

"It is necessary for the preservation of the Empire. It is a sacrifice, I know, but duty requires sacrifices of us all." Xa-hneem cast an eye toward the silent Ishda. "The purpose of life is to learn, we are told, and my scholarly young brother would prefer to be pursuing that goal, for example, but I need his talents and so he leaves his libraries for the sake of his house. Since this is your new homeland, you have a duty to it, too."

She folded her arms. "How does imprisoning my people preserve the Empire?"

Xa-hneem sent a glance at Ishda, as though to say: *Are you sure this person is so intelligent?* Aloud, he said, "Stability is balance. The Kings must both adore and fear me, must like and dislike each other. The armies must maintain equal strength."

"Fine. Go on."

His scalp furrowed. "It is an endless, delicate task, requiring great skill, and sometimes covert manipulation." He paced away to the shelves again, reaching out to touch a wooden cup. "I regret what I must do, but what choice do I have when the metal and weapons your people bring into this society could plunge the Empire into the chaos of imbalance?" He turned to focus the pearly green eyes on her. "For the safety of my people, I must either become your keeper, or destroy you."

Despite the heat, goosebumps raised all over her body. Now she knew why Ishda had brought the imperial army to Gthe-ge. "Send us away."

A jeweled, pointed ear flicked. "Where? Or is it also untrue that you can't return to your homeland?"

Should she tell him about the north? Temptation prodded her. Caution pulled back harder, however. "We can't go home. That's absolutely true. But if we could find somewhere else, would you let us go?"

He regarded her steadily. "You are my guests. Enjoy the hospitality of the house. Tour the city if you like, taking along my brother and an escort to safeguard you, of course. Make use of the library. There is a formal lastmeal tonight, at which I look forward to seeing you. I've taken the liberty of ordering clothing altered to fit your party. Please honor me by accepting it as a gift."

"Would you let us go?" Liberty repeated.

He hesitated a moment before replying. "When you know of a place, ask me again."

He turned away and moved down the shelves in a rustle of clothing.

Ishda led Liberty out and back toward the guest courts. She sighed. So they could not depend on the Emperor to voluntarily release them. They had better keep preparing for an escape. At least they had somewhere to go and a means to take them there.

She glanced sideways at Ishda, walking stiff and silent beside her. "Do you like your brother?"

He cast a surprised eye toward her. "Xa-hneem has been Emperor since before I was born. He is like God. One does not like or dislike God."

Their concept of God combined both good and evil, she recalled. "Do you like working for him?"

"The question is meaningless. It is my duty to serve. It justifies my existence."

House before *everything*, even personal desires or needs, then. She must never forget that in dealing with hees.

They passed an archway guarded by a husky woman in yellow-and-green armor. A couple stood in the loggia beyond the archway. Liberty had just a glimpse in passing and might never have paid attention to a man in court clothes speaking with a women in blue-and-white servants' dress, except that for that glimpse, the woman's ear showed in sharp relief against her creamy-pale hide, an ear with its graceful crop marred by notches cut in the back edge. Liberty sucked in her lower lip, frowning. The Emperor used convicts as servants?

She opened her mouth to ask, but they had arrived back at her court and a more interesting question posed itself. "Why is it called the Court of Lost Souls?"

Ishda pointed to the knobby black pieces of wood around the pool. "Those come from a water forest in Gtheen, where legend says a certain village fell into disfavor with the earth goddess Dsa, a different religion from the Five where Mio is earth goddess, and were all turned into trees. If you look closely, you can see the villagers' faces in the grain."

Liberty noted that his stiffness eased as he spoke. He liked lecturing. That was something to remember, too.

Looking, she did see faces in the wood. They peered back at her when she bent close, tortured heest faces with wide-spaced, distorted eyes and screaming mouths. She grimaced. Enjoy the palace . . . with a convict servant in the next court and petrified faces howling in soundless horror outside her door?

Sighing, she went inside to tell the men about the meeting.

Chapter Eight

Liberty had to admire the speed of the palace seamstress, or tailor. The altered clothing arrived before the end of the afternoon. It fit remarkably well, too, which had to mean that among his other talents, Ishda also possessed a keen eye for distance. She knew of no one else who could have given the tailor human dimensions. Had he chosen the colors, too? Her, Noel, and Dalyn's vests and loose wrap-around trousers were brilliant red-orange, moss green, and aqua, respectively, complimenting their individual coloring.

"These are much cooler than our clothes," Noel had Liberty tell Ishda as the hees led them through the formal elegance of the State courts toward the dining hall.

And top-dink of any clothes Liberty had ever worn. She felt like a glad in them. On the other hand, softer material would have been nice. The embroidery and stiff collar rising high behind her head made the vest chafe. Though what she *really* needed was something to keep the vest closed in front.

Their entrance stopped all conversation. Around the room with its large circle of cushions and low tables, heest eyes snapped toward them. Liberty made sure she stood carefully erect, holding the vest against her sides with her upper arms.

Dalyn moved with a certain stiffness, too, but for a

113

different reason. His gun was strapped to his leg under his trousers, where someone going through their room would not find it.

A servant appeared in the doorway and clapped his hands sharply. "May it please the lords and ladies. His Most Imperial Highness, the Emperor Xa-hneem, comes." He sang on, reciting a string of titles and honorifics that more than made up for the afternoon's lack of ceremony. And it outdid any fanfare of trumpets. Liberty felt like shouting: "Hallelujah!"

At the servant's first cry, the assembly had rushed to form a line on each side of the doorway. Arms slapped across chests, except those of the house headwoman He-po and an elderly man beside her at the head of the line. The headman?

The Emperor appeared as the sound of his last title faded. Together with another man and two women, he moved down the lines speaking to everyone. He stopped before the humans. "I'm honored you wear the clothing. May I present another of my guests, a most honored ally, His Royal Majesty Hana-Kaem, King of Shapeen, and two of his wives, Hana-Nue and Hana-Ba-ta."

Liberty found herself facing the ruddy-hided man she had seen in the next court, looking into eyes the color of molten copper. The oval pupils dilated and his mouth worked soundlessly, astonishment obviously robbing him of words for a moment. Liberty jumped into the gap, grinning inwardly at the idea of an ex-stablegirl putting a King at ease. "It's a pleasure to meet you, Your Majesty. I enjoyed what I saw of your kingdom from the Three Rivers Canal."

The King managed to find his voice. "Our northern provinces and those around the Xapu Lakesea are even more beautiful." His nostrils flared. "You should visit them. Perhaps this autumn. The war with Gthe-ge will begin after the border fields are harvested and since Po-xan and I have planned it to include our entire common frontier, I can promise you wonderful fighting spectacle by day and evening entertainment by some of the leading acting troupes in the Empire."

Now Liberty stared speechless. *Planned* the war?

"Join us," Xa-hneem said, and continued on down the long line, introducing her and the men along with Kaem and the King's wives.

At first she tried to remember the names but as the stream of them passed . . . wives, brothers, sisters, mothers, fathers, elder sisters—any mature woman who had not won the breeding right, Ishda whispered—not to mention more of Kaem's entourage, nobles, and other non-house members of the court, Liberty stopped listening. Ishda dropped out somewhere along the way. She glanced back to see him in conversation with a middle-aged elder sister, and obviously enjoying what she had to say; his nostrils quivered, listening to her, and he brought her to sit beside him when they all took their places at the circle of tables. Liberty sat on one side of the Emperor while Kaem took the cushion to Xa-hneem's left.

She sat stiffly at first, but stopped caring about the vest's open front when the food arrived. One could not judge heest cooking by what she had eaten in the Gthe-get camp and on the boat, it became quickly apparent. This might have the same elements—fruits, half-raw vegetables, grain cakes—but cooked differently, and meat had been added. A servant even set a shallow cup of what looked like coffee beside that of the usual tea to wash it all down.

"*Koem*, my lord," the servant said.

Liberty almost strangled on the first swallow. Not coffee!

"Jesus. I didn't know you could make hundred-proof beer," Noel said.

Dalyn grinned. "It almost makes up for its being warm and flat."

Almost. Liberty savored it swallow by swallow and listened to Kaem's conversation with Xa-hneem.

"The money brought in by spectators will increase the profits even more for the provinces involved," the King was saying.

"I still wonder about involving the entire border." The Emperor's scalp furrowed. "The loser's forfeit would be smaller if the northern half fought this year and the southern half next year."

Kaem's eyes glittered. "I intend to collect that forfeit, not pay it out. You and your court should come, and bring the humans with you. I would be interested in hearing their ideas on battle strategy."

Would he now. Anger flared in her. Was that all Kings thought about when they saw humans—power?

A shrill whistle broke through her thoughts. He-po stood up at her place across the circle. "Honored guests, husbands, sons, daughters, and nobles. For your entertainment tonight we have a troupe from the Ha-bui-nu acting company, but before they begin, I take great pleasure in bringing "The Raising Of the Wall," as danced by members of this house, with my sons Zhu-diu, Hdeth, and Dth'is as Shada, Ga-xe-ke, and Bethee, and my daughters Shiu and Ibas as Mio and Kon-wa."

As with the dancing in camp, Liberty found the performance interesting without understanding the stylized moves. Presumably the group danced well. Tongues trilled around the circle and some hees held up hands with the fingers folded, leaving the thumbs extended. She had a better appreciation of the tumbling and juggling which followed. A pantomimed play ended the display, narrated by a member of the troupe. From the trills that greeted the announcement of the title, Liberty gathered that "The Census-taker's Night" must be a popular classic.

It began with a young census-taker caught by night

between villages and seeking a bed at a private family compound.

"Do you wish more beer, my lord?" a voice murmured in her ear.

"Pl—" She broke off as the servantman leaned over her. His uncropped ears unfolded to reveal notches cut in the edge. "Please," she finished, and stared after him as he moved on around the circle. Another convict.

A muffled flutter of nostrils brought her attention back to the play. One after another, three generations of the house's wives were slapping on the guest room door, begging admittance to bring water or check the night jar. But once inside, each in turn pounced on the weary census-taker. The stylized depiction of heest sex struck her as more educational than comic, but she watched fascinated. Half the jokes the soldiers told dealt with adultery, too, she recalled.

"How often does something like this happen?" she whispered to Xa-hneem.

"Only in jokes and plays," he replied.

Beyond the actors, the convict refilled He-po's beer cup. Liberty eyed him. "Is using convicts as servants customary?"

Xa-hneem's scalp furrowed, distorting the designs painted on it. "Convicts? You mean Kud? He isn't a convict. See how the notches are on the rear of the ear, not the bottom? Misfortunately, he is *hes-gena*."

She had never heard the term before. "What's that?"

The furrows in the Emperor's scalp deepened. "It is— there are no other words that mean the same. It refers to one without a house, but because that house was betrayed from within and in betrayal, destroyed, even to its ancestors. It is one who has ceased to be a person and become property."

Property? Liberty stiffened. "You mean . . . you *own* that man?" A slave! Revulsion flooded her.

"Of course. Being the imperial house does not exempt us from moral responsibility. Ah. Watch. It is the next morning. Here comes the final joke." His eyes focused on the play again.

Moral responsibility! How the hell was owning slaves morally responsible? "Your Highness—"

But his attention was entirely on the actors, where the young civil servant rode away and the headman exclaimed in admiration over the census-taker's knowledge of the number of married women in the house without appearing to count them.

The narrator said, "But the headman shakes his head, too, for the young man seems so tired. As he says to his wives, daughters, and granddaughters, 'I had no idea census-taking was such hard work.' "

The dining hall erupted into a deafening trilling of tongues. Courtiers thrust out both hands, all four thumbs extended.

"Superbly witty," Xa-hneem said. "The Ha-bui-nu never disappoints me."

Liberty could think of nothing but the slave. Urgently, she began, "Your Highness, about the *hes-gena*, the slaves—"

A pearly green eye swung toward her. "We can speak tomorrow, honored guest." Standing, he formally and lengthily thanked everyone responsible for the entertainment, then started around the table personally wishing everyone good night.

Liberty swore under her breath.

"What's wrong?" Dalyn asked.

She told him.

Noel sighed. "Well, there's no sense getting upset. We can't do anything."

"We can try. Ishda." She started around the men to where Ishda still talked with the elder sister.

Dalyn caught her arm. "This isn't the time to climb on your free person soapbox," he hissed.

She jerked her arm free. "Don't touch me with anything you don't want to lose, leo!"

Ishda turned around. "Is there a problem?"

"No problem," Liberty said quickly. For of course Dalyn was right. She was supposed to be observing and learning, not interfering. "Will you take us back to our court?"

He spoke briefly to the elder sister, then led them out of the dining hall. Back at the Court of Lost Souls the servant who greeted them was not Adee, but another woman with cream-colored hide and slave-notched ears. Liberty sucked in her lower lip. How many did Xa-hneem own?

The slavewoman crossed her arms over her chest. "I am Xtas. A cart struck one of Adee's fathers in the streets tonight and He-po sent her to help her mothers tend him. If you will come in, I have tea for you. It will prevent morning misery from the beer."

Liberty eyed her. "How did you become a slave?"

Noel groaned. Dalyn glared. Even Ishda started.

"I'm just asking," she told them in English, widening her eyes innocently.

"It was God's evil, my lord," Xtas replied. She sounded eager to talk about it. "True, my father slew a guest in our house, but that person abused our hospitality by seducing one of my mothers. It was unjust to condemn my father to labor for that and sell the rest of the house."

Ishda sighed. "Xtas, when a woman unpegs the guest room door and begs admittance, the man is not the seducer, and your father did not even challenge the man to a duel, just cut his throat on the pallet. His house was certainly entitled to be indemnified for the loss of him. Now, please attend your charges and do not disturb their peace by dwelling on the tragedies of the past."

Xtas's scalp furrowed. "I shouldn't have gone to the block. In four more days I would have been married. I was leaving the house. It wasn't fair to sell me, too."

Liberty's sympathy withered before the self-pitying whine. She stared, shocked. "You don't care what happened to the rest of your house?" So not everyone was as devoted as Ishda.

His nostrils pinched. "I beg your forgiveness for her, honored guests. Xtas, you will please—"

"You." Teeth bared in the lamplight. "Fine nobleman with your luxury and power. I'd like to see how you would react if evil ever touched you!"

He stiffened as though stabbed and his eyes hardened to ice. "Slaves' Rights protect you from abuse; they don't permit you to inflict it. Tend to your duties and say nothing more of the past or I will report every word of this to He-po."

Xtas glared at him, then flung away into the room. "The tea waits."

Ishda looked after her a moment, then flicked an eye toward Liberty. "Please come with me. We're only going to walk on the wall," he added as Dalyn frowned.

"I'll be all right," Liberty said, and followed Ishda out of the court.

He said nothing as they wound through the courtyards and climbed a set of deep-tread/shallow-riser steps to the top of the wall, except to greet hees they met and acknowledged the crossed arms of a guard on the wall. Beyond the shoulder-high battlement the oval moon slipping west turned the countryside silver and ebony. A gentle night wind brought a medly of scents and the distant whoop of a ha-gho-wu.

Liberty started to take a deep breath, but it turned to a gasp as the wall shrugged beneath her. Light danced across the patterned stones of the plaza as the lamps outside the wall swung. "Damn. Ishda, what are the chances of one of these knocking down the palace?"

His nostrils quivered. "It is written in the plaza."

"What?" But leaning out on the wall she saw what he

meant. The pattern, clearly visible from the wall, made groups of vertical and oblique lines . . . heest letters, repeated over and over down the plaza. "What does it say?"

" 'Glory lasts but a breath.' "

She grimaced. How reassuring. "That sounds like something the venerable Pe would write." But what an interesting message to meet the Emperor's eyes each time he looked out over his domain.

"You recognize the style?" He sounded pleased. Then his voice went somber. "Why did you ask Xtas that question?"

She might as well answer. "I wanted to know about slavery. Among my people it's considered an abomination. Why do you have it?"

He turned one eye toward her and another toward the guard down the wall, then looked out over the city, hidden beneath its walltop hedges. "How else are we to raise compensation for the houses of murder victims?"

"You could just sell off property."

He turned toward her. "And leave the house homeless, to become beggars, or bandits? We are not so cruel. What do your people do about killers and compensating the victim's house?"

Liberty began to wish she had not brought up the subject. "We imprison or execute the killer."

"*Execute!*" He recoiled. "Yet you call *slavery* an abomination? That is barbaric!"

Anger flared in her. "You can't tell me you don't believe in execution. What do you call what you intended to do to us? And I don't believe that a very rich house would let one of its members go to trial for murder. Tell me the truth, don't accused murders sometimes vanish before they can be tried and convicted? I'll bet there's been a little quiet fratricide."

His scalp furrowed. "Sometimes houses find it necessary to cleanse themselves, it is true."

"And you don't call that execution?"

The furrows deepened. "I call it a private matter concerning only the house. Why should the world be told of the shame of a brother killing a brother, or of a girl so irresponsible she has become pregnant without earning the right to be?"

She stiffened. How had pregnancy come into this? Slowly, she asked, "What does happen to pregnant girls?"

He turned to look out over the city. "Stoning is traditional."

It hit her like a punch in the stomach. "Oh, my god."

He went on, "That way the entire house expresses its disapproval and shares in the pain of destroying part of itself. The offender is usually cremated hide and all, then her name cup broken so that no one will remember her in prayer and her existence will be forgotten. She is erased from the house."

Liberty leaned against the battlement, sickened. Stoning unwed mothers. Slaves. Wars for sport and economic gain. Maybe she knew as much about the hees she as she cared or dared to. Tomorrow she must see if she could send word to Jaes to rush the blimp project. The sooner they left for the north, the better.

Dimly, she became aware of shouting from somewhere inside the palace, but not until Ishda whirled, nostrils and eyes widening, did she listen.

"Fire!"

Stable-trained reflexes brought her spinning around, too, adrenalin pumping icy heat through her. Red glowed in smoke rising from one court.

"Lost Souls!" Ishda cried.

Liberty bolted for the steps.

"This way is faster, Ib-ih-tee."

Ishda swung down the inside of the wall onto the roof

below. Liberty quickly followed. The slippery tiles and loose trousers tangling around her legs made footing treacherous but she just cursed each skid and kept moving, on all fours when necessary. Fire. Some disasters afflicted every culture. Had one of the men accidentally started this one?

Hees already filled the court when she and Ishda dropped over the edge of the loggia roof. A servantwoman and two palace guards tugged gingerly at the handle of the door.

"It's pegged," a guard said.

Liberty choked. "You mean they're still *in there*?" Memory crashed through her, bringing back the agonized shrieks of the horses trapped inside during the stable fire she once helped fight. "Dal!" She hurled herself at the door. "Noel!"

Flame licked out of the wall vents beside her and the heat in the door seared her hands as she pounded on the smoking wood. "*Dal*. Damn you, leo, *wake up*!" How could they sleep so soundly? Had they drunk that much. "Dalyn Thomas McIntyre, *answer me*!"

No sound came from the room, nothing but the crackle of flame.

Hands caught and dragged her backward . . . Ishda. A double bucket line had formed, she saw, made up of guards, soldiers, servants, and even children and members of the imperial family. Liberty recognized faces from the dining hall. Kaem and his entourage were there, too, shoulder to shoulder with slaves and servants. The line vanished out of the court down the arcade to some court with a well.

"Let me help, too."

With a quick lift of his chin, Ishda shoved her into the front of one line. A guard had set a ladder against the roof of the loggia and climbed halfway up. She handed buckets from Liberty to hees on the roof. One brawny servantwoman carried an axe with a solid metal head. She swung it, shattering the tiles. Where they broke, another servant poured water.

The other line doused the door and vents.

"If anyone is alive, the roof is the only way to reach them," Ishda said, handing Liberty another bucket. "Failing that, we must keep the fire from spreading along the roof."

More tiles shattered. Shards skated clattering down over the edge into the court. With every swing of the blade, the servantwoman chopped deeper through wood and plaster beneath the tiles. Still, Liberty willed her to chop faster. There could not be much time left to save the men.

"Almost through," someone on the roof called, then yelped.

Flame spouted into the air. The circle on the roof retreated. "It's too hot to stand on anymore!"

Liberty went numb. The men had run out of time. Increasingly, the smell of burning meat mixed with that of woodsmoke. Her stomach churned in threat.

"I grieve for your loss," Ishda said.

"Thank you." Taking the next bucket from him, she passed it up to the guard on the ladder. They still had the palace to save, after all.

Tears blurred her vision but she made no effort to shake them away. She had no real right to grieve for the men. For all the time they spent together these past weeks and months, she barely knew them. Her fault, probably, walking her own wild way like the cat in the Kipling story, who walked alone. Still, she could feel a sense of loss. They had been her people, and somehow, inexplicably, she felt she had failed them. Would they be dead if she had stayed instead of walking with Ishda?

Ishda jogged her and handed her another bucket. Shaking herself, she handed it on and reached for another. The time for reflection was later.

The roof group poured bucket after bucket on the roof

while the second line soaked the walls. With more axes, they chopped through the tile at the edges of the burning room and doused the beams beneath. They soaked the under side of the loggia by tossing water up from beneath. Liberty's arms soon ached. From weary quivering, pain like fire set in, but she ignored it, teeth set in her lower lip, and worked doggedly, determined to keep up with the hees.

When observers reported flame in the ceiling of adjoining rooms, the axe wielders chopped the burning roof free of the rest. It broke over the partitioning walls and collapsed into the three affected rooms in a spectacular geiser of flame and sparks, driving back axewomen and water carriers.

Now, finally, the water went directly on the flame. If fought back, hissing, but as dawn approached, the water finally triumphed. Flame died to smoldering coals. A rising sun found only wisps of smoke curling up from the blackened rubble in the roofless shell that had been a guest room.

A child handed Liberty a mug of water. She drank, though every swallow tortured a throat raw and rasped. Her eyes felt filled with sand. She ached in bone-deep pain.

Slumping to the ground under the tree, she eyed the faces in the wood pieces. Their frozen cries screamed back at her. Court of Lost Souls indeed, she reflected wearily.

Someone touched her shoulder. Liberty looked up into the face of the elder sister with whom Ishda had sat at dinner.

"I am Shu-the. Let me tend you," she said.

Shu-the held out a wet cloth. Like a nurse tending a child, she used it to wipe Liberty's face, arms, and chest, then followed it with a clove-scented salve that she rubbed on numerous small burns Liberty had not even been conscious of receiving.

Liberty sighed in relief. "Thank you. I don't know where Ishda is, but he probably needs you, too." The smoke had left her voice only a hoarse whisper.

The seamed chin tucked in. "I saw to my young brother first of all. He asked me to find you. God's good, my brother," she said, looking up past Liberty.

Liberty looked around. Xa-hneem stood behind her, sweat stains streaking his bare torso. She blinked in surprise. Had even he worked the bucket line?

He crossed his arms over his chest. "Honored guest, I cannot adequately express the sorrow I feel for your loss, but I beg you to please accept the most profound apologies of my house. It will be to our everlasting shame that God's evil should have come to you while within our walls and protection."

"I don't blame you," she managed to say.

"You are a most kind guest. And humans are an extraordinary people," he added. "You only look fragile."

But he could not see how she felt: she wanted to sleep for a week. Nor were humans fireproof, unfortunately.

That started her thoughts churning. How had the fire started? Why had the men been trapped in it? Looking up at the Emperor moving away, suspicion hissed in her. Had it been an accident, or had the men died because they were human? Perhaps she ought to find out.

Chapter Nine

A full day had cooled the ruins. Heat still filled the room as Liberty helped soldiers and Ishda move aside the blackened remains of beams and ceiling plaster, but it came from the sun, this time. Like the hees, she wore only a loincloth. The sun glistened on sweat making vertical tracks through the soot darkening her bare trunk. Ashes rose at every step, swirling around them with the scents of burned wood and flesh.

Beneath the beams, the remains of furniture emerged: the shattered night jar, the cabinet holding the sleeping pallets, and the desk table, against the wall behind the door.

Then Ishda, working near the door, straightened and turned, shaking off the sweat running into his eyes. "Ib-ih-tee, a body."

She ran to join him, chest tightening. The blackened lump lay with its skull and several charred ribs showing where the flesh had burned away. It still looked broad, though. Noel? Then she saw the hand stretched toward a broken lamp. It had two thumbs. Xtas, then. Liberty frowned. The slavewoman had been trapped, too? How was *that* possible? Suspicion sharpened in her.

Minutes later they found the men's bodies. Each lay on a layer of ashes still retaining the rectangular outline of pallets. Liberty knelt down between the two with a frown. After the stable fire, the bodies of the horses had remained clearly horses, but this residue could scarcely be identified. Only the boots, a twisted and blackened metal belt buckle, and a few thin, charred bones protruding from the lumps of ash told her these had been the men she knew. Pensively, she prodded the crushed rib cage of one body. Did the difference lie in the size of the body, or maybe the heat of the fire . . . only if that were so, why should this fire be so much hotter? "What do you think happened, Ishda?"

"I think it started here. The room reeks of lamp oil." His nostrils flared as he sniffed. Squatting, he picked up a fragment of lamp by Xtas's hand. "She must have fallen asleep waiting for you to return and knocked over the lamp. It's happened before."

Now that he mentioned it, she smelled the oil, too, faintly sweet beneath the scents of burned wood and meat. The combination brought back memories of the Gthe-get camp. How ironic, to have so much disaster from one small lamp. So much smell, too . . . like a funeral pyre. Pyre.

The hair raised on Liberty's neck. Swiftly, she bent close to the men's bodies and sniffed, and stiffened. No wonder she smelled so much oil. It was all over these bodies. Now, how could one lamp spread oil this far? It could not. She crawled toward the lamp, sniffing the floor.

From the corner of her eye she saw soldiers staring in astonishment, and discovered the reason as she met Ishda head-on halfway to the lamp. They sat back on their heels, eyeing each other.

"There's lamp oil back there," Liberty said, "but—"

"None on the floor between the men and the lamp," Ishda finished.

Which meant one thing—murder. Liberty stood, eyeing the space where the pegged door had blocked rescue.

"What reason could Xtas have for killing the men and destroying herself with them?"

Ishda stood, too. "To shame our house while escaping a life she hated. She probably drugged or poisoned the tea, and drank some herself to avoid pain."

Any remaining sympathy Liberty felt for the slavewoman vanished.

A pale eye turned down toward the bodies. "In death, your people look more like birds than ever."

They did. Liberty's throat tightened. Who would ever have thought that someone as husky as Noel could look so fragile, or that she would be unable to tell his body from Dalyn's.

Retracing her steps to them, she knelt again and felt around the remains of the pallet, hunting the gun. That would identify which one was Dalyn. Thinking of the gun, she bit her lip. They were lucky the ammunition had not exploded in the fire.

No gun around that body. It must be Noel, then. She turned to the other body.

But five minutes later she sat back on her heels in perplexity. The gun was not around this pallet, either. Could Dalyn have stashed it somewhere else? No. They had no luggage and he had slept with it every night since they left the ship, to make sure it stayed out of heest hands. Apprehension knotted her stomach. Where could it be?

"May I ask what you're hunting?" Ishda asked.

"A—" Think fast. "A good luck charm Dalyn always carried."

The gun could *not* be gone. It must be somewhere near. Unless—the thought exploded in her—unless the gun was not here because *Dalyn* was not.

With her heart pounding, she leaned over a body and examined it more closely. Those bones . . . Liberty felt along the collapsed rib cage, tracing the sharp, keel-like

edge of the sternum.   Since when had humans a keel?
But to confirm her suspicion, she explored the skull, too,
testing the shape of the bones through the blackened flesh.
Wrong, all wrong. The bones of the second body felt the
same.

Suspicion became conviction, striking an anger that overwhelmed her initial relief. Now the question was, had Xtas
been a part of the plot?

Liberty scrambled across to the slavewoman's body.
Even burned, the neck looked odd. She shoved at the
shoulders.

The soldiers gaped at her. Even Ishda blinked. "What
are you doing?"

"Looking for something like this," she replied grimly.

The body broke apart, bones pulling free from a layer of
flesh fused to the floor. The neck remained intact, however,
and on the downward side, the underlying muscles and
tendons had suffered less damage. Less fire damage. A
deep, straight slash severed them almost to the spine.

Liberty flung up her head to stare accusingly at Ishda.
"Would you care to explain all this?"

He turned toward the soldiers. "I thank you very much
for your help. You may all return to the barracks now."
He watched them leave, then bent over the "men's"
bodies. His ears flicked. "Greatlegs. They're probably
some of ours, from the park."

"Probably?" Liberty stood, frowning. "Are you trying
to tell me you didn't arrange this?"

The pale eyes glinted up at her. "Why should I? Xa-
hneem already has custody of you."

Conviction faltered. Still . . . "Whoever did this has to
be connected with the palace," she maintained stubbornly.
"How could any outsider come in past all those guards
and family members and servants and remove someone as
conspicuous as Dalyn and—" She broke off, jolted by a
sudden thought. "Kaem! He's in the next court, and com-

ing back from the audience with Xa-hneem, I saw him talking to a slavewoman with a cream-colored hide. It could have been Xtas.''

Ishda's hide twitched. "Kaem and his entourage left yesterday while you and I were sleeping. They would have trunks for their clothing.'' He hurried for the door.

Liberty followed. "If you're going to see Xa-hneem, I'm coming, too. I discovered the abduction and it's my people who've been taken.''

A pale eye rayed back toward her. "Come, then.''

They found the Emperor in his receiving court listening to petitioners who had managed to talk their way past the gauntlet of civil servants. Seeing Ishda and Liberty slipping in at the back, however, he declared a recess and led the way down a narrow corridor to a secluded study. Shutters making up one entire wall of it had been slid back to open the room to an enclosed garden. He sat on a cushion in the loggia and motioned them to others.

"What is it that brings you to the State courts looking like Conscripts, my young brother and honored guest?''

Ishda told him quickly and tersely.

Xa-hneem's face froze. When his brother finished, he asked rapid questions in another language.

Ishda replied in Akansh. "I humbly ask that we include Ib-ih-tee in our discussion, my brother, since without her, we might never have discovered the abduction.''

Xa-hneem's scalp rippled, then he lifted his chin. "Very well. You think Kaem is responsible?''

Ishda crossed his arms over his chest. "I have no proof, my brother, but—''

"Who else could it be? We know he would like human weapons to insure a victory against Gthe-ge and having been ruthless enough to dispose of his own brother for Shapeen's throne, why should he hesitate at abuction or killing a slave? But how could he peg the door from the inside?''

Liberty had been wondering about that, too. Now as the Emperor asked the question, she remembered the desk table against the wall. "I don't think he did. I think he or his accomplices looped cord around the legs of the desk table and ran the cords out between the door and wall. With the door closed, they could pull the table up tight behind it. That would be enough to make it seem pegged by the time it heated up enough that no one would pull very hard on the handle."

A pearly green eye measured her. "Humans are clever as well as sturdy." His focus returned to Ishda. "Kaem was here for nearly a month before you arrived, ample time to hear from his spies that you were bringing the humans, to find a servant he could use, and to learn which of the servants might be assigned to the humans so that he could arrange to substitute his agent at the crucial time."

"Why use Xtas at all; why not just bribe Adee?" Liberty asked, then sighed as the two hees faces went blandly expressionless. Of course. The servants assigned would be only those absolutely loyal, so they could spy on her. "Hadn't we better start after Kaem? He has a whole day's start."

Xa-hneem turned an eye back toward her. "We? I think it better that Ishda tend to this matter while you remain here. Or were you speaking figuratively?"

Liberty clenched her fists. "I'm speaking of me coming along! I wouldn't let Nui-kopa have my people even if I had to burn down his camp single-handed, and I won't let Kaem take them now. If you lock me up to keep me here, I'll tear down the walls with my bare hands!"

Xa-hneem turned an eye toward Ishda, whose nasal bulge seemed to have developed an itch that required the complete covering of his nostrils while he scratched it. "You were so correct, my brother." He focused both eyes on her. "Honored Ib-ih-tee, I appreciate your sense of duty, but this matter requires inconspicuous pursuit."

She thought fast. "I can be inconspicuous. Your people look at clothes before the person in them. Put me in armor with a helmet over my head and who will look twice at me?"

"Imperial armor is hardly inconspicuous, either, even if we could arrange for some to fit you. Kaem will be watching for pursuit."

"Post riders," Ishda said suddenly.

Xa-hneem turned to look at him with both eyes. "One might question whom you serve, my brother."

Ishda stiffened. Crossing his arms over his chest, he spoke in another language.

Xa-hneem shot a thoughtful eye toward Liberty. "My young brother suggests that permitting you to assist him might generate good will and more willing compliance with the restrictions on your people. Perhaps he's right. See how quickly a post rider's uniform can be altered to fit her and have Miun saddle two dxee. I'll pray to our ancestors to send God's good with you." He regarded Liberty gravely. "What a great deal of trouble your people are to host. I wonder if you're worth it."

Even with icy claws clenched in her spine—the company had to go north soon!—the post uniform interested her. She saw why Ishda suggested it as a disguise. Not only did it have a loose blue shirt and narrow breeches similar to camp clothes, but a vest of multiple layers of leather, flexible but tough, and a leather helmet, both blue with the Emperor's insignia in white. She examined the vest, hefting the weight of it. So heest mail carriers had to wear body armor as did their human counterparts.

The palace tailor had impressed her with his speed again. She and Ishda packed saddlebags, including some food the kitchen staff made up while the two of them ate a meal, and were bathing in a servants' bath close to the stable courts when a boy appeared with the altered clothing.

"Are you sure magic is only myth here?" she asked Ishda.

While he helped her into the uniform, tying the shirt cuffs and showing her how to wrap and tie the calf flap of her boots, he told a story about how he had ridden in from a mission one night, still dressed in the disguise of a messenger, and for a joke lived in the servants' courts for two days before anyone discovered his identity.

Liberty eyed him. Her guts tied in knots worrying if Xa-hneem was about to decide he could not afford humans as guests and Ishda looked and sounded happier than he had since nearing Ku-wen. Joy at leaving the palace?

The boots were a child's. Even so, they had to be stuffed with cottony material to fill the width and the flap wrapped as tight as possible. Her sword belt needed two wraps to stay up but a chin strap kept her helmet on.

Ishda regarded her critically. "You look like someone took a normal man and divided him in half, but I think you're right, people will see the uniform and never notice your face or hands." He put on his own uniform and picked up the saddlebags. "Let's ride."

A stablegirl held two dxee for them at the stable gate, steel grays with black leg and neck stripes. Ishda patted them. "Shuman are *the* post breed, fast but with great stamina."

They led the animals out of the palace and down through the city to the quay, where they boarded a ferry barge and crossed the river to the sister city, Th'a-xoba, the capital of the central kingdom Tho-ba, Ishda told her. Liberty kept close to her mount and Ishda and kept her head down, but cautious side glances showed no one even looking at her. She breathed easier.

They mounted beside the walls of Th'a-xoba. Liberty remembered to mount from the right as everyone here did, and to keep her dxee's nose pulled around against her knee until she had settled in her saddle and stirrups. However, only the years of riding horses catapulting out of starting gates kept her on the beast's back as she freed its head and it exploded forward after Ishda's mount.

Ishda not only clung to his dxee; he urged it faster.

"Shouldn't we rate them to save their strength?" she called ahead to him.

He glanced back. "They only have to reach the next post station. We'll be relay riding."

In that case . . . Liberty hunched forward, close to the chunky neck, and urged the dxee on with hands and voice, giving herself to the exhilaration of the race. Carts and pedestrians with wheelbarrows pulled aside on the highway to give them room. Straw-hatted peasants looked up from vines and bushes in the hilly fields to watch them pass and sometimes trill encouragement.

Even with the excitement of racing, though, Liberty did not forget that this time she rode for more than a share of the purse. When they pounded into the post station, a private compound, she asked, "From our direction, I assume we're trying to intercept Kaem. How far do we have to go?"

He gulped a cup of the beer a child of the house brought them. "To HNusen, three marches away. But we must be there by tomorrow morning if we want to catch the royal barges. Otherwise, we'll be chasing them, and could be seen."

Three marches! Liberty stared at him. He expected to cover two hundred and forty kilometers in *one night*! Could they do it?

She figured quickly. Maybe they could, maintaining this pace and riding nonstop, except . . . the sun would set in a few hours and the moon follow in a few more, leaving them in darkness with more than a third of the distance yet to cover.

Their fresh mounts came out of the stable. Liberty took her reins. On the other hand, the farther they went while they had light, the closer they would be. She vaulted into the saddle and slapped the dxee's neck. "Make tracks, kid."

They thundered on north and west, using the road as much as possible, but taking the paths between fields when it saved ground. With the shadows lengthening, every meter counted.

They changed mounts again, and a third time, and Liberty began to wonder if she would be able to ride the distance even if they had the light. It had been months since she spent this long in the saddle at one stretch. The small of her back ached and the muscles in her thighs. By the fourth change her knees had begun to stiffen and she almost collapsed when she slid to the ground. After that, when roughness of the road or traffic slowed them, she swung down and ran beside her mount.

The sun had vanished over the horizon. They were alone on the road. As the light faded, only that from the crescent of moon remained to see by.

"Have you made a ride like this before?" she called across to Ishda.

"One or two times."

"In the dark?"

His hesitation told her he had not. After a bit he said, "I've prayed for guidance."

Liberty sighed. "With all due respect to your ancestors, I'd prefer headlights on the dxee." At least they had another hour or so of moonlight.

She just completed the thought when the moon vanished behind a cloud. It reappeared quickly, but moonlight reflecting off more clouds revealed a heavy front moving in rapidly from the west. Liberty swore. They would not even have moonlight much longer.

"Your ancestors better go to work soon."

Either he did not appreciate her humor or he was beginning to feel some pain himself. He did not reply. Liberty slapped her mount's neck, sending the animal racing up the field path they followed, determined to cover as much ground as possible before they were forced to stop.

A moment later she found herself sailing through the air to land in a field of bushes with knife-edged leaves.

"Ib-ih-tee!" Ishda vaulted off his mount and raced over to her.

She crawled out of the bush onto her feet, shrugging off his hands. "I'm fine." Only thoroughly disgusted with herself. "The bush broke my fall."

Her worry was the dxee. Hurrying over to where it struggled to its feet, she saw with a sinking stomach that her instincts had been right. The dxee put no weight on the right foreleg. Kneeling beside it, she palpated the bones and tendons with swift, sure fingers . . . and swore. "The fetlock is sprained. No one will be riding this kid for weeks, I'm afraid. How close is the next post station?"

"Three hikes."

She sighed. Twenty-four kilometers. Too far to walk a lame mount.

"There's a compound just ahead, though," Ishda said. "We'll ask for the loan of another mount."

Liberty coaxed and cajoled the dxee through every hobbling step toward the compound, but at the same time, cursed the minutes lost. For all the good those few minutes would have been. By the time they reached the compound gates, clouds had completely swallowed the moon. The only light came from a lamp held by someone on the wall.

She patted the dxee's neck while Ishda and the person on the wall called back and forth in the local language and bit her lip in an agony of impatience. If they did not hurry, she and Ishda would miss the barges at HNusen.

Finally the gates creaked up and a mustard-hided man stepped out. "I am headman Adas-him of the house of Pem-a-zhu-Dsho," he said in Akansh. "I welcome the honored post riders to our house, wishing only that more fortunate circumstances brought this meeting."

Liberty glanced down at the dxee's leg and frowned. The fetlock was swelling fast. "My mount needs care. Do you have cloth to wrap its legs?"

"We have herbal bandages that will reduce the pain and swelling. Please bring him inside." He led the way through the gates to stable courts where sleek dxee paced behind rope webbing in open-fronted stalls. "After we tend your mounts, may we share our last meal with you before showing you to your room?"

A room. Liberty bit her lip. Lying down would be heaven!

Ishda said, "We thank you, honorable headman, but we don't require either food or pallets. We carry urgent messages that must reach HNusen by dawn. Do you have a dxee and lamp that we may borrow to reach the post station?"

Adas turned his entire head to stare at Ishda. "You intend to ride on? In the dark? With all respect, post rider, this is a house of tea growers, nor a livery stable, and we take pride in our care of our animals. We could not think of letting one of them risk an injury such as your mount has already suffered." He paused. "Of course, if you were to *purchase* the animal, it would be yours to do with as you wish."

Liberty snapped around. Why that pirate!

Ice glittered in Ishda's eyes, though his voice went silken. "Buy it with what? Honorable headman, we're post riders, not nobles."

A sound rumbled in the distance, like a gate lowering. It stopped before Liberty could identify it.

Adas crossed his arms over his chest. "Most unfortunate. Perhaps we could barter."

The sound came again and this time Liberty recognized the rumble of thunder. She grimaced. On top of everything else, rain was going to make a mire of the road.

"Let us examine your saddlebags," Adas purred. "It

may be that you carry something valuable enough to buy not only a dxee but your lives.''

Liberty forgot thunder. She forgot her dxee. Wishing for a hees's ability to splay her eyes, she froze in the courtyard and tried to count the archers who appeared in the stalls without moving her head. Anger flared even as her spine went cold. Bastards! Now what would happen to Noel and Dalyn? "I see why there are pegs inside guest room doors," she said in English.

The headman reached out. "Please, give me your swords and any knives in your boots or sleeves.''

The thunder growled louder.

"Give him your sword," Ishda said, adding in broken English, "I think the archers lower their weapons, then. Run for next court.''

She spotted the archway while she unbuckled her sword and handed it to Adas. It looked a long way away, but not farther than an arrow flight.

He gaped at her hand. Looking into her face, his jaw dropped still farther, obviously *seeing* her for the first time. "Who—who are you? Where are you from?''

Maybe here was a way for at least one of them to escape. "From Gtheen, the Forest of Lost Souls," Liberty replied, and pulled off her helmet so they could see how strange she really was. "I'll distract them; you bolt," she told Ishda in English. "Honorable headman, you'll no doubt want this, too." Pulling out her shirttail, she untied the string of money. Every reflex screamed against giving it up, but she made herself bring it out. "Only, you'll *have to pick it up, you bloody pirate!*" She snapped the string like a whip, scattering square and round coins across the court in a glittering, ringing shower. And as heads turned and hands reached for the shine and sound, Liberty leaped for the archway.

Something tugged at the vest over one shoulder. Another arrow clattered off the paving behind her. Footsteps raced after her, too, but she did not pause to make sure they belonged to Ishda.

Then his voice reassured her. "Look for stairs to the wall."

She saw none in this court, only more stalls. But a cart stood near the edge of the roof extending out from the stalls. She scrambled into that and from there up to the roof.

"Take this," Ishda called.

She turned in time to catch the tool he tossed up. Form follows function, she reflected. It had only two wooden tines and they came off the end of the curved handle in a V shape, but it had to be a pitchfork.

Dsho's poured into the court behind Ishda.

"Watch out!" Liberty yelled.

He spun, swinging his sword. It caught Adas on the side of the head and sent the headman sprawling. Ishda whirled away and clambered to the roof after Liberty. Lightning arced overhead, followed moment later by a deafening crash of thunder. Ishda shouted, "Thank you, my ancestors!"

Liberty glanced back in her struggle up the slick roof tiles. "You think this is your ancestors' answer to your prayer?"

"It's light, isn't it? Run!"

The wall loomed ahead. Unfortunately, so did half a dozen squat figures, vaguely visible in the lamplight shining up from the court below. Liberty forced herself to keep heading straight for them. It was dark and she made a small target, after all.

With the next zigzag of lightning, however, an arrow hissed past her to clatter on the roof tiles. Fear and anger washed her in a deluge of ice and fire. Baring her teeth, she lunged for the nearest hees.

This close the archer did not try to nock another arrow, but used his bow to deflect the tines he anticipated. What he did not anticipate was that Liberty's two-handed grip on the pitchfork, copying a leo's hold on his baton, let her suddenly spin it to ram the end of the handle in under his sternum. He collapsed in an agonized explosion of breath. Liberty spun the pitchfork again to rake the tines across the face of a second attacker, and kept the tool spinning until the handle met the hees's throat with all the strength Liberty could put into the blow. The tines slowed down a third attacker, too, as they sank into her leg.

Liberty left the fork there and scrambled past the woman onto the wall. There she looked back for Ishda.

A strobe-like series of lightning showed him clawing his way between two female opponents, using the blade of the sword on one, sinking the pommel into the stomach of the other.

"Do you need help?"

"Jump!" he yelled. "Now!"

Beyond him another member of the house had climbed on the roof and was nocking an arrow in her bow, raising it toward Liberty. Liberty dropped over the edge of the wall, hung there by her hands a moment, then took a breath and let go.

Roll, she reminded herself as she hit the ground, and when an arrow buried itself not half a meter away, she kept rolling, right into the rows of bushes near the walls.

The first drops of rain hit . . . large, heavy, lazy. Through them, Liberty saw someone else drop from the wall and scramble four-legged for the bushes. "Ib-ih-tee, where are you?"

She stood up.

He pointed north. "Run."

She did, though she wondered what it would accomplish. House gates creaked up behind them. Mounted riders would be chasing them any minute and the two of them made easy quarry here in the open. Still, she ran, driven by anger and fear, fighting gravity. Breath scorched her throat.

The rain came harder and faster. Lightning flashed so

bright that for an instant, the countryside stood out with the sharpness of midday. It must also have clearly shown their position to the riders and people on the wall, Liberty realized sourly.

Ishda shoved her hard sideways, into the bushes. "Down. Now that they've seen what direction we're headed, we'll hide and let them chase that direction." He sighed. "I apologize for this misfortune. Most houses are more hospitable."

She shrugged. "We have recorded instances of families who not only robbed and killed guests but ate them, too."

"In the great famines of the Second Darkness," he began, then, as the rainfall became heavier still and the hoofbeats grew louder, broke off. "Once they're past, we can run for the post station."

"Run *three hikes?*" Liberty shook her head emphatically. "Not me, jon."

She edged to the end of the row and keeping flat, peered around a bush down the pathway. Lightning showed her a dozen riders pounding in her direction. Pulling back, she pressed into the sharp leaves and waited.

The riders swept past. Liberty counted. Ten . . . eleven . . . twelve. She sprang, grabbing both the reins and the last rider's near arm. The dxee reacted exactly as she expected. It leaped straight sideways, out from under its equally startled rider. He landed sprawling, where Liberty kicked him hard under the chin then hauled in the reins of the squealing dxee. It bounded forward, trying to escape her, but she let herself be dragged and used the momentum to vault into the saddle, giving thanks dxee were not as tall as thoroughbreds.

Several riders splayed eyes back at the commotion, turning their heads. Liberty prayed that through the rain and lightning, they would see only the dxee with a shape on its back and assume the animal was merely behaving like a dxee. A sharp slap on the neck sent the beast out after the other riders.

Now to find a mount for Ishda.

Her mount pulled even with the hindmost rider. She edged it sideways until her stirrup almost touched the hees's. Bush track racing had taught her a great deal, not all of it nice. A well-aimed kick knocked the other rider's stirrup off his foot. At the same time, she sank her outside heel into her dxee's side and drove it hard into the other animal while stiff-arming the rider. He vanished over the far side of his mount.

Liberty caught the flying reins. Without slowing, she wheeled her mount and dragged the other with her.

Ishda was already running to meet her. "I am indebted."

File that for the future. "Do we still have a chance to make HNusen or have we lost too much time?"

He vaulted into the saddle and wheeled the animal into the field, slapping it into a gallop. "I don't know. We'll just have to see."

Chapter Ten

The dxee stumbled under Liberty. At the jerk, she stiffened. "Hey, kid, you okay?"

Through a fog of weariness, her body listened to her mount. Its ribs worked like a bellows between her knees and as it labored up the hill, the roar of its breathing reached her clearly above the hammering rain. However, its gait resumed a normal rhythm a stride later. Liberty sighed in relief. The stumble had been tiredness, then, not lameness.

She patted the sodden neck in apology. "Sorry, babe. I'd get off and run, but it would slow both of us down." She had not felt anything below her knees for the past hour, nothing, that is, except the pain that burned like flame in every muscle and bone of her body. She doubted she could stand well enough to walk, let alone run.

How far had they come? How close were they to HNusen? She had lost track of the post stations after the one following their escape from the bandit house. They told the station master to pass the story of their experience on to the provincial judge, she thought, somewhere between snatching a few bites of food and gulping down a cup of beer. Since then the monotonous drum of rain and a countryside that existed only intermittently in strobe flickers of lightning had reduced the ride to the unreality of a dream. At least the roads had not become the mire she feared. Someone who built them knew about drainage and despite the downpour, the surface remained firm and free of excess water, faster riding than the fields.

The dxee stumbled again.

"How far to the next post station, Ishda?" she called in concern.

Ahead of her, he stopped at the crest of the hill. "Let him rest. Look."

Liberty halted beside him. The dxee dropped its head and stood with sides pumping. Lightning cast town walls below into sharp relief, but more important, the flash showed Liberty an inky ribbon of water below.

"HNusen?" In the next burst of light, she tried to study all the boats moored along the canal. "Do you see Kaem's barge?"

"He has three for his entourage, but I don't—wait. There."

He pointed to the south. Almost hidden by a cut through a hill and anchored just this side of lock gates sat the broad outlines of three barges. The figures of armored guards stood around the decks, illuminated by lightning and lamps hung on the cabins.

"Which one do you think Noel and Dalyn are on?"

Ishda tapped his dxee's neck, urging it down the hill at a walk. "If I were Kaem, I would keep them as close to me as possible to maintain the secrecy of their presence and reduce the chances of betrayal."

Liberty sucked in her lower lip. "Speaking of betrayal, how could Kaem talk Xtas into helping him? What could he offer a slave other than a chance to spite her masters?"

"Freedom."

Liberty frowned. "Then slaves *can* be freed?"

"They cannot, but he could offer transport to the highlands. The Bethxim are said to welcome women of childbearing age. Their own women bear few children."

Liberty nodded. "It's probably due to the stress of decreased oxygen." Damn! Exhaustion was making her careless. "Pregnant girls must try to run away there, too, then."

He turned off the road into a field. "We'll go this way."

On the far side of the field stretched a band of trees. The canal lay beyond them, with the barges anchored in the middle. Ishda halted and dismounted in the trees.

Liberty almost fell, sliding off her dxee. Her knees barely held her. Lurching over to a tree, she grabbed the shaggy trunk for support while she worked feeling back into her legs. Ishda also took advantage of a tree, she noticed. The sag of his body against it made him look as exhausted as she felt.

Liberty sighed. They had reached Kaem, but did they have any energy left for a rescue?

She shed her vest. That at least lightened the weight on her a little. Pushing her dripping hair out of her eyes, she peered out of the trees at the barges. "Can you tell which one Kaem is on?"

All three looked alike to her . . . the same number of soldiers patrolling each deck, reed curtains concealing the cabin interiors.

Ishda sighed. "I had hoped he would mount an extra guard on your men, but he's cleverer than that. We may have to go aboard and look. This rain is good cover for activity like that."

Except they would stumble over a bizillion soldiers and courtiers, Liberty reflected wryly. There must be a safer way to find the men. Her mind raced and presently she smiled. Maybe there was.

Pushing away from the tree, she limped over to join Ishda. "It would be simpler if I just ask Kaem where they are." His head snapped around but before he could voice surprise or objections, she began explaining her idea.

*　　　*　　　*

Gooseflesh rose on Liberty's bare arms and legs as she slithered down the facing rock into the canal. To prevent recognition of the shirt and breeches as a post rider's uniform, she had ripped off the legs and sleeves. The chill of the water helped revive her, though, and she welcomed the shivering. Dog-paddling, she struck out for the central barge.

Flotsam, she thought, bobbing like a piece of vegetation knocked into the water by the storm. Being invisible had never been more important.

Maybe she did look like flotsam. She reached the stern of the barge without being challenged. Pulling herself up on the rudder, she peered over the gunwale. A soldier stood less than a meter away, staring out through the rain. Liberty sank back into the water and worked around to the side of the stern. There she took another peek.

This time the soldier had turned away, talking to another soldier around the aft corner of the cabin.

Liberty moved swiftly, and when the soldier turned around again, she found a small, wet, grotesquely thin creature perched on the helmsman's bench, one-thumbed hands spread on spindly thighs.

"Am I too early for my audience with His Majesty?"

The dramatic effect was all Liberty could have hoped for. The soldier gaped in dumbfounded astonishment. Only belatedly did she remember to whistle a warning for her fellow guards and reach for her sword.

Liberty shook her head. "I wouldn't use that if I were you, not until you've told the King I'm here." She used a crisp Polite Formal.

The sword stopped halfway out of its sheath.

Other soldiers dashed around the rear of the cabin with swords already drawn. Liberty's gut knotted. She made herself lean back casually against the gunwale and stare down her nose at them. "Where is your watch commander?"

They ploughed to a nonplused halt. After a moment a

soldier with a green collar shouldered through them. "Who are you?" he demanded. "How did you get aboard? Nin?"

The soldier on duty at the stern winced. "Sergeant, I—"

"Humans have a gift of invisibility," Liberty said. "Please tell King Kaem that Liberty of the house of Ibarra has arrived."

The sergeant stared hard at her, then responded to the authorative speech forms and tone with a terse order to several soldiers around her. Those stationed themselves with swords ready to swing. The rest dispersed back to their posts. The watch commander vaulted the gunwale onto the northmost of the barges.

Liberty settled back against the tied tiller, blinking the rain out of her eyes. Carefully, she avoided glancing down at the water behind her. She just had to trust that Ishda was there.

"The leading barge," she said in English in a conversational tone.

The watch commander returned quickly. Crossing his arms over his chest, he addressed her in Deferential Formal. "If you please, honored visitor, His Majesty King Kaem awaits you."

Did she see a shadow slip on board behind the staring guards as she crossed to the northern barge? Could Ishda reach the roof of the cabin without making any noise? She kept her eyes ahead and ducked under the reed curtain the sergeant lifted for her.

Kaem could not have been awake for more than a few minutes, yet he had managed to scramble into a court vest and trousers and sat behind a desk table. Above him, the oil-fed flame of a ceramic lamp flickered inside its colored glass chimney, like an echo of the lightning beyond the curtains. It cast dancing, distorted shadows on the curtains and on wicker screens dividing this central section of the cabin from the rest. A sleeping pallet still spread open on the deck.

Had Kaem also spent those minutes arranging his face? He regarded her with a perfect composure she had to admire, considering that she had dropped out of the night on him and must look like a drowned cat. "God's good, honored visitor. I'm pleased to welcome you aboard, despite the surprising method and hour of your arrival."

Oh, how relentlessly courteous they were. Liberty deliberately addressed him in the mode a master would a servant, only terser. "Surprising? I don't know why you think so. You stole something from me, Kaem, and I want them back."

His expression never flickered. "With all respect, this is bewildering. I stole something? I am insulted."

"*I'm* insulted that you think so little of my intelligence," she snapped. "Did you think I wouldn't know my own people from greatlegs, even burned? You're fortunate that I left without telling the Emperor about this fraud. Now, where are my wives?"

Kaem sat upright. "I'm glad you didn't falsely accuse me, but why did the Emperor send you here, then?"

For all his prostestations, he had lowered his voice, Liberty noticed. To avoid being heard by his entourage? She smiled thinly. "Send me? Why should I wait for the Emperor to send me after my own wives? I simply left and came on my own."

His scalp furrowed. "That is impossible."

"Would you say it is also impossible to board your barges without being seen by the guards?"

A flicker in the molten copper eyes told her she made her point.

"Kaem, we humans are impatient people. I want my wives, and unless you return them immediately, alive and unharmed, I'll tear this barge apart looking for them."

He tilted back his head to look her over slowly. "That is a daring threat for one who comes here alone and unarmed."

She bared her teeth. "How can you be sure I'm unarmed?" While he digested that, pupils dilating, nostrils pinching, she went on, "How much do you want to win the war with Gthe-ge?"

His face and body froze into stillness.

Liberty's grin widened. This might be great fun if the men were safe. "If my wives are returned, I'll consider helping you . . . for a price beyond their return, though."

A jewel-studded ear twitched. "What price would that be?"

She pretended to study him before answering. "Is winning one war all you want?" She lowered her voice to almost a whisper. "If you had more ambition and daring, my power could make you Emperor."

His head flung up. "Emperor . . ." His eyes flared. "That is half-souled. Still, what would your price be?"

Where was Ishda? She heard nothing above them. "Land . . . not just an estate but a kingdom, enough for my people to live by ourselves and by our own laws, as the Bethxim do."

The lamplight went fever-bright in his eyes. "Would you settle for one of the central kingdoms? They're small but surely adequate for your people. You could serve a useful function for me there, too. The Thim emperors use the central kingdoms for protection. Being dependent on the imperial army to augment their military, they pose no threat to the imperial throne, but they stand between Kuwen and the armies of large kingdoms. With your people in possession of a central kingdom, your powers could guarantee the security of my capital even more than the present arrangement."

Saying her lines, Liberty almost believed the role she played, that they could make him Emperor, that a kingdom would be room enough to protect hees and humans from each other, but Kaem brought her sharply back to reality. *My* capital . . . as though the end were accomplished. He succombed to imperial fever with dismaying abruptness. Was he already planning his coronation, too?

She hissed, "I guarantee nothing until I have my wives back."

"Of course, and I shall produce them presently, but first—"

She had seen one eye twitch toward the aft screens, however, and she started toward them. "Produce them *now*!"

Kaem drew a breath and opened his mouth.

She spun toward him. "Don't call for the guards if you want to be Emperor. Only *I* can convince my people to help you and I warn you, king, my patience is at an end."

She folded back a screen. Behind him, baggage surrounded the mast mount, and foremost among it sat several wicker trunks. Kaem hurried past her to throw back the lids of two.

"Here are your wives, unharmed, only sleeping from a drug to keep them quiet."

Liberty bent over the chests. The men curled inside, still dressed in the clothes they had worn to the dinner, and looking anything but unharmed. Cold, gray skin made them look and feel like corpses. Only a faint movement of their chests and a thready pulse in their necks reassured her that they still lived. She slapped Dalyn's face with a force that left a white outline of her fingers on his skin, but he did not even twitch in reaction.

Anger hissed up through her and she whirled on Kaem. "Sleeping! What the hell did you give them? Don't you have any better sense than to use the same drugs on different species? They're comatose, maybe dying!"

In a way, she almost wished they were dead, because now how could she take them off the barge? Her plan had been for all of them to race for the rail and dive overboard.

She shook Dalyn by the shoulders. "Dal, wake up. Come *on*, leo! We have to get out of here before daylight," she said in English.

"That isn't possible any longer." Ishda's voice spoke overhead in Akansh. A circle of roof where the mast would rise lifted clear and he dropped through. "It's almost dawn now."

He wore only breeches but instant recognition flashed in Kaem's eyes. "You *did* tell the Emperor." His hand reached into his other sleeve and came out with blade protruding from each side of his fist. He lunged for Ishda.

Liberty scrabbled under Dalyn's trousers for the gun strapped to his thigh and swung to point it at Kaem. "Stop right there."

But he never paused and staring at his blade gleaming in the lamplight, she realized that he did not recognize the gun as a weapon. With no time to tell him, she thumbed off the safety and fired past his head.

The report boomed like a cannon blast. It left Liberty's ears ringing, and rain drizzling in through the hole the bullet tore in the roof. Kaem stopped like someone slamming into a wall. Only his eyes moved, splaying sideways to the gun. Ishda stared, too.

Liberty swore, her mind racing. They would have every guard on all three barges in here now. Could she frighten them back?

She braced herself for the effort . . . but no one came. After a minute, she let out her breath. Of course. A gunshot meant nothing dangerous to people who had never heard one before. The sound may even have been taken for thunder.

Kaem relaxed, too. He turned to fix one eye on the gun and the other up toward the hole in the roof. "That is an impressive weapon."

His voice reflected more greed than awe. Liberty pointed the barrel at his chest. "It makes an even larger hole through people. So you will please arrange for Ishda and me to disembark with the trunks at HNusen.''

Kaem tucked his chin. ''I think not. I prefer that you join me in Shapeen for the war.''

Liberty hefted the gun.

Kaem's nostrils flared. ''You can't threaten me with that. Harm me and my guards will kill you in turn. Even should you escape, your wives can't.''

Ishda said, ''We don't threaten you with the weapon. We threaten you with Huat. Make us prisoners and your house will learn how and why he died. You will lose not only your throne but your life and identity.''

Liberty had never seen a hees go pale before. Kaem's hide did not resume its normal color for several minutes. His nostrils pinched tight. ''Very well; we will dock at HNusen. Ride splay-eyed from now, though, because I intend to give your hides to my watch axa for whelping blankets.''

Ishda crossed his arms over his chest. ''You may try, Your Majesty.''

They disembarked on HNusen's dripping quay in a gray dawn. The thunder and lightning were passing, except for an occasional distant grumble, but the slow drizzle persisted. Soldiers carried the wicker trunks down the gangway and set them on the quay while Kaem watched under the rolled reed curtain from his private portion of the cabin.

Liberty sighed as the barge pushed off and paddled north. Either the Kings coveted human powers and weapons or they hated her guts, and that latter group increased every day. Oh, to go north!

''What?'' she asked, realizing belatedly that Ishda had been speaking.

''I said, imperial troops are stationed here. We'll send someone after the post mounts and go back to Ku-wen by military cutter.''

He pointed at a moored boat, a slender lance of a craft, light and low and sharp-prowed. Her gut knotted, looking at it. Ku-wen. If she and the men returned to the Imperial Palace, how could the Emperor see them and not remember that far from his protection squelching the Kings' ambitions, one had even violated the sanctity of the Imperial Palace itself to steal them. And he must seriously wonder if they were worth protecting. She had to warn Jaes, so they could leave for the north just as soon as possible.

"I think we should go to Swordwood."

A pale eye glanced toward her. "My brother expectes us in Ku-wen."

"But you see what Kaem's drugs have done to Noel and Dalyn. They need medical care, and what can your healers do for them? They need *human* care. They'll be safer at Swordwood with the imperial army, too. Send a message to Xa-hneem telling him where you've gone and why. He has to understand, under the circumstances." She bit her tongue to keep from adding: *You don't really want to go back to Ku-wen, do you*?

Ishda squatted down beside a trunk and peeked in under the lid. He glanced south, then into the trunk again, then west. Finally he stood. "I'll take you to Swordwood."

Chapter Eleven

The cutter bucked violently. At the height of its leap toward the strip of pewter afternoon sky visible overhead, it hung suspended for a breathless moment, then slammed down again with a force that lifted passengers and crew from the deck and drenched them in sheets of spray. Someone needed to tell these people about lifejackets, Liberty reflected grimly. With the nails of one hand digging into the stern gunwale, she wrapped the other arm around Dalyn to keep him from being flung overboard. And Ishda should have told her that after they left the Three Rivers Canals, the Winding Water River would dive between the sheer walls of a gorge, becoming a gauntlet of swift whitewater and glistening rocks. She often enjoyed risk, an EVA walk off the Glenn platform or galloping a greenbroken horse, but not while she was responsible for Noel and Dalyn. Two full days after their rescue they still remained no nearer consciousness than an occasional mutter and stir. Urgency pulsed in her, too. North. North.

The crew's whoops and trills indicated they found the trip exhilarating, but across from her Ishda hung on to Noel with a distant expression, divorced from everything around him. It was not quite the same as if he had been approaching Ku-wen, however. He glanced up at the gorge walls from time to time with softened lines in his face that reminded her of the contentment he showed talking to Elder Sister Shu-the at the banquet. Having grown up on the estate, could this be a homecoming to him?

The cutter's commander shouted a sharp warning. The crew dug their paddles into the water in time to scrape around a stony fang that thrust up in their path. More spray washed over the gunwales.

Liberty blinked the water out of her eyes. "How long does this go on?" She had to shout to be heard above the roar of water.

Ishda's nostrils flared. "We're almost there."

The crew's paddles warded off a mid-stream chain of boulders. They brought the cutter around it and plunging through the edge of a whirlpool, into . . . a calm pool. Through the shock of the sudden peace, they paddled across the pool toward a rock slab jutting into the water from the eastern cliff.

Ishda laid Noel down. "We'll walk from here."

What? Liberty blinked at him. The rock slab might suffice for a landing stage, but where could they go from there? Surely not up that rock face?

One of the sailors leaped onto the slab with the bow rope. Before she could secure it, however, a voice boomed around them. "I would welcome you, travelers and soldiers, but you have come to private property and so I must respectfully inquire your purpose here before permitting you to disembark."

Even with the polite rules of war, did one group sometimes pretend to be their opponents? Liberty wondered. Or could the guard be afraid of bandits? Where *was* the guard, anyway? Liberty saw no one and the echo made the voice impossible to locate.

Ishda stood up. "Guard, I am Lord E-do-Ishda of this house, bringing three humans where swordwood shapes strong and true."

The sentence had the sound of a password. Perhaps it

was. Moments later a soldier stepped out of what looked like a vertical crack in the rock face. She crossed her arms over her chest. "Welcome to Swordwood, my lord."

Half a dozen more soldiers marched out of the crack. They helped secure the cutter long enough to remove the unconscious men and let Liberty and Ishda climb onto the landing stage. Two burly women shouldered the men and all marched back toward the crack while the cutter crew pushed off again. Wondering, Liberty followed.

The opening may have actually begun as a fault in the rock, but now, hidden from the river, a stairway rose upward, cut through the stone. Narrow and steep by heest standards, just about comfortable for a human, it came out on top of the gorge amid large boulders balanced where an easy shove would send them crashing down the stair slot.

Liberty barely glanced at the defenses, though. Beyond them to the east and south lay the estate itself. Looking out across the treeless hills, she felt a surge of astonishment, and joy. Except for the lack of limestone rimrock, the rolling hills could have been part of Kansas' Flint Hills. They shared the same far horizons and a feeling of infinite breathing room that made her ache for a long ride on a bold horse. No wonder Ishda looked forward to coming here.

Then she grimaced. Wonderful . . . to come to a place where she felt instantly at home but where she could not stay. Swordwood offered no home to her and the other humans, only imprisonment and peril.

And thinking of home, where was the compound? No sign of it showed on the hills around her.

When she asked Ishda, he pointed south. "It's beyond those hills. I'm afraid that since we're unexpected, we'll have to walk there."

He headed down a path between the hills. Liberty hurried after him, followed by the two soldiers carrying Noel and Dalyn. Liberty glanced back at them in concern, but they strode along as though the men weighed nothing.

Ishda had not lied about the size of the estate, she decided. They walked for what she estimated to be over an hour at a brisk pace before even sighting the compound on a distant hilltop. Between river and compound lay untouched land, no buildings, no fences, just an undulating sea of knee-deep grass and wildflowers. Instead of people, animals populated it, coveys of field birds, small bands of dxee—wild, judging by the wary curiosity with which they stopped grazing to watch the hikers pass—and two communities of creatures that reminded her of prairie dogs, except these had small horns growing just above their nostrils.

But he had lied, also. No plough had ever touched this land because none ever should. The rocky topsoil might make good grazing but would be hell for cultivation. It was just as well the colonists did not have to stay here and try to coax crops from the land. Shutting out the smells of grass and flowers and the medly of insect and bird songs, she stepped up her pace, hurrying toward the compound.

They reached it as the sun vanished over the horizon, a scarlet globe showing for a moment between earth and the cloud ceiling, then slipping out of sight. It left a crimson sky arching over the sprawling walls above Liberty. Like the Imperial Palace, its size had been dwarfed by distance. Up close, the walls reached wide enough to enfold several villages and almost filled the pleateau-like top of the hill.

A shout from the walls indicated they had been seen. The gates creaked up and Frank Riggs came running down the path to meet them, eyes on the two limp forms over the soldiers' shoulders.

"Are they dead?"

"Not yet, but I need the doctor."

Frank shouted back at the heads visible above the wall. One vanished.

The guard must have run at light speed. In the few minutes necessary to reach the courtyard inside the gates, Dr. Ramon Duarte had joined the gathering crowd of curious, concerned colonists. Liberty breathed deeply. Humans. She did not remember people smelling this acid, but what did that matter when she was back among her own kind?

Then she saw Jaes in the crowd, frowning at her. She stiffened. What was wrong?

"Tell them to put the men down there," Duarte said. Liberty relayed the instruction and the doctor knelt beside Noel and Dalyn, feeling pulses and peeling back eyelids. "What happened?"

"They've been drugged with some local sedative. I don't know what kind." Kaem had not been at all interested in telling her when she asked him just before the barge docked at HNusen. "They've been like this for at least two days."

Noel rolled his head and groaned.

Duarte touched the gray skin, frowning. "I guess I'll take blood samples and see what the computer can find in them. In the meantime, we can try stimulants to help catabolize the drug faster. Will someone move them to my quarters?"

"Are you sure you ought to give them anything?" Jaes asked. "We can't be sure how it will react with what's already in them."

Duarte smiled. "Whatever it is probably isn't too exotic. I don't think these people are chemists yet and the basic compound are very similar on all Earth-type—"

"Watch out!" Liberty warned in Spanish. "The envoy understands English."

Jaes turned to Ishda. "Thank you for bringing them home, Lord Ishda. Welcome to Swordwood. Though the compound is crowded, we'll find space for you to sleep."

"Thank you," Ishda replied in English, "but I will not

impose. I am content to find a pallet in the military courts.
So if you will excuse me, I'll go present myself to General
Be-ed."

He left, not by the gate but climbing the steps to the
wall and disappearing along it with the two soldiers.

Jaes watched him leave, then said abruptly, "Let's walk,
Liberty."

He climbed the steps, too. Liberty followed, eyeing
him. She did not like the curt tone of his voice. Had she
done something wrong?

On the wall she discovered why Ishda had not left by
the gate. Far ahead, he and the soldiers were descending
into other courtyards. The imperial and military courts did
not sit quite adjacent, however. Between them lay a sand-
surfaced arena so large it could have contained the *Invictus*
twice over. It already held stacks of crates and tarp-covered
piles she recognized as frame and hull panels from the
ship. It also contained four soldiers leading u-tse in slow
circles while several human children clinging to each broad
back pleaded in shrill Akansh to go faster.

Jaes stared broodingly down at the group. "Why the
hell did you bring Ishda here?"

Anger flared in Liberty. What a warm welcome. "I
didn't," she snapped. "He brought *me*, at my asking. I
didn't want Noel and Dalyn to die, and I had to warn
you."

His head jerked around. "Warn? What's happened?"

"First, how is the blimp coming?"

He shook his head. "We came in early yesterday. All
we've had time to do is activate the computer." He pointed
back toward the human courts, to solar cells set up on the
roof in one court. "Now, what happened?"

She told him, in detail, Jaes's muttered curses punctuat-
ing the recitation.

At the end he turned to lean on the wall and stare west
toward the fading strip of light. A fist tapped the wall.

"The universe seems to have us marked to annihilation, one way or another, doesn't it?" He turned back to look down at the children, then at Liberty. "I'll get the blimp project rolling. You go back to Ku-wen and—"

"Ku-wen!" She stared at him. "I can't. Don't you understand? Xa-hneem—"

"I do understand," he interrupted, "but it's a risk we have to take. We can't afford to have Ishda around here. It'll be trouble enough building the blimp in the compound with the soldiers doting like grandparents on the kids." He pointed at the group below. "I don't know what it is about the kids that appeals to them so much."

"They're women, Jaes. In the *compound*!" she exclaimed, suddenly hearing the rest of what he said. "Jaes, that's brainbent!"

"Maybe not." He smiled thinly. "Which seems more suspicious, people sneaking off into the hills every day, or building openly, especially when the guards have no experience with flying machines to tell them the project isn't something innocent, like a greenhouse, say? We can warn the older children not to talk and keep our mouths shut around the younger ones. We can even lie convincingly to Tsebe. She's so easygoing and inclined to take things at face value. Ishda is another matter. He's bright and observant, obviously, and a lateral thinker. He's dangerous."

She could not dispute that. "All right. It's back to Ku-wen. We'll see if I still know how to be invisible."

Jaes smiled. "Good girl. With luck, we won't need more than a month. Now, speaking of risks, where's that damn gun of Dalyn's? I'm going to put it somewhere before it has another chance to fall into the wrong hands."

Liberty stiffened. She saw Jaes's point, but surely any decision about Dalyn's gun should be his to make when he woke. With the hard edges of the weapon biting into her spine where she had shoved it down her shorts under the loose shirt, she looked straight at Jaes and lied. "You're too late. After Kaem put us off the barge, I threw it in the canal. Now, what can I do to help with the Habitent and where do I sleep tonight?''

Instead of answering, he glanced past her. Liberty turned to find Tsebe standing a dozen meters down the wall with arms folded over her chest, obviously waiting to be noticed.

Jaes invited her forward with a wave of his arm and she ran to join them, lime eyes bright. ''God's good, friend Ib-ih-tee. Please forgive my absence at the gate but class had not yet adjourned.'' She spoke better English than when Liberty had left, though l's and r's still eluded her.

''What class?'' Liberty asked.

The lime eyes brightened still more. ''Captain Zhes has asked me to teach the reading and writing of Akansh to your children.''

Liberty glanced sideways at an expressionless Jaes. What was this, a ploy to keep the heest girl out of the way? ''It's very kind of you to take the time.''

''I am honored. Swordwood possesses such a fine library with all the classical writings. I'll show you in the days ahead if you like.''

The books Ishda quoted from. For a moment, Liberty regretted not being able to browse through the library. ''Thank you, but I'm afraid I won't be here. I have to go back to Ku-wen.''

The heest girl's expression drooped. She sighed. ''Of course. May I confess to disappointment? I had looked forward to visiting with you. It is very amusing, discovering that you are female, too.''

Jaes said, ''Tsebe, Liberty needs sleeping space tonight. If you don't mind sharing your room with her, that will give you time to talk.''

The girl's nostrils flared. ''Please, Captain Zhes. I am most honored to share.''

''That's settled, then. Will you tell the children it's time for them to get off the u-tse and eat supper?''

As the girl hurried away Liberty turned angrily. "Jaes, no one makes my decisions for me!"

He regarded her with grave eyes. "You'll be more comfortable there than anywhere else, and if she's busy with you, I can hold a company meeting without worrying about being overheard. We need to organize the work groups so we can start on the blimp the moment Ishda is gone."

Liberty glared at him in frustration. Why did helping her people always mean being haltered and led here and there at someone else's pleasure? Once this was over and they were settled in the north, she was going to become a hermit!

"Will you help?" Jaes prompted.

She sighed. "Of course." As long as they needed her, how could she refuse?

Dinner came camp-style, with all four-hundred-odd colonists lining up, plates in hand, to be served from a vat of stew. Because the compound had no dining hall large enough for everyone, though, they spread out through the courts around the kitchen, sitting wherever they could. It gave the compound the same rabbit warren look of the Imperial Palace. Liberty and Tsebe perched on the edge of a loggia, feet down in a little garden courtyard.

No formal gourmet meal could have pleased her more, though. Picnic or not, she was eating human food again at last, thoroughly cooked with meat and real raised bread to soak up the gravy. The generous tan slab still smelled fragrant and warm from baking. She savored every bite.

Tsebe, however, nibbled at the bread and stew with uncertainty.

Liberty raised a brow. "You've been with my people for weeks. Haven't you eaten human cooking before?"

The broad jaw tucked in. "On the barges, the army

cooks prepared meals from food bought at villages along the way. This is very interesting, very different.''

Liberty smiled. Trust a hees to be polite. ''The only trouble is, in an hour you're hungry again. That's an old human joke,'' she explained when Tsebe splayed a puzzled eye toward her.

''A joke?'' Tsebe sighed. ''There remains so much yet to understand about your people.''

Liberty bit her lip. The girl's wistful tone brought a stab of guilt at having to prevent that understanding. She made herself lie. ''You'll learn. You have two years here in service to the Emperor.''

She lapsed into silence, glancing around the court for someone else to talk to, but saw no one she knew well. The fragments of conversation she overheard did not interest her anyway, complaints about the crowded conditions and gossip about the effect of the situation on individuals and marriage. The usual. Liberty sighed. She was home all right, and nothing had changed.

''You'd think they'd be panting to hear about Dalyn and Noel, or about the Emperor and Imperial Palace, wouldn't you?'' she told Tsebe.

''I would like to hear about the Emperor,'' Tsebe said. ''What is the palace like? Did you meet any of the imperial family?'' She leaned toward Liberty, voice rising. ''The Emperor's wife Shiu was a famous dancer with the Ha-bui-sono acting company, and his wife Meta is the historian who located the ruins of Asu-sewa, the Usurper Tu-Nan-see's capital. Did you know it's just four or five days from here? I think it's interesting that every dynasty has built its capital in the Central Kingdoms, even the Usurper. Did you meet the Emperor?''

Liberty grinned secretly. The girl sounded like a human teenager talking about an actor or pop music star. Fine. As long as she had to keep Tsebe occupied, she could use that.

She talked through the meal, describing everything she could remember about the city, palace, and people, down to a recapitulation of the dinner entertainment. The recitation carried them into examining the crates in the riding arena for the carton of her personal belongings, which she lugged to Tsebe's room to unpack in search of scissors and clothes.

Tsebe picked up several books. "How small these are, and what strange writing. What is this one?"

In horror, Liberty realized the girl had her photograph album. Moving with deliberate speed, she gently removed the album from Tsebe's hands and closed it. "That's a very private book, Tsebe." She buried it and Dalyn's gun at the bottom of the carton and tried to distract the girl with more description of the Emperor and palace.

That lasted her through cutting her hair back to the boyish cap she preferred and sluicing away hair and travel dirt in the nearest bath. She managed to still be talking when she pulled on a tank top and shorts and padded back to Tsebe's room, though by that time Tsebe's interest in the scissors and Liberty's mirror eclipsed her desire to hear about royalty.

The girl played with the scissors, using them on the mutilated post rider's uniform Liberty discarded until it lay around her cushion in shreds. "This is a wonderful device."

Liberty nodded absently. All the time she had been rattling on to Tsebe, she kept thinking of the company meeting. How had it gone? she wondered now. How soon could the blimp be finished? Given that the Habitent would not make a very large blimp, how many trips would it take to move the entire company with it? *Could* they move without being caught?

Presuming the north proved habitable, of course. She crossed her fingers.

Tsebe's head began to droop. Liberty took away the scissors. "You ought to go to bed."

Tsebe yawned. "I think you are right." She picked up the scraps and put them on the pallet cabinet, then pulled out her pallet and unrolled it. She looked up in surprise as Liberty strolled toward the door. "Aren't you going to sleep?"

"I think I'll take a walk on the wall first. Don't peg the door."

The meeting must be over by now. She was anxious to find Jaes and ask how it had gone.

A woman whose name she could not remember sat in the court outside, dangling bare toes in the pool. She gave Liberty directions to Jaes's room. Padding down the loggias, Liberty noticed that the clouds had broken. The oval of cracked-egg moon shone through, filling the courts with silver light. Along the loggias, the light of lamps shone out through the ventilation vents and snatches of voices reached her. Sometimes a door stood open and she could see half a dozen people or so in a room.

The door she thought should be Jaes's, however, was closed and no light showed through the vents beside it.

She rapped at a door that did show lights. "Is Jaes gone?"

"Jaes is in the next court," the man answering the door said. "That's the library."

Library. Liberty could not resist taking a peek into it before finding Jaes.

A lamp near the door lighted with matches some human had left on its bracket. By the light she saw shelves lining the long room, shelves similar to those in the shrine room of the Imperial Palace. But ledger-sized books filled these. She pulled one from its place and opened it under the lamp. She had expected something like books in Earth's Middle Ages, copied by hand and ornately illuminated. Instead, though the rows of vertical and diagonal lines covered only one side of each heavy sheet, they looked printed . . . or embossed. The lines felt raised under her

fingers. The drawings in this book, detailing the workings
of a cylinder-type clock, were as neat and precise as a
draughtsman's.

"God's good to you, Ib-ih-tee. I see you've discovered
my personal shrine. How are your men now?"

She spun around. Ishda sat on a stool at the far end of
the room. Had he been sitting there in the dark when she
came in? She did not remember seeing him.

"I haven't seen them since we arrived." She closed the
book and returned it to its place. "Do you often read in the
dark?"

His nostrils quivered. "I was just sitting and remembering the hours Shu-the and I spent here when I was a boy.
Your guards were kind enough to let me come into the
courts at this late hour."

Liberty looked around. "You've quoted from these books
so much, I'm sorry I can't read them for myself. When
we're back in Ku-wen, would it be imposing to ask you to
teach me?"

He stood and came along the shelves, pausing now and
then to touch a book. "Not at all, but why wait until
Ku-wen?"

She frowned, suspicion chilling her. "Isn't that the
soonest we'll be near a library? I'm assuming that now that
the men are safe, you'll be wanting to start back as soon as
possible. I'm prepared to leave first thing in the morning."

"I'm not," he said. "I'm not planning to leave soon at
all."

Liberty kept her voice even with difficulty. "But there's
no need to stay any longer. Won't your brother be anxious
to have us back?"

"Don't you think we should make sure your men are all
right?" he replied. "Xa-hneem will want to know." In the
lamplight his eyes did look blind, and as opaquely unreadable as gemstones. "Besides, I think you're right; you're
safer here than anywhere else. I'll send Xa-hneem a report

by messenger and wait until he sends word of his wishes. That will take a week or more, ample time to begin teaching you to read. It may be even longer if he has more pressing business than instructions to me.''

A week or more? She could not even think of a polite reply, only stare at him in dismay. How would they work on the blimp now?

Chapter Twelve

"It's going to be up to you, Liberty. You'll have to keep him too busy to notice our activities," Jaes said.

She stared at him in dismay. Was that the best he could come up with after a whole night to think on it? Liberty looked around the room at the boardmembers meeting here in Jaes's quarters. "Does anyone have any suggestions, short of chaining Ishda up somewhere?"

One after another, Matt Hedinger, the Lindemuths, and Bea Laurent only shook their heads. Behind the desk table, Jaes fondled the ears of the two Labradors lying with their chins on his lap. "All those weeks you've spent with him must have taught you something you can use to manipulate him."

"Manipulate?" The word soured on her tongue. Manipulation was not something free people were supposed to do to each other. "Jaes, he's schooled in court intrigue." She sighed. "But of course I'll do my best."

Jaes smiled. "Thank you. You'd better go find him and get started because one group is unpacking the Habitent this morning and another is gathering material for the gondola, elevators, rudders, and the blimp's internal structures. There's no way for him to avoid seeing the main balloon in the arena, just see he doesn't linger there too long, but the mechanical parts will all be built in our private courtyards so keep him out of here, or be very careful how you two go to the library.''

''What do I tell him when he asks why we're working around the clock on a greenhouse?''

Jaes did not answer immediately. Instead, he looked down at the dogs. The bitch pushed against his hand and he rubbed the dog behind her ears. ''We won't be working at night, at least not on the outer envelope.''

''Not—'' She stiffened in alarm. ''Why *not!*''

He looked up but Bea answered. ''It's hard to believe the situation is as urgent as you claim. Look at them, falling all over themselves playing with our children. And if they want our weapons and technology, aren't they much more likely to take good care of us until they have them?''

Liberty sighed in exasperation. ''But the Emperor *doesn't* want them, and he's the power here, not the Kings or some soldiers who will stop being doting the minute they're ordered to destroy us. Look.'' She ran her hands through her hair and tried to organize her thoughts. ''You have to understand hees. They have rigid priorities and the first loyalty of any individual is always to his house. I've seen example after example of that. Unless a person is a renegade or some sociopath, personal desires are *always* secondary. Xa-hneem stood in that shrine pointing at *six hundred years* of Thims whom he firmly believes are watching everything he says and does. Do you think he's going to risk betraying them by letting a group of foreigners destroy the Empire all those ancestors spent their lives maintaining? Never! The minute he feels threatened, he'll order us wiped out. Ishda was prepared to at the landing site.''

Cara Lindemuth glanced at Jaes. ''I'm convinced on the basis of that fact alone.''

''But it's only her opinion that the Emperor is ready to carry through with that any moment,'' Matt said, ''and these are aliens, who don't think the way we do. Liberty, are you sure you're not letting your in-bred distrust of Authority influence you?''

Liberty hissed. ''God! What does it take to convince you, the army pouring in here with weapons drawn?''

Jaes said, ''It isn't us you have to convince. I think we're agreed the situation is really serious, but we're trying to point out the attitude out there.'' He waved toward the door. ''You have to pursuade four hundred plus ordinary company members that our life supports are still in jeopardy, but without causing a panic that the hees are sure to detect.'' He looked around the room. ''I think talking one-to-one will be more effective than all the argument at the meeting last night. Each of you circulate and see what you can do. Liberty, you'd better attach yourself to Ishda.'' He stood up and started for the door with the dogs following. ''Meeting adjourned.''

Liberty did not immediately hunt for Ishda. Instead, she asked the way to Dr. Duarte's quarters and stopped there. To her relief, both Noel and Dalyn were awake.

''Welcome back, gentlemen.''

Noel frowned up at her in an obvious effort to focus. ''Liberty? God, this heest beer gives a hell of a hangover. Where am I, and where did the doc come from?''

She raised a brow at Duarte. ''Haven't you told them yet?''

He smiled. ''I've tried . . . several times. They're still drifting in and out, especially McIntyre.'' He frowned past her at Dalyn, who lay muttering and alternatively patting his trunk and legs and groping around his sleeping pallet. ''I don't know if the restlessness is an individual reaction to the drug or is symptomatic of another problem. Dalyn, what's wrong?'' he called.

''Where is it?'' Dalyn muttered. ''Where is it?''

It? Understanding flooded Liberty. The *gun*. Of course it would be his first concern, finding himself waking in a strange place. She knelt down beside him. "Don't worry, leo. Your habit's safe. I have it and I'll return it as soon as you're on your feet again."

He went still. "No, keep it." Suddenly he sounded strong and coherent. "Hold it for me until we go north."

She patted his shoulder.

As she stood to leave, Duarte said, "Whatever that was about seems to have solved the problem. Gracias, señorita."

She shrugged. "De nada." And left in search of Ishda.

Not that he proved very hard to find. As she expected, his camp clothes-clad figure stood in the arena, where he had a close view of the colonists unrolling the Habitent's long sections of translucent, kevfiber-impregnated plastic. Tsebe accompanied him, her broad-shouldered bulk making her look like an u-tse with a dxee.

She turned as Liberty strolled up to join them. "God's good, friend Ib-ih-tee. My lord Ishda was just wondering what your people are doing."

"I asked someone," Ishda said, splaying a pale eye at Liberty, "but the answer puzzles me, since this is neither green nor a house." He leaned down to finger the edge of a strip. "What is this material?"

Liberty made her voice casual. "Green refers to what will be inside: plants. We have some delicate seedlings that must be started in a controlled environment. I've seen Dalyn and Noel and they appear to be recovering quickly."

Ishda stepped back for a pair of colonists unrolling another section of Habitent. "Tsebe said someone remarked to that effect at firstmeal, but I'm glad to hear you confirm it."

Tsebe said. Liberty sucked in her lower lip. How much other human activity and conversation had the girl reported? She had better keep Ishda away from Tsebe as well as the blimp. "Lord Ishda, I have a favor to beg. Jaes has asked me to locate areas on the estate suitable for planting. Will you guide me?"

"Of course." He glanced at her bare legs and feet. "If you will find clothing more suitable for riding, I'll ask Major Kus for mounts."

Kus, the officer in charge of the military stable, gave them u-tse instead of dxee, but Liberty found no difficulty riding the big animal. She strongly suspected that the major, faced with a request he could not refuse and one rider of unknown ability, had assigned them school mounts, rider-wise and trail-wise. Her Kxa plodded along placidly beside Ishda's mount, a rusty-colored beast more finely boned than most u-tse Liberty had seen. The heavy body under her absorbed most of the shock of its stride, leaving Liberty with little to do but hang on, be grateful for her boots and breeches in a saddle designed for heest width, and enjoy the scenery.

They rode east, saying little for a long time, each alone with his thoughts in the grass, bright sunlight, and breeze. Liberty's lingered back at the compound, willing the colonists to use Ishda's absence well.

Bands of dxee lifted horned heads to watch the riders pass. Several coveys of birds exploded from the grass in a whirring thunder of wings. Once both u-tse stopped short, planting their legs wide. Liberty clutched at her saddle until the vibration under her subsided, then resumed breathing with a grimace. Would she ever acclimate to the ground playing periodic hopscotch? Otherwise, the ride proceeded in lazy peace.

"I can't understand why Xa-hneem uses this land for military training," she said. "If I owned it, it would be my hideaway for rest and relaxation."

Ishda scratched at his mount's neck. "It has been in the past. When my father Tseth' was Emperor, he called it Wilderness and came here to hunt. My great-grandfather Ees named the estate Solitude and meditated here. He stocked the library with duplicates of all the books in the library at the Imperial Palace. Every owner has looked at it differently. The known history of this land goes back to the Second Dynasty and the Thims are the Fifth Dynasty.''

Liberty stared around at the hills in awe, feeling time and history even more acutely than she had in the shrine at the Imperial Palace. Suddenly she realized she *had* learned something about Ishda that would let her manipulate him. He was a scholar at heart. ''This place has seen a lot of history, then. Do you know any of it?''

When he looked around with his eyes lighting, she knew she had pushed the right button. ''I know everything that is recorded.''

With very little encouragement, he told her, and Liberty discovered he was not exaggerating. He did know the estate's history, from its seizure from peasants by the Xab emperors through divisions and reformations as dynasties passed, occupation by warlords in the First and Second Darkness . . . battles and power struggles, feuds, plots, treachery, and the shedding of generations of royal blood. EtA-ShEaHon had cut the stairs in the gorge, she learned, after a general like Nui-kopa deposed him and the estate became his base in the struggle to regain the throne.

''The Third Dynasty is actually two, the Early EtA emperors and the Later EtA, though it's counted as one,'' Ishda said. They sat on the slope above a small lake, eating a lunch of fruit and grain cakes while the u-tse grazed below them. ''ShEaHon never regained his throne. His son TAnshanAn restored their line, though, so the succession is intact except for the AnnAmMin Hiatus.''

They finished eating and remounted to continue the ride. Liberty gave thanks that Ishda knew how to tell a story well, otherwise this could have been torture. As it was, she listened to the saga, fascinated, astonished. How had a boy raised in a military camp—intended from birth, perhaps, for his brother's service?—managed to become such a scholar?

About mid-afternoon she began recognizing names, or rather, one name, Tu-Nan-see, and she began to understand why, of all the usurpers in history, it appended to his name in capitals. A heest Genghis Khan.

"Ah. The boundary," Ishda said, breaking off his story. "We're farther south than I thought."

Liberty looked down the hill and felt her blood congeal. If she ever had doubts about this being a prison, they vanished now. At two meters high and almost as thick, with thorns she could see even from where she sat, the hedge below made a wall that should confine humans as efficiently as it did the bands of dxee. She thought again of the colonists at the compound and tightened her grip on her reins. "Tsebe says that the ruins of his capital are near here. Could we go see them?" Four or five days away, Tsebe had said. With travel time up and back plus however long they spent in the ruins themselves, that should buy the project nearly two weeks.

Ishda's nostrils flared. "I would enjoy visiting Asusewa ag—" He broke off, staring past her, then continued with a sigh, "However, it might not be wise to leave Swordwood."

She started to look down the hill again to see what changed his mind.

"Don't," he said. "There's a man on a dxee talking to peasants and watching us."

So? Hees stared at her all the time. "What makes you think he's any more than a holder checking on his sharecroppers?"

"I know the holders of all the land around Swordwood and he is a stranger. He is dressed as a scholar but his ears are soldier-cropped with tips split to give them a double point." His nostrils pinched. "That crop is popular among Shapeen's Royal Palace Guards."

Liberty fought not to turn and look. "You think he's a spy from Kaem?"

"I think it wise to find out. He's leaving now. Wait here while I go talk to the peasants." He vaulted off his u-tse and tossed her the reins.

She glanced down at the hedge. "Won't that interfere with reaching them?"

His nostrils quivered. "It never has before."

He trotted down the hill and dropped to his hands and knees beside the hedge. Crawling, he peered under the thorny branches and presently stopped where a shallow depression dipped into the hedge. Dropping flat, he wiggled head-first beneath the thorns, reappearing on the other side a minute later, slapping the dust out of his clothes.

Vines curved around the hillside beyond the hedge in contour planting. Liberty's thoughts churned as she watched Ishda make his way up through the rows chatting with the peasants grooming the vines and hoeing between the rows. Could the stranger really be from Kaem's personal corps of guards? If so, was he here to make good the King's threat, or did Kaem intend to make another try for "military advisers"? She sucked in her lower lip, biting down hard on it. If Kaem did attack Swordwood, if not even the Imperial Army deterred him, then Xa-hneem would have nowhere he could consider the humans secure.

Ishda came jogging back down the hill. "Return to the compound," he shouted across at her. "I'm going to follow that rider."

Liberty set her jaw. Go back? Sit passive, letting someone else's actions decide her future? "I will not; I'm coming with you!" she called back. She saw his chin tuck and quickly added, "If he suspects you saw him and he *is* a spy, he may be watching for you. I can guard your back."

The golden copper scalp furrowed deeply and he vanished behind the hedge. Liberty urged the u-tse downhill so that she was there to meet him when he wiggled out from under the hedge again. Sucking a cut on his lateral left thumb, he caught the reins she tossed him, then climbed the girth loops to his saddle.

"A little tighter fit than when you dug it as a boy?" she asked.

He looked across at her with eyes that had a predator's opacity. "The wild axa and ha-gho-wu dig the spaces. I cannot force you to return to the compound without taking you myself, so come." Hauling his u-tse's head around, he headed the animal uphill at a canter.

Liberty booted her mount after him. "What did the peasants say?"

"He told them his name was Kandath-Azh-min, a student at the Te-shan school." He flung the words over his shoulder. "He claims to be studying the history of Swordwood and wants to talk with people who have worked here."

A scholar might do that, Liberty reflected, but a spy certainly would, looking for information on the layout of the compound and the routine of the personnel there. She frowned. So which was he?

"Where are we going?"

"Xoso, the closer of the villages that always provided our servants." He slapped the u-tse's neck, urging it into a thunderous gallop.

Closer than others, maybe, but not close. Even pushing the u-tse, they did not reach the estate's wooden-barred gate until nearly sunset. Even then Liberty wondered if they would reach the village before its gates closed for the night. The sergeant of the troopers at the gate eyed her dubiously.

"My lord, my orders forbid allowing humans to leave the estate. Only you may pass."

"I'll crawl under the hedge and follow," Liberty threatened in English.

His nostrils pinched fractionally but he continued to

look straight at the sergeant with both eyes. "*Unaccompanied* humans, sergeant. This one, as you see, will be with me. Now, open the gate."

He could sound very much the imperious noble when he wanted. The sergeant jumped aside, shouting orders at her troopers.

Outside they slapped the u-tse into a brisk trot. Ishda pointed out their destination, a village about four kilometers ahead. For the first time, Liberty wondered if her presence would handicap Ishda. She and the u-tse made a subtle approach to this Azh-min out of the question.

"What do you want me to do when we find Azh-min?"

He splayed an eye toward her, still remote and opaque. "Follow my lead. The direct approach worked so well with Kaem, I think I'll ask this 'scholar' if he wishes to talk to someone who knows all about Swordwood. We might even invite him back to the compound."

Liberty grinned without amusement. A scholar should be deliriously happy, but what an interesting dilemma that presented to a spy. To keep in character and learn about the compound, he should accept, but he must also be aware that if they suspected him, once inside he might never be able to leave again.

They slowed to a walk for the last kilometer. Ishda pulled a double-pointed knife out of his boot and handed it across to her. "If you plan to guard my back, you'll need a weapon."

Her fingers closed around the grip in the middle. He had few doubts about Azh-min, then. Grimly, she checked the sheaths on both points then slipped the knife into her own boot.

The village gates had not been built with headroom for mounted riders, but following Ishda's lead, Liberty flattened on her u-tse's neck and rode through anyway. The guards' whistles shrilled. That sound cut off the shrill jabber of peasants around the market booths with knife-edged suddenness. Heads and bodies snapped around toward the gate, knives half drawn. Then motion stopped, too, at the sight of Liberty. Eyes and nostrils widened in astonishment. Some jaws dropped.

She pretended not to notice their gawking. "God's good," she murmured, and looked out over them for someone with a scholar's vest and split-tip ears.

A garrison soldier pushed through the crowd. He stared at Liberty for a moment but fastened ultimately on Ishda's collarless, rankless shirt. "Trooper, I demand to know why—"

"My lord Ishda," interrupted a second soldier, this one wearing an officer's collar. The arms of both soldiers snapped across their chests. "I welcome you back to Xoso. However, I must inquire why you ride war mounts into the village."

Ishda slid to the ground. "Haste, lieutenant. I offer humble apologies to the people of Xoso for alarming them, but I need to find someone here before your gates close. He is a scholar named Kandath-Azh-min."

What kind of dxee had he been riding? Liberty wondered. A cream-colored one with chestnut leg and neck stripes stood tethered near the gate. "Ishda." She pointed to the animal.

A lift of his chin indicated he had seen it. "It's my desire to help this scholar with his research."

"He was talking to Geso-Wen at the weaver's booth," the first soldier said. "There." Turning, he pointed.

The villagers pulled aside, leaving a path straight to a dun-hided man with the long, many-pocketed vest of a scholar and split-tipped ears. If the exposure dismayed Azh-min, he covered beautifully. Hurrying forward, he crossed his arms over his chest. "You wish to help me? My lord, I am honored. Where did you hear about me?"

"We saw you near the estate this afternoon and I talked

to the peasants a short while later. Please, will you use our library at Swordwood?"

Liberty watched their man closely for his reaction. With the invitation offered in front of the entire village, he must be very careful how he responded . . . if he were a spy. Did he hesitate a moment too long before answering?

His nostrils flared. "My lord, I am overwhelmed. I'm not worthy."

"It is little enough my house can do in support of scholarship. I have a great deal of interest in history myself and have accumulated information on Swordwood you may find nowhere else."

"I would not wish to impose. I've heard that—" He splayed an eye at Liberty. "—that the compound already hosts a great many guests."

Was that a probe, or just a repetition of local gossip?

"You are no imposition, I assure you, honored scholar," Ishda purred.

"Then I gratefully accept your most kind invitation."

Liberty lay flat on her u-tse to ride under the gates. The men led their mounts outside before mounting.

One villager followed them out, speaking to Ishda in an urgent tone. Ishda, however, pulled in his chin, made some reply, and climbed the girth loops to his saddle.

"What was that?" Liberty asked in English as they turned up the road toward the estate.

"The village headman urged me to spend the night and not ride home in the dark. I told him that since we are less than a hike from the estate gate and that the moon will be rising almost as soon as the last light has faded, there's little danger. All we have to be concerned about is our honorable scholar."

They sandwiched the dxee between their u-tse. If that disturbed Azh-min, though, he successfully hid all signs of it. "This is truly God's good," he said. "I expected all my information on recent history to have to come from former servants."

"Tell me, how did you become interested in Sword-wood?" Liberty asked.

"Oh, it is described in record fragments found at Asu-sewa."

Liberty raised a brow at Ishda above Azh-min's head. Ishda lifted his chin. "Is that common knowledge?" she asked in English.

Ishda's head tilted back and forth. No help there. Liberty bit her lip.

"I thought, what history estates such as these have seen and decided I must make a study of them," Azh-min rattled on. "I hope to solve such mysteries as why Emperor Xa-hneem stopped hunting here and gave it over to military use."

Xa-hneem hunted here? She glanced at Ishda but he stared straight ahead and in the rapidly fading light she could distinguish little of his expression. "That's interesting. How long ago did it happen?"

"About pentafive-and-three—"

"Have you come across the story of Sth'e-Teu yet?" Ishda interrupted. "When it looked inevitable that his throne would fall to Tu-Nan-see, this became his last retreat. The Usurper's forces surrounded the estate, but Teu had had his few remaining followers chop a stairway down the Ha-ban Gorge cliff to the river and he escaped in a peasant's reed boat."

The moon peeked over the eastern horizon, bringing a new twilight. It was not enough to see Azh-min's expression, though, and Liberty waited tensely for his response.

"I've seen a few references, of course, but haven't studied them in detail. It struck me as a gallant but futile act, since the Usurper eventually caught him anyway."

Her stomach plunged. So he was a spy. The only question was his mission.

"Kaem should have briefed you better," Ishda said. "The river stair is Third not Fourth Dynasty."

Azh-min's slap on his dxee's neck sounded like a gunshot. The animal shot forward and bolted up the road.

"Ishda!"

But Ishda was already slapping his u-tse. School mount or not, it remembered war training. Keening, it rolled into a thunderous gallop and after the dxee. Liberty followed, cursing. They would never catch Azh-min, not on u-tse. Why had Ishda given him this chance to escape before they reached the estate?

Compounding his advantage of having a faster, more agile mount, Azh-min turned the dxee off the road through a field. Liberty hauled at her u-tse's head to follow.

"Not on an u-tse!" Ishda called. "You'll damage the crop! Follow the base of the hill. I'll go around from the other side."

Now he *would* escape, damn it! But she headed the u-tse downhill to follow a path between the field and a strip of timber flanking a stream. She could still see Azh-min, silhouetted against the moonlit sky, but far ahead on the crest of the next hill. Hopeless! She fumed in frustration. Still, she kept her mount racing through the brightening night, her ears and body drowning in the thunder of its hooves. Maybe the dxee would fall. "Stumble, damn it!" she yelled at the distant form.

It did not, but after a few minutes Liberty thought it might be tiring. It no longer seemed to be drawing away.

Her u-tse keened. She patted the heavy neck. "Keep it up, kid. We don't want that vacuum-brained horn factory getting the best of us, do we?"

Looking up again, she found the shape ahead growing larger. Losing ground? She whooped. "You should have chosen something Shuman-bred instead of a sprinter!"

The dxee turned downhill. Liberty raced to intercept. The dxee still had some energy reserve, though. Azh-min slapped it again and it stretched out . . . and vanished into the timber just ahead of Liberty.

Swearing, she hauled on her reins. The u-tse ploughed around and crashed between the trees in pursuit. Moonlight did not penetrate the woods. She had to follow the dxee's sound. Water splashed. Moment later her u-tse lumbered through the stream, too, and up the opposite bank.

Ahead, the dxee broke from the timber, but as the moonlight outside showed Liberty the animal no longer carried a rider, hands closed on her left ankle and jerked. So she was not the only one who knew that trick, she thought in a flash, grabbing by reflex for mane. Too late she remembered that u-tse had none. Her nails scraped over the thick hide and she came flying out of the saddle to land with a jolt in a thick carpet of humus. She kicked with her free leg. An exclamation and vanishing grip on her ankle told her she connected, but before she could roll to her feet, Azh-min grabbed her again, this time by the hair. He jerked her to her knees. The tearing pain in her scalp brought tears. She snarled, clawing at his wrist. "Bastard! Squatty hairless four-thumbed son of a bitch! Ugazh!"

The latter was the only word he could have understood. It was enough. Seemingly oblivious to her nails, he dragged her forward on her knees with another vicious jerk. "Fortunately, you are not. I don't know how you've angered His Majesty, but he is offering a reward for word of you and Lord Ishda, and will pay a rich bonus for delivery of you, or your hides, or even just your heads."

Liberty stopped clawing to stare up at the shadow of him above her. Then his bolt had not been out of panic. He deliberately drew them into a chase and let her catch up. After killing her, no doubt he intended to lie in wait for Ishda, too.

Letting her hands fall to her sides, she reached slowly

for the knife in her boot. "Then we're the reason you came to Swordwood."

Above her, the darkness of his arm moved against the greater darkness of the trees. A thin spear of moonlight coming through the branches from the east reflected off the blade of a T-knife protruding between his fingers. "One of them."

She jerked the knife from her boot with a flick that bared both blades.

He saw the knife or guessed the meaning of her movement, or perhaps he merely reacted to a sense of danger, but he hauled her sideways just as she struck. The blade went wide, missing its target, and before she could recover to try again, his fist with the blade stabbed at her.

Liberty twisted in his grip, ignoring the pain in her scalp, and kicked at his hand. Her toe connected with his elbow. Yelping, Azh-min dropped the T-knife. Now she had the bastard! She slashed with her knife again.

This time she found him. He screamed in pain . . . but still did not let go. Instead, his hand smashed across her face.

Pain set off novas and comets in Liberty's vision. She tasted blood. Then she felt him grab the back of her breeches and lift upward. Déjà vu. Oh, god, not again! This time there was no river to land in.

Sure enough, he threw her. She smashed broadside into a tree. Ribs gave with a *crack* and excruciating pain and she dropped to the ground fighting for breath that would not come. She lay paralyzed, listening to the sound of his feet scuffing through the humus toward her.

"Azh-min! Do Kaem's Royal Guards now collect hides like bandits?"

Ishda! Liberty tried to shout a warning but found only enough air for a whisper.

Azh-min snatched the knife she somehow still held in her hand and moved away. Moments later water splashed.

"Only hides with a royal bounty, my lord. Come let me take yours."

She struggled to sit up. The effort brought a thousand knives of exquisite pain and sent a wave of nausea through her. Setting teeth into a swelling lip, she clawed her way up the tree until she leaned against it, breathing in short, agonized gasps she tried to take without moving her chest.

Across the stream, Ishda and Azh-min faced off, though in the shadows it was impossible to tell the crouched forms apart. The arm of one slashed a figure-8 in the air, forcing the other back. Azh-min with her knife? But Ishda had given it to her. He might have a twin.

They circled, feinting at each other, parrying, retreating. They taunted, too, but the voices came so close together they did not help with identity. She needed to be closer. She could not very well guard Ishda's back from over here anyway.

If she could move. Changing position brought fresh pain. Her ears rang and sweat broke out on her forehead.

Across the stream, one form lunged. The other man cried out in Azh-min's voice.

"Go, Ishda," Liberty whispered.

Ishda pressed forward. "*You* may be the one to become saddle leather."

Azh-min sidestepped, ducking the swinging blades. "But I will have learned such interesting things." He stepped forward, arm slashing backhanded. His blade met Ishda's in a shower of sparks. "Like this change at the estate. It came so suddenly."

Ishda circled sideways, feinting.

Azh-min kept his distance. "The imperial house had been there for hunting and when it left, two women remained behind, an elder sister and the wife Tu-fen. They remained there for months, doing research in the library, and it became obvious that Tu-fen was pregnant."

Ishda lunged forward. "If you want my hide, you cannot talk it off."

But Azh-min only danced away. "But you haven't heard the most mysterious part that the villagers in Xoso told me. Tu-fen spent her entire pregnancy there and when she delivered, a triplet birth, of course the chief steward sent word of it to Ku-wen. Within a week the entire imperial house arrived without warning and dismissed the whole staff as they rode in the gates. When a bare minimum of servants were recalled several days later, the household had left. Only the elder sister and three infants remained. Tu-fen had gone, too. Oh, there were the ashes of a pyre in the tanning court. The next month, the mounted divisions of the army moved their headquarters, built onto the compound, and announced that it had been renamed. Isn't that fascinating?"

"Ishda, don't let him rattle you!" Liberty forced herself to call. Why else could he be telling a story Ishda must know all too well? She pushed herself away from the tree and shuffled toward the stream. "Ishda!"

But how could he hear her wheeze, even if he were listening? So he lunged, and Azh-min met him with a slash that sent Ishda reeling. The spy pressed his advantage with a forehand pass and from Ishda's cry, it connected, too.

A weapon. Liberty staggered forward. She needed a weapon.

The stream bank gave way, spilling her full length into the water. Cold and blackness washed over her. Damn. Why did such a warm world always have cold water? It revived her, though, and reminded her that she had better get out before she drowned.

Pulling her knees under her, she tried, but it was as though she dragged herself through glue. Swords impaled her chest. Damn! Above her Ishda had fallen, was barely managing to roll away from Azh-min, and she could not move fast enough to help him, nor did she have a weapon.

Her fingers closed over a rock in the stream bed.

Rock!

Straining, she pulled it loose and stood. The effort felt like it tore every muscle in her side and sawed her ribs into her lungs, but cursing and whimpering, she pulled the rock back over her head and heaved it at Azh-min. The child Liberty could hit a tormentor half a block away with a stone. This enemy, barely four meters from her, seemed a kilometer away. Could she come anywhere near him?

The rock struck the spy squarely on the temple. He dropped like a marionette with its strings cut.

Liberty crawled out of the stream and over to Ishda. "How bad are you hurt?" Her eyes had accommodated enough that she could see blood streaming from his neck and shoulder.

"It seems I did. Need you to guard my back," he added. "I thank you for doing so well."

She probed at his wounds. He gasped. "Not well," she said. "Not soon enough."

Azh-min groaned.

She looked over at him. "I ought to tie him up before he regains consciousness."

Ishda sighed wearily. "That's too much trouble. I think Kaem may benefit from a reminder of the Emperor's invicibility." And before Liberty realized what he intended, he rolled onto his stomach, reached out, and plunged one blade of his knife into the spy's throat. Then he rolled back again, clutching at his shoulder and gasping in agony.

After a minute, Liberty retrieved the blade to use in cutting off Ishda's shirt for bandages. "We'd better stop this bleeding and then see if either of us can manage to ride."

Ishda opened his eyes. "We'll have to. Major Kus will flay us alive if we don't bring back his u-tse."

She almost laughed, except that it hurt too much and fear sat too cold in her gut. She pressed a wad of cloth against his shoulder and tied it in place with another strip. "Do you have to tell your brother about this? Except, he's really your uncle. Your mother was his sister, wasn't she? That's why they killed her." No wonder he was uncomfortable around his family except Shu-the, who shared his childhood exile here and tried to help his mother.

Ishda opened his eyes. "My brother. The house adopted me, which makes me the son of the headman. But I must report this to Xa-hneem. Are you afraid it may prevent you from finishing your flying device and leaving in it to explore the north?"

Liberty froze. She opened her mouth but no sound came out. He knew! He must have been using those passages and spy holes he spent the day telling her about. Her gaze dropped to the knife on the ground beside her knee. She could say Azh-min, a bandit, had killed him.

Ishda's hand closed over the knife. "Please do not act rashly. You are strange and powerful people and for the sake of my house and people, I must know what you're doing. That doesn't mean I necessarily intend to interfere. Under the proper conditions, you can even have my full cooperation in building your device."

She stared at him in utter bewilderment, fighting for breath. Cooperation? Somewhere she found enough air and coherence of thought to ask, "What conditions?"

With an effort he sat up and looked straight into her eyes. "Participation. You will be allowed to continue construction provided that it is understood that the Emperor must share in learning about the north. I will accompany you on the flight as his eyes. Otherwise, I regret that it will be necessary for me to destroy this device and any others you may attempt to build."

Chapter Thirteen

"I can't believe we're actually giving in to this blackmail," a woman on the far side of Tsebe said.

Liberty sighed. The act still hurt, though not as much as it had nine days ago. What choice did they have? Without agreeing to Ishda's conditions the *Northern Hope* before her in the arena could never have been finished.

Liberty regarded the blimp with satisfaction. She did not quite look like an air ship yet, true. Only the ballonets fore and aft inside had been filled and those with air to keep the balloon rigid while the air pressure at lower altitudes compressed the hydrogen in the main envelope. So the balloon still lay on the ground to the side of the gondola, partially swelling at both ends but flat on the arena sand in the middle.

That should change by tonight. The power group had set up their windmill outside and strung cable to the generator and electrolysis apparatus in the arena. The first hydrogen was pumping into the envelope now, an activity which had brought all the colonists into the arena and packed the wall with goggle-eyed troopers.

Liberty searched the burly forms and flat faces for Ishda, and found him above the military entrance with a group of officers that also included General Be-ed, the commandant. She had to admit that Ishda had kept his side of the bargain well enough, providing maps of the country between here and the northeast coast and arranging with Be-ed for troopers to lend their muscle when a task required physical labor, all the while remaining discreetly away from the human courts. Did he suspect—or had he been hidden somewhere listening and knew—the bitterness in the company meeting the morning after she and Ishda came home half-conscious on their u-tse?

The adults and older children had crowded into the court and onto the roof of the central stable court. Liberty stayed near the entry archway, moving as little as possible lest she stress her fractured ribs, taped under her tank top. Around her she felt the surge of anger and despair.

"What's the point of going on with it if the Emperor knows?" one woman demanded. "The idea was to escape."

Jaes stood at the edge of the covered walkway along the stalls opposite Liberty. "And now we may have the Emperor's help. It's to his advantage to have us beyond the mountains where the Kings can't reach us."

"But we don't know he'll think that. We don't even have a guarantee we can finish the blimp or take off," someone else objected. "Ishda may say so, but can't the Emperor countermand that any time?"

Across the width of the court, Liberty watched Jaes nod acknowledgment of the possibility. "This is a risk, yes, but what else have we done but risk everything time and time again? Succeed or fail, at least *we've* made the choices. The only other alternative is to give up, to lie down and let the Emperor do what he wants with us. We're not that kind of people or we wouldn't have left Earth in the first place."

"As I understand it, we aren't promising anything except to take Ishda along on the exploration flight," someone behind Liberty said. "That gives us plenty of leeway to take advantage of opportunities for our own benefit along the way."

Liberty glanced around and saw Dalyn, a bit leaner than

usual but otherwise looking recovered from his long sleep.
He nodded at her.

In the end, the company voted for the agreement . . .
not willingly, not even with good grace. An adolescent
boy near Liberty muttered, "We'll show those bastards
yet," characterizing the mood. But . . . they voted themselves the opportunity to finish the blimp.

"Next order of business is the crew," Jaes said.
"Obviously we're no longer planning to leave in advance
party on the other side. I won't chance stranding anyone.
Since the board refuses to let me go, Noel Hedinger will
pilot, and since Ishda will be along, Liberty must be there
to handle him. She can also spend time in the second seat
at the controls."

Handle Ishda? Liberty almost snorted aloud. She welcomed the excuse to be on the flight, though. Excitement
and curiosity stirred in her just thinking of the north.

"But we need two people at the controls, so there must
be a relief pilot to spell Noel and a fourth person to take
the watch with him and provide some general muscle for
repairs."

Dalyn raised his hand. "I'll go so no family man has
to."

From around the edge of the court somewhere, Frank
Riggs' voice called. "I'll be relief pilot."

Jaes acknowledged the offers with a nod. "After the
meeting, I'd like to see the crew in my quarters. We'll set
up some computer simulations in lieu of training flights."

They dealt with a few more minor pieces of business,
then adjourned. Liberty pressed against the wall, letting
the crowd file out past her. Across the court Noel and
Frank joined Jaes. Dalyn stood aside near her, also waiting
out the crowd. So, with one exception, the crew of the
blimp would be made up of people from the *Invictus*'s
crew. Perhaps that was predictable. People who had not
volunteered and qualified for the supposedly simple job of

crewing the ramjet were not likely to volunteer for a much more dangerous flight.

Only, staying was equally perilous now, Liberty reflected, watching the *Hope* inflate. The more she thought about Xa-hneem, the more she wondered why he had sent neither confirmation of nor a countermand to Ishda's agreement. Considering how much ground she and Ishda had covered that one night, there should have been time for any urgent communication to have reached here days ago.

"Excuse me, Tsebe," she said.

The heest girl was too entranced watching the blimp and electrolysis apparatus to hear her. Liberty slid back through the crowd of colonists and between the stacks of cargo to the steps. Up them, she made her way around the wall to Ishda.

He no longer wore bandages on his neck and shoulder and Duarte had recently removed the stitches he put in that night under the fascinated eyes of the military surgeon, but Ishda still moved with some stiffness.

After proper greetings to him, Be-ed, and the other officers, Liberty asked in English, "What do you hear from Ku-wen?"

Both eyes remained on the blimp below. "I've had no communication yet." He spoke Akansh. "My brother is a busy man and each matter must wait its turn for disposition. Will filling take long?"

Liberty lifted a brow. Did she hear an anxious note in his voice? "Is there a chance a message could arrive at the last minute forbidding us to lift off?"

A pale eye rolled toward her. "I cannot imagine you obeying such an order without great physical restraint, but be at peace. My brother will not deny you. The purpose of life is to learn."

But some sought knowledge more than others. "I wonder if being your brother's eyes is your real reason for going," she said in English.

He turned opaque eyes on her. "What other reason could there be?"

The poetry did not readily translate into English. Liberty quoted it in Akansh. " *'I dream of shadow wings,/Of unseen talons lifting me/Past bird and cloud/And sky-high rise of Mio's Wall/To the lands where Wonder dwells.'* "

She left him staring after her.

The blimp inflated slowly. At noon it began to lift off the sand. Tiedowns were tightened. At sunset it floated fully upright but flabby, the ends drooping to make a crescent shape above the gondola. The troopers stared rapt. Tsebe joined the colonists loading supplies into the gondola.

The blimp kept filling while its crew went to bed early.

Liberty wondered how she could sleep when so much depended on this flight, but her life-long ability to sleep anytime and anywhere remained true. It seemed only moments from the time she stretched out on the sleeping pallet until the rumble of an opening door brought her sitting upright. Tsebe's burly figure filled the doorway, silhouetted against lamplight outside.

"Ib-ih-tee, Captain Zhes says I should bring you."

Her pulse jumped. She reached for shorts and a tee-shirt. "What time is it?"

"About half-past the second hour."

"Your time or mine?" Liberty rolled up a bundle of clothes, including her riding boots, some slacks, and turtlenecks, in case altitude lowered the temperature.

Tsebe put away the sleeping pallet. "It is half-past the third hour your time."

Which meant about three hours to dawn. Liberty tucked her bundle under her arm and headed for the arena.

Beside her, Tsebe fairly skipped. "This is so exciting! It seems like magic that you can travel to the highlands and back in just five-and-three days! I wish I could go along. The Emperor should be very pleased with this gift."

"If it works." The agreed-on lie did not come without a twinge of conscience, but while revelation of the blimp's true nature made building it easier, she agreed with Ishda's suggestion that its purpose and the existence of the north should continue to remain a secret until the Emperor had a full report on the flight.

"I have faith you will succeed. I've prayed twice a day to my ancestors, especially to my father Denath, who met you. I explained that success will bring honor to everyone involved, which includes my house. They will help protect you for that reason, though I also asked because you are my friend. This is a most auspicious time to embark, too. At dawn, the last night of the year is gone and the world is born anew. Surely it will bring you nothing but God's good."

If it did not bring massacre, Liberty reflected. Cold settled into her spine even as Tsebe's kindness gouged Liberty's conscience deeper. She stopped to turn and look up at the heest girl. "I thank you very sincerely, but . . . how can you consider me your friend? I've lied to you about things like the blimp. All my people have, and will again if we think we need to."

The cream-colored scalp furrowed. "Of course, but you have never hurt me or my house, and my house is a part of history now." The lime eyes gleamed. "When books are written about the strangers from across the sea, they will say Bhada-wu-tsebe of the house of Btha-u-tse-Kxa was there!"

Liberty laughed wryly. What a highly pragmatic, quintessentially *heest* reason for friendship. On impulse, she threw her arms around the broad torso in an affectionate hug. "I wish you a prosperous new year, too, and many mentions in history books." Then retrieving the clothing bundle she had dropped, she hurried on toward the arena.

Mentally, she reviewed the course they would take . . .

north following the Winding Water River to the highlands, then east along the highlands. Four thousand kilometers to the coast—two days' flying with luck and some good tail winds—then another estimated two thousand more to inland in the north. They would have to swing out to sea to avoid the storms Ishda said occurred off the highlands. Three days up, three back, and who could say how many in actual exploration, and meanwhile most of the time they would have no way of knowing what was happening back here. God, what she would give for a jet! "Pray for everyone back here to stay safe, too, will you, Tsebe?"

The *Hope* was small compared with the *Invictus*, only sixty meters long, but she dominated the arena as she floated, straining at her ties, the wheels on her gondola and lower rudder fin barely touching the ground. Word of the takeoff must have swept through the entire compound because it looked to Liberty as though despite the hour, every human and hees had crowded into the arena or onto the wall around it. Ishda climbed the stirrup step to the hatch of the gondola, but Dalyn and Noel stood by the near engine with Jaes and his dogs, obviously waiting for Liberty, and for Frank, who was still hugging Vona and their children.

As they joined the group, Jaes said, "We'll keep radio contact as long as we can and after that, activate for half an hour at seven, fourteen, twenty-one, and twenty-eight hundred hours each day until you re-establish contact. I hope you don't have to be out of range too long."

Liberty could not help glancing toward the troopers on the walls.

Jaes shook hands with each of them. "Godspeed."

Climbing into the gondola, Liberty's heart raced. They had spent the last three days living in it around the work crews testing the engines cannibalized from the chopper and its spare parts and attaching it to the balloon by lines coming down from the catenary curtains on the top of the inside of the envelope. But with the balloon taut and straining above them, the *Hope* suddenly felt *real*. Liberty checked the securing of the supplies at the rear of the gondola while Frank and Noel ran through the checkout. The gondola vibrated with the roar of the engines. Through a window, Liberty watched the prop wash kick up a small sandstorm that sent humans and hees behind the blimp scurrying from the sting of flying grains.

"Liberty, we're ready to go," Dalyn called.

She hurried forward. Five moulded-foam chairs from the *Invictus*'s wardroom gave the portion of the gondola behind the control section the look of a lounge. She sat down in an empty seat next to Ishda.

The cabin lights dimmed into a faint red glow.

"Up ship!" Noel called out the window by him.

Jaes signaled to the men at the tiedowns, then gave the gondola a V-for-victory sign. Behind him with the colonists, Tsebe held out a spread hand.

Liberty felt no motion, not even a quiver to indicate they were ascending, but outside the compound fell away, shrinking. The excited barking of dogs followed them but human and heest forms and upturned faces dwindled and faded into the sand and wall. In the moonless night, the compound quickly became only a cluster of yellow lights floating in the blackness of the surrounding land. Liberty drew a deep breath. The gondola hung in a void, suspended in silence between darkness below and immediately above, where the balloon blocked out the sky. Laterally from them, though, the hard brilliance of alien constellations spilled like broken glass over the horizon.

"Lines," Noel said.

Those of them not at the control console hurried to pull the tiedowns in at the four corners of the gondola. The engines whined and roared into life, running off energy gathered all day by the horizontal strip of solar cells on each side of the balloon. With a slight vibration the *Hope* glided forward, leaving the glow of the compound quickly behind. Liberty pressed against a window, once part of a sleeper pod, watching until the lights vanished. After that, only darkness lay beneath.

"Good evening, lady and gentlemen."

She looked around to find Noel with one hand on the rudder control wheel and the other cupped near his mouth like someone adjusting the microphone wand of his headset. "Welcome aboard Dauntless Airways Flight 001, nonstop from Swordwood to Back-of-beyond. We are cruising at a speed of forty-three-and-a-half knots and will shortly reach an altitude of three hundred meters, if we've calibrated this altimeter correctly for a hard atmosphere. *Please* observe the *no smoking* rule at *all* times, and try to ignore lurches of the ship and curses from the pilots. We will still have everything under control . . . we hope." He looked back at them and grinned. "Enjoy your flight."

Dalyn grimaced. "Eighty klicks an hour? Back home I used to *drive* faster than that."

Below them lights appeared occasionally, but were few at this time of night and as they were neither bright nor numerous enough to show above the walls enclosing them, they vanished as soon as the *Hope* passed over. No wonder the ship's cameras had failed to detect cities as they came in, Liberty mused.

She leaned back in her chair, wanting to sleep, but for once, sleep eluded her. Time passed with tedious slowness. Dalyn could not relax either, she noticed. He paced or stood at Noel's shoulder. Only Ishda seemed to be enjoying every minute, staring around the ruby twilight of the gondola or pressing against a window to look out into the darkness.

"Sight-seeing will be more fun in daylight," she said.

"That should be soon."

Liberty glanced out the starboard windows. Yes, the sky was lightening on the eastern horizon . . . red, then gold, then white. As the landscape became visible, Ishda took an audible breath. The world spread out in a broad panorama: the glimmering race of the Winding Water to the east, patchwork fields covering gentle hills, villages like nested boxes.

"I can see the people laying out the New Year's feast in their markets," Ishda said. "Some of them see us, too. They look excited. I wonder if they think we're an Uo."

"New Year's." Noel looked around. "My god, think of it . . . New Year's from now on without a Rose Bowl Parade or Game. Sacriledge."

Frank shrugged. "We gave up watching after the soccer leagues bought the rights to the date. My father and grand-father would take all us kids out in the yard, or to an empty end of the hay barn if there was snow on the ground, and we'd play football, the Nostalgia Bowl, my brother Tom called it."

The deck dropped. Swearing, Noel and Frank whipped back toward their rudder and elevator wheels. After several more bumpy minutes, the ride smoothed again.

Noel shook his head. "Sorry about the turbulence. Now I see why the computer said the old dirigible captains didn't like flying over land in the daylight. We'll probably have more, but there's no need to worry about it."

Ishda did not look reassured, Liberty saw. His hide twitched under his shirt and he eyed the humans and gondola with . . . what? Uneasiness?

"You don't have to be nervous, Ishda. He's right. We may have trouble with bumpy air or maneuvering, but unless we ignite the hydrogen or rip open the envelope, we aren't likely to fall out of the sky."

A pale eye splayed toward her. "Thank you, but I'm not worried about that. If all of you are so much at ease, then there must be nothing to fear."

Yet something bothered him. That was obvious.

Handing out breakfast a short time later, the answer

came. They had brought along the last packaged meals from the *Invictus*'s crew rations. Ishda stared at his with the white-rimmed eyes of a shying horse, tentatively poking a finger into steaming sections that had been cool when Liberty ripped off the cover. She smiled in amused sympathy. So that was it: Ishda had just realized where and what he was. Unlike the surface, where humans were aliens, the *Hope* produced a pocket of human environment, and in it, *he* became the alien.

She left him alone with the discovery.

The radio murmured, "Base to *Hope*."

Frank had the main controls with Dalyn at the elevator wheel while Noel slept in one of the sleeping bags at the rear of the cabin. He punched the mike button. "*Hope* here."

Jaes's voice came over the air. "I thought you ought to know that a courier just rode in from Ku-wen with a message from the Emperor for Ishda."

Liberty straightened in her chair.

"General Be-ed opened it. It orders Ishda to prevent us from building or using any kind of flying machine."

"We're lucky we left when we did," Dalyn said.

Liberty glanced at Ishda, but he showed no change of expression. Perhaps he did not understand what was said. Radio voices were difficult enough to understand when one was fluent in the language being broadcast.

"Luckier than you know," Jaes replied. "According to Tsebe, who took the courier to Be-ed and managed to read the message over the general's shoulder, the report arrived at Ku-wen long after it should have. Somehow it went first to the capital of the local kingdom in a pouch of non-priority agricultural reports from this province. It wasn't discovered until a few days ago."

Liberty eyed Ishda again. Really? She translated the

transmission and watched Ishda grow very still in his chair.

"No wonder we heard nothing from my brother. I sent a special courier to Ku-wen, however. I wonder what he delivered?"

Liberty thought back over Ishda's calm acceptance of the silence from Ku-wen and that tense note in his voice asking how soon the blimp would fill. "A non-priority agricultural report intended for the King of Th'apu, perhaps."

"Ah. An unfortunate confusion of pouches." Ishda turned to the window to look down at the landscape.

"Are you going to order us to turn around?" Dalyn asked.

A serene eye splayed toward the control panel. "How could I enforce such an order? If you choose to go on, there is nothing I can do to stop you."

Frowning, Frank crooked a beckoning finger at Liberty. "I don't like this," he muttered. "Why should he help us?"

"Maybe he wants to see how the blimp operates and take a look at the north so he can hand both over to his brother," Dalyn said.

Liberty sucked in her lower lip. "I don't think so. He's spent more time looking out the window than at the controls and he would have discussed a plan like that with Xa-hneem. Why don't I just ask?"

Before she even sat down on the chair beside him he turned to face her, as though anticipating the question. She did not disappoint him.

"Ishda, let's stop pretending. That report didn't go astray by accident. Why did you do it? I can't believe you would go against your house."

A soldier-cropped ear flicked. "I haven't! I do exactly as I must, taking steps to learn about things which touch the Empire, no matter how . . . strange, and frightening, they seem."

Did she hear him saying that he suspected Xa-hneem would shy away from some learning opportunities through fear?

"I could serve better," he went on, "and we could learn more from each other if we *would* stop all pretense." Ishda took a square of stiff paper from a pocket of his shirt and laid it on her lap.

The breath froze in Liberty's chest. It was a photograph of herself at the age of eight, taken with her great-grandfather on the reservation one summer evening. She snatched it up. "Where did you get this!"

"The day after we encountered Azh-min Tsebe mentioned that you had a book of wonderful small drawings of humans and strange buildings and machines. I arranged to look at it, of course."

Tsebe. *Friend* Tsebe! "I know where my next pair of riding boots is coming from!"

His nostrils quivered. "You begin to sound hees. But don't blame the girl too much. I drew the information out of her." His nostrils pinched. "I don't understand what those pictures are, but they aren't drawings. I think they are true images of where you come from. And where *is* that?"

Liberty made herself look straight into the pale eyes. "We've told you."

"I think you lied." Leaning toward her, he reached out to point a single finger at the 2-D photograph's background.

Liberty caught her breath. Behind her and her great-grandfather rose a full moon, its craters and seas clearly visible.

"That is not this world's moon," Ishda said. "Now will you tell me where you really come from?"

Chapter Fourteen

Jaes's voice came over the radio raspy with exasperation. "Unfortunately, Ishda seems to be every bit as bright as I gave him credit for."

"Do you want us to chuck him out the hatch?" Noel asked.

Liberty stiffened. "*Noel—*"

"I don't think that would solve anything," Jaes said calmly. "If he found that photo and put everything together right after the incident with Kaem's spy, his conclusions were in his report to the Emperor. Which might explain a certain note of hysteria in those orders to Ishda. The Emperor can't enjoy having his well-ordered world and universe suddenly become very large and complicated. No, just keep additional revelations to a minimum, please."

"Why?" Liberty asked thoughtfully, mind racing. "Why not answer questions except those about advanced science or weapons? What's to be gained by silence now?"

"We're trying to save them from culture shock," Jaes reminded her.

She rolled her eyes. "I'm not talking about broadcasting to the whole Empire; I'm talking about *one man*, a *thinking* man who talks only to Emperor if he talks to anyone."

Dalyn's eyes narrowed. "I see wheels turning. What are you up to, woman?"

"Survival, maybe."

"Go on," Jaes said.

Liberty glanced back toward Ishda, who sat looking out the window, seeming to ignore the conversation at the front of the gondola. "We need an advocate, someone with influence with the Emperor. Xa-hneem must trust and respect Ishda or he wouldn't give him the free rein he does. That report finagle shows Ishda differentiates between what his brother wants and what he believes is good for the house, though. What if we offer him unlimited learning? Do you think he might want to keep us around?"

Frank frowned dubiously, but Noel and Dalyn grinned. Jaes's voice sounded thoughtful. "It's worth a try. Don't bother keeping the answers to his questions simple, either. That way if he's like my kids, the answers will generate more questions."

Now Frank grinned.

"Oh, I just got word from our people on the wall that a rider has left the military side riding hard. I think we can assume it's a courier headed for Ku-wen. I'll keep you posted."

All grins faded abruptly. Frank tugged at an ear. "Jaes . . . if you had to, could you hold off the troopers with rifles long enough to airlift everyone out?"

"At a payload of fifteen hundred kilos a trip?" His sigh reached them over the distance. "Not long enough. I have people working on strategy with dynamite and guerilla tricks but I'd rather talk us free than resort to fighting our way out. Neither will work unless you find somewhere for us to live, though. So, good luck . . . with everything."

Liberty walked back to join Ishda. "No more pretense. I'll answer your questions."

*   *   *

Their first glimpse of the Wall came at mid-morning the next day. The plains beneath had been rising steadily, forcing Noel to take the *Hope* continually higher to maintain altitude. Now the rise sharpened and soon the pattern of villages and fields changed to groves of scrubby trees and meadows carpeted in deep grass and a rainbow of wildflowers: red, blue, yellow, purple. The *Hope* shook and bucked in the turbulence of the southeast trades from the warm lowlands meeting cold air from the north. They turned east, and north of them the land continued to rise, climbing in folds and stairstep escarpments, until snow covered the slopes, then stretching *still* farther skyward through the crystal air, mercilessly, endlessly. Some places the Wall vanished into the clouds, but as the day wore on and the sun burned away any overcast, Liberty could see the top many thousands of meters above them, capped in a blinding-bright crest of ice.

No one spoke. Liberty wondered if they even breathed. She was not conscious of doing so and the only sound in the gondola was the muted roar of the engines. That glacier had to be twice as high as Mount Everest, and it did not even mark the edge of the mountains, just the approach to the "foothills." The mountains lay an estimated several hundred kilometers farther north yet.

She breathed deep and tasted a clean, arctic edge on the air. It sent her back to her bundle of clothes to change into something warmer.

"No King or Emperor has ever taken possession of the highlands," Ishda said. "Some of the records found in Asu-sewa describe an attempt Tu-Nan-see made. The commanding officer's journal said they would wake in the morning to find themselves covered in a white substance that turned to water in their hands but burned like flame to touch. By mid-morning it would all be gone and by noon the heat had become so fierce that the air above the meadows danced and shimmered. But storms rolled down on them in the afternoon, bringing drenching cold rain that turned to spear-hard pellets of water and back to the white stuff during the night. The Bethxim retreated before Tu-Nan-see's army, but always higher, until the army labored for breath just to take a single step. Then the Bethxim swooped down and slaughtered the army.''

"Nice country," Dalyn murmured.

But the words echoed in Liberty. She sucked in her lower lip. Perhaps this could be a sanctuary for humans as it had been for slaves and pregnant girls, a temporary campsite. They could airlift everyone from Swordwood to here, shortening the most critical period, then ferry the company on around the mountains at greater leisure.

"Speaking of storms," Noel said. "If our estimations are right, we'll reach the coast about midnight. I guess we'd better plan on tieing down there until daylight."

Protest rose in Liberty. Tie down! That would lose them eight or twelve hours of flying time, maybe a thousand kilometers! But she said nothing. What other choice did they have with those storms off the end of the wall? Night Rages, the people of Gtheen called them, Ishda had said when he told Jaes about the storms during the blimp's construction. *The thunder shakes the ground like a groundshiver,* he had said.

The fierceness had to do with winds being funnelled west by the costal cliffs and having nowhere to go but into cold upper atmosphere when they hit the end of the mountains. The storm was not something they dared to fly through. Trying to go around on a route they had never flown before would be just as dangerous.

They kept flying as long as possible, even after sunset, though Noel took them down to a hundred meters and used the spotlight on the front of the gondola to watch the ground. The bright circle raced ahead of them, briefly throwing rocks, trees, and bands of startled grazers into sharp relief.

"I want to be as close to the coast as possible in the morning," Noel said, "just in case we need every minute of daylight to find our way across to the north shore."

No one argued with him.

As midnight neared, everyone crowded up behind Noel and Frank, watching the sky and the bright circle on the ground. Presently, Liberty felt the gondola sway. The deck hopped underfoot.

"Picking up increased headwinds," Frank said.

Ahead of them a brilliant chain of lightning traced down to the horizon.

Noel throttled back. "That's it. Frank, elevators. Dal, Liberty, Ishda . . . man the lines."

The *Hope* angled earthward. Liberty hurried for her tiedown.

The wind bit into her as she slid open the window and leaned out to drop the coils, first making sure the end remained securely lashed through the ring on the balloon. Above the rush past her ears came the distant grumble of thunder.

With the lines down fore and aft, they slid open the hatch and dropped out a rope ladder. Liberty wiped her palms on her jeans. Without a ground crew, they had to go down and catch the lines themselves. She waited for Noel's signal.

Dalyn sat down in the hatch with his legs dangling out.

"Not yet," Noel said.

Liberty peered out the hatch over Dalyn. The spotlight slid across a meadow so close below them the end of the lines danced along the top of the grass. Something gleamed pale beyond the edge of the light on the upland side . . . steam rising from a lake, she realized moments later. Hot spring fed?

"Scattered trees coming, people. Go, Dal."

The engine noise died away and as the *Hope* lost forward movement, Dalyn dropped down the ladder hand over hand.

Liberty was swinging out the hatch when a suddenly stronger gust of wind kicked the blimp sideways to port. The movement hurled her back inside over Frank and Ishda behind her, but she forgot all about the knifing pain in her ribs as she realized they were not only moving sideways but *up*, and with the speed of an express elevator! Air hissed out of the ballonets collapsing under the pressure of expanding hydrogen.

"Updraft over the lake!" Noel shouted. "Frank, get the elevators while I restart the engines!"

"Can't we just ride it out?"

"Internal pressure could split the balloon or we could run out of air before we're at the top."

Liberty was already finding breathing difficult. Her pulse hammered in ringing ears.

Blood gushed from Ishda's nostrils. Frank tried to reach the controls but went down on hands and knees, his nose bleeding, too.

The engines whined then ground to silence again. With vision blurring, Liberty crawled across the gondola for the co-pilot chair.

"Get the elevators," Noel gasped.

The engines whined fruitlessly again.

Catch, Liberty prayed. Elevators would do no good without power. She hauled at the wheel.

"Not that way, the other! We want to go down, not up!"

The engines whined . . . and caught. Liberty hauled harder at the wheel. Her muscles seemed to have become low-test tissue paper.

Overhead, the envelope creaked. Warmth streamed down Liberty's upper lip. Gasping, she ignored the blood, ignored the tearing pain in her ribs . . . ignored everything but the elevator wheel and the agonizing slowness with which it turned.

The envelope screamed under the strain of internal pressure.

"For god's sake, *pull*, Liberty!"

She pulled. She hauled at it desperately as the envelope shrieked overhead. Then suddenly the wheel was spinning. She looked over to see a blood-soaked camp shirt and a squat figure pushing up on one side of the wheel as she pulled down on her side. Eyes gleamed garnet-colored in the gondola's night lighting.

Noel shoved the throttle all the way forward. Propellors howled as they clawed at the rarified atmosphere.

Liberty felt as if her ears were bursting. Her vision dimmed.

Then they hit the edge of the updraft and broke free. It was like diving out a window. Air screamed past the gondola and Liberty floated, lighter than she had been since planetfall, and each breath came easier than the last. Vision cleared.

Noel eased up on the throttle. "Level off a little."

"*Oh, my God!*"

Liberty whirled at the groan to see Frank by the open hatch, staring out. Her stomach lurched. Dalyn! Oh, no!

Frank slumped back against the bulkhead wiping blood from his face. "The ladder's empty," he said hoarsely. "We've lost McIntyre."

They tied down in a little ripple-like valley, uneventfully this time. No one spoke while they checked the blimp and themselves for damage. The *Hope* seemed all right. Outwardly, they, too, seemed to have suffered no serious harm. Inwardly . . . who could say? Liberty's throat ached and her guts felt leaden. Noel stared into a cup of coffee with an expression that made it clear he wished the mug held something much stronger. Frank stared out a window into the soundless night.

"The universe is a bitch," Liberty said.

Frank grimaced. "Amen. Shall I raise Jaes, Noel?"

"No." Noel leaned back in the moulded foam chair pressing the heels of his hands against his eyes. "Tomorrow is soon enough."

Ishda watched them with silent puzzlement, she saw. Mystified by their reaction to death, no doubt. She would not have minded believing in his religion right now. "Are we going to look for his body?"

Noel sighed. "I'm not fond of the idea of leaving him to be some predator's breakfast, but there's a little problem knowing where to look. Do you know where we were and where we are now?"

The radio crackled forward. "Base to *Hope*."

"Maybe I'll tell Jaes tonight after all," Noel said. He crossed to the console and punched on the transmitter. "*Hope* here."

There was a pause, then Jaes's voice came back? "What's wrong, Noel?"

Noel told him. "I'd like to find his body if possible. Any suggestions?"

"Well . . . ." Even at this distance, the hesitant note sent a prickle of apprehension up Liberty's spine. "I can understand your feelings, but there's trouble here, too. A courier rode in about an hour ago. General Be-ed was kind enough to let us know the message he carried. The Emperor is on his way here. Noel." The voice became slow and emphatic. "We need to know about the north before he arrives."

Liberty whipped toward Ishda. He sat on his bedroll with head tilted, scalp furrowed, obviously straining to hear. "Your brother's coming to Swordwood. How long will the trip take him?"

A soldier-cropped ear flicked. "An Emperor's retinue travels slowly. Five days, probably."

She passed the figure on to Frank and Noel. The two men exchanged grim glances. She could almost read their thoughts. Five days meant no dawdling, no time for anything but straight, hard flying. No time for hunting bodies.

Noel swore softly. "All right, Jaes. We'll do our best to be back in time." He stabbed off the radio. "We probably couldn't have found him anyway."

They lifted at the first graying in the east and flew straight for the coast. An hour after sunrise, they reached it.

The sight stunned all of them. At this point in the highlands, the coastal cliff had grown from thirty meters to two thousand. The rock face plunged precipitously into the cobalt sea with a young river spilling down it like smoke. Though the night's storm had abated, new anvil clouds were already forming, and the blimp bucked in the brine-scented winds rushing in from the sea. Noel fought the *Hope* through them, heading east.

Not until they turnd north and could look back toward land, however, did they finally see the actual mountains. Liberty stared in awe, forgetting for a moment the pain of Dalyn's loss and the urgency of their mission. Noel had just said they were a hundred kilometers out, yet she *still saw the mountains* . . . not lying on the horizon, either. They reached high into the sky even from here. The towering heights of the highlands dwarfed before the needle-sharp peaks, whose lower half tended to vanish' in the atmospheric haze but whose tops showed clearly. Could she be looking up out of the atmosphere at them? They shone the same silver-blue as the crescent moon trailing the sun.

"How tall are those monsters anyway?" she asked.

"A hell of a lot taller than I would have thought something could be in this gravity," Noel replied.

Ishda pressed both hands against one window, as though

he wanted to touch the mountains. "I am humbled. This voyage is one of learning, of wonder, yet I have no words to describe the terror I felt last night and none at all adequate for this, the top of the world, the stuff of myth."

Frank said softly, " *'This world is a miracle; wonderful, inscrutable, magical.'* " Then he flushed as everyone turned to stare at the ex-rancher. "It's something I read once."

"Very nice," Ishda said.

Liberty mused that it would be nice if the hees were right about dying, if Dalyn were still consciously somewhere, looking down on them and seeing what they saw. *Don't forget that you lived, Dal. Don't forget who you were.*

By noon the spectacle had ended. The sun's angle of reflection on the tops had changed and they faded, too, leaving the towers of clouds as the only show. Then a northwest trade became a brisk tail wind, booting their speed to almost seventy knots and putting them in sight of the northern cliffs by mid-afternoon. Half a dozen rivers crashed into the sea within their view, four boiling directly down thirty meters of rock, the remaining two spewing as cataracts from canyons they were cutting into the continent.

"The north has water," Frank said.

Once over the cliffs, Liberty saw the reason for so much spillage. The entire forest below them sat rooted in water. Reflections of the *Hope* rippled below between each grove of trees and chain of islands they passed over.

"I'm not fond of bayous, but it's a start," Noel murmured.

A start. Liberty looked down on fish darting through the water, on wading birds and tree birds with riotous tropical plumage, on white-ruffed, deerlike animals that fled the *Hope*'s shadow in great springing bounds. She watched Ishda watching the landscape with childlike raptness. "Are you enjoying the lands where Wonder dwells?"

He splayed an eye toward her. "Very much, though it seems little different from a water forest in Gtheen."

While the *Hope* flew west toward drier land, she tried to explain the effects of environment on evolution.

The land rose quickly and as it dried and the temperature dropped, the landscape changed from swamp to rainforest to thorn forest to mountain meadows. Near sunset Noel guided the *Hope* down into one bisected by one of the streams feeding the swamps downland. Their approach frightened off a band of shaggy black grazers.

With the blimp tethered to trees bordering the meadow, they walked through the grove to where they could look down over the land falling away to the east and north. Liberty breathed in the crisp sweetness of the air. It made her ache with longing. This looked like a beautiful continent to live on.

"So far, so good," Frank said.

Noel grunted. "We'll see after we've looked over the lower highlands tomorrow, and then . . . we'll see."

They glanced at Ishda and fell silent.

Liberty watched them for a moment, then bit her lip. Were they thinking about the Emperor? "Ishda, I feel grimy. Let's see if there's a place for bathing in that stream."

He must know that the water would be glacial, but he lifted his chin and followed her back through the trees and across the meadow to the stream. And he squatted beside her as she knelt to scoop up water in her hands to drink. His nostrils flared.

"We have a legend about a warlord who chose his generals by the way they drank from a stream. Those who drank as you are, he said, were more cautious and alert to their surroundings than those who bent down to drink directly from the water."

Liberty looked around in surprise. "We have a similar story." She sat back on her heels, hugging her aching ribs. Good; he had given her her opening. "Our two peoples share another similarity, too . . . a desire to survive, to grow crops and raise children and live out their lives in peace. Right now this looks like someplace my people could do that. It's also a place where not even the greediest King can find us. Here, we can't disturb the stability of the Empire; that is, if Xa-hneem doesn't interfere with leaving Swordwood.''

Ishda said nothing, only stared across the stream toward the setting sun.

The breeze was growing colder. Liberty pushed the turtle neck of her sweater higher toward her ears. "Will you help us?"

His scalp twitched. "How can I do that?"

"Reason with your brother. Show him why we should be allowed to leave."

"I'm sure that he has considered every aspect of the problem since you first suggested that and will make a wise decision without my aid."

She frowned. "*I'm* not sure. If you think his decisions are always wise, why did that report go astray?"

An ear flicked sharply, but he repeated, "My brother knows what he is doing."

She tried to hold down the exasperation rising in her. "Does that mean you can say nothing? Does house loyalty forbid *any* kind of varying viewpoints? Can't you even offer advice?"

He stiffened. "Of course I may give him information."

"That's all I ask of you, certainly not that you advocate for us against your brother. Let him know that if we live our knowledge will be available when he wishes to share it. Dead, that opportunity is gone forever. Tell him we understand his fears for his people and share those fears. We want to live our way and let you live yours. Will you tell him that?"

"I will if he asks."

If he *asks*. Fear and anger flared in her. "Judas! I don't understand you at all. Loyalty is one thing, but you *crawl*

for your house! How can you do that when you hate them
so much?''

He jerked around. "Hate them? What do you mean? How
could I ever hate them?''

She stared, nonplussed by his bewilderment. "They
killed your mother.''

His scalp rippled. "Why would I hate them for that? It
was a necessary and correct action.''

"But—'' Now *she* floundered in bewilderment. "Why
do you dislike being around them, then?''

For a minute she thought he might refuse to answer.
That remote, opaque expression closed over his face. But
he did speak, though in a voice so flat and deliberate that
the words seemed to be torn from him one at a time.
"Ib-ih-tee, how could I possibly want to thrust my presence on them when it must constantly remind them of the
shame brought on our house and recall the pain of remov-
ing that offender? How could I be that cruel? I should
never have been born. If Shu-the had not been so half-
souled as to aid her birthmate, I would not have been. I
should not have lived through childhood, either. I don't
know how I survived the illness that took my birthmates. I
have prayed endlessly, asking to be told the reason. I have
prayed for death . . . and received neither. I must therefore assume that I am intended for some purpose, and what
else could that be but serving the house so that I may
expiate the shame of my birth?''

He had mentioned that once before, she recalled now,
that service justified his existence.

"So I serve, Ib-ih-tee. I serve and I try to remember that
it is not my place to question those who deserve to exist,
and I keep from their sight as much as possible.''

Liberty's stomach plunged. Lord, how she had misread
him, though she should not have. It explained so much
about his behavior, and utterly destroyed the humans'
chance for an advocate. Unless their survival happened to

be vital to his house, she could not expect him to say a word for them.

"Ishda, I'm sorry if I've caused you pain bringing this up, but you can understand that—"

She broke off. He had not heard a word. He peered past her at something across the stream. She turned to look. "What is it?"

"Something is watching us from those trees."

"An animal, perhaps?"

"I don't know. It looked—there. See?"

She saw movement, but in the twilight shadows of the grove, the shape making it remained vague.

Ishda stood and waded the stream.

Liberty scrambled after him, swearing. "Don't be half-souled. You don't know what that thing is. It could be dangerous."

"We have knives."

Much they might do against a bear-size predator. Still, she reached down into her boot for it and stayed beside him.

Shadows moved in the grove again, but this time Liberty saw the shape more clearly. To her relief, it moved away from them.

But relief died in an icy purge. Flight took the shape to a more recognizable one on the far side of the grove, a horned, four-legged animal like those they had frightened off by landing, this one silhouetted against the fading light. The watcher scrambled onto the back of the four-legged animal and kicked the beast into a gallop.

"People," Ishda said in a tone of delight. "There are people on this side of the wall, too." He broke into a run after the rider.

People.

"No!" Her howl echoed back at her from the rocks upland of the meadow. "*No!* There can't be!" They could not have gone to so much trouble to come, not lost Dalyn, all for nothing. *"No!"*

But even as she screamed her fury and despair, she was sprinting after Ishda. She had to see, had to know for certain.

She overtook him on the far side of the grove, jogging down a narrow game trail. "If there are people, let's just confirm that and leave. We don't want to charge in on them when we have no idea what they're like."

He splayed an eye at her. "Of course not, but I would like to see them, at least."

She lifted her chin, saving her breath for jogging. At this altitude, the exertion had both of them gasping like fish out of water, and every intake of breath plunged a knife into Liberty's chest.

The rider's mount had left hoofprints distinguishable even in this light. She and Ishda tracked them along the trail that followed the curve of the hillside then climbed to another meadow where they circled a small lake and disappeared into a grove of scrubby trees. Broken branches and the angry calls of disturbed birds marked the rider's passage between the trees.

At the far edge, the two of them stopped. A herd of shaggy black grazers spread over the slope beyond and past them, almost too far to see details in this light, sat a group of square black tents, each with smoke curling out the top. The smells of wood and cooking drifted across the meadow toward Liberty.

People. She swore bitterly.

"Let's see if we can get closer," Ishda said.

"Be careful. I see mounted guards on the edges of the herd. "We—oh, shit," she breathed.

The herd scattered before a group of torch-carrying riders pounding toward the grove where she and Ishda stood.

"God's evil," Ishda echoed.

Liberty whirled and bolted back into the woods.

"We can't outrun them," Ishda called after her. "Hide."

She flung back, "I can't let them reach the *Hope* and catch Noel and Frank flat, either!"

His footsteps raced after her.

Adrenalin helped even in his gravity and altitude, despite the stabs of pain that each breath brought. They reached the far side of the lake and started downslope before the riders overtook them.

At the closing thunder of hooves, she pulled her knife from her boot again, but held it so the blade lay flat along the under side of her forearm, not immediately visible. Turning, she faced the riders. Ishda had done the same with his knife, she saw.

The riders circled them.

Liberty spun back-to-back with Ishda. Against her shoulder blades the motion of his ribs felt like a pumping bellows. So did her own, but with a saw inside and the air scorching her throat. She fought to control the panting so her knife arm would be steady.

For several minutes the riders said nothing, just circled, staring. Liberty stared back. They looked like hees, and not like hees. Body size and build remained unknown inside the baggy, shaggy black coats they wore—made from the hide of animals like the ones they rode, surely— but the hands showed three fingers and medial and lateral thumbs, and the wide-spaced lime or green-black eyes could splay as heest eyes did. The heads looked narrower, though, the ears smaller, the nasal bulge thin and sharp enough that it resembled one of the broader varieties of human noses. A crest of short, stiff hair grew back across the top of the scalp and down the neck, disappearing under the cowl-like collar of their coats. This was not parallel evolution, then. Once upon a time, before the mountains went up, these and the hees had been a single species.

The riders halted and swung their mounts to face the two in the center. One spoke.

"Sorry, we don't understand," Liberty replied.

The rider spoke again, louder this time.

"Do you have any language in the Empire that sounds that that?" she asked Ishda.

"None."

The speaker vaulted off his—her? its?—mount and cautiously approached, holding his torch across in front of him like a sword and keeping up a running stream of comments. He stood just slightly taller than Ishda.

At the thought of weapons Liberty noticed that the rider carried only a knife, and that remained shoved beneath the belt gathering his coat around his hips. A quick glance around the circle confirmed that no one had a weapon drawn.

"Maybe they don't mean us harm, Ishda."

The speaker did not sound friendly, all the same. His voice rose with each sentence until he was shouting, and waving his torch almost under Liberty's nose.

Anger flared in her. "Why don't you quiet down, you ugly little toad. Shouting doesn't make your language any more intelligible." She shrank away from the torch.

The speaker fell silent. He stared at her a moment, then tentatively poked the torch at her again. Liberty held up her arm to protect her face. Too late, she realized that she used her right arm, the one with the knife tucked against it. Shouting, the speaker reached for his own knife.

"Ishda!" Liberty yelled, and charged the speaker. As he went down, bowled over, she grabbed his torch and flung it at the downslope riders.

Bellowing in fear, their mounts plunged sideways. Liberty dived for the gap. One rider had dropped his torch. She paused long enough to pick it up and hurl it back at the other riders charging after her. In her peripheral vision Ishda pulled a rider from his mount and sent the animal bolting. Should they try to catch some riderless animals? Liberty wondered, but quickly discarded the idea. This was not the time to learn to ride a new species of animal.

She sprinted down the trail on foot, Ishda right behind.

The chaos they left reorganized quickly, however. Hoofbeats resumed behind them. Liberty strained to run faster, pouring her desperation into her feet. They had to reach the *Hope*, had to—

Around a bend just before the watcher's grove she ran squarely into Frank.

"Liberty, what the hell?" We heard you screaming and have been look—"

"Run!" she gasped.

He stared past her one frozen moment before flinging around and dragging her behind him toward the grove. Ishda's footsteps thudded behind Liberty.

Noel came out of the grove just as the riders caught them. Liberty heard him breath, "Holy shit," as she whirled and crouched to make herself a small target for the knives. "Maybe we can back into the trees."

But the knives remained in the riders' belts. The speaker held something in his hand to a torch and threw the object. It landed at Ishda's feet where Liberty could see it by the light of the torches: a small clay bottle with scored sides and a burning cord vanishing into a hole at one end. Ishda bent to pick it up.

Liberty heard Noel shout but recognition and horror were already galvanizing her. "Oh, my god, *no*, Ishda!" She hit him broadside, sending them both sprawling.

The explosion was not a large one, but it sounded louder than a rifle shot and Liberty felt small objects bounce off her boots and shower her back. The smell of sulfur permeated the air. Glancing up at the riders, she saw the speaker lighting another fuse.

She somersaulted onto her feet. "Run for the blimp!"

Noel and Frank matched her stride for stride in the

woods, but . . . where was Ishda? She started to slow.
"Ishda!"

Noel caught her arm. "He's coming. Don't stop."

They broke out of the grove. Moments later Ishda did,
too. Relieved, Liberty concentrated on keeping her footing
in the stream, then on tearing loose tiedowns and hauling
herself up the rope ladder. Only when they were in the air,
rising safely out of the meadow, did she look down and
see that the riders had not pursued beyond the grove.

She turned and slid down the bulkhead to the deck.
From the controls, Noel and Frank looked around at her
bleakly.

"The north is populated, too?" Frank ran a hand through
his hair and echoed Liberty's thoughts, even with the same
note of hopelessness. "Now where can we go?"

Chapter Fifteen

Soon now. Liberty sucked in her lower lip. Below them the Winding Water River plunged into the shadows of the Hu-ban Gorge. Home lay just minutes away.

Home.

She snorted. Home ought to be a place you wanted to go, somewhere offering warmth and security. Not even Ishda looked forward to Swordwood. He sat stiff in his chair, face frozen.

"The Emperor is here," Indra had said when they re-established radio contact.

That had been just what they needed to hear on the heels of the exhausting night crossing. Swinging out to sea escaped the brunt of the Night Rage, but the maelstrom filled the western horizon all night, its thunder reverberating around them and lightning creating a false twilight as continuous bolts raced from the towering top of the storm to the foaming seas beneath. The *Hope* shook and creaked and groaned in the pull of the winds . . . as if she, too, wept bitterly. The external and internal storms drained all of them by the time they reached the southern cliffs, so that hearing the news about the Emperor, Noel had turned snarling on Ishda.

"You said he'd need five days!"

Ishda stiffened. Ice glinted in the pale eyes.

Indra saved him from answering. "We didn't even realize who he was at first. He looked like just another courier riding in yesterday, except he had five troopers with him."

Consternation flooded Ishda's eyes. "Xa-hneem rode like a courier!" He congealed, as though the life drained out of him, leaving him a golden copper statue.

Liberty's gut knotted in sudden fear. If that arrival startled even Ishda, then it must be totally out of character, which meant this matter had profoundly disturbed Xa-hneem.

She saw her dismay reflected in Noel and Frank's eyes. Frank asked sharply, "What's he doing?"

"Not much, just talking to people, using Tsebe as interpreter." The distant voice paused. "He's very pleasant. I wonder if we've misjudged him."

"Come on, Indra," Noel said. "Did you ever see a politician who *wasn't* charming?"

Liberty eyed Ishda. "He's waiting for us, isn't he?"

One pale eye turned toward her. "And for me."

At the time and for the two days since, Liberty had shrugged when she thought about the remark. After all, what could happen to him that compared to the annihilation threatening the colonists? But now, within sight of the estate, concern pricked her. He had bought enough time to finish the blimp and leave before he could receive orders forbidding it. From Xa-hneem's point of view, that might be interpreted as an act against the house.

She sat down in a chair by Ishda. "Can you make Xa-hneem understand that you only did what you thought you had to for your house?"

He sat unmoving, staring out the window. "I don't know."

She bit her lip. "What can he do to you? He can't have you stoned, can he?"

"Unfortunately not."

Liberty grimaced. If only there were some way to help.

Even though he had not helped them for their sake, he still helped. "Is there anything I can do?"

"I see the compound."

A whole new set of knots tied in her gut.

Pressing against the window, Liberty saw that their homecoming had not attracted the crowd the send-off had. Troopers riding practice maneuvers in the hills craned around in their saddles to stare up at the *Hope* passing overhead and some remaining at the compound scrambled onto the walls, but few humans were in the arena except those on guard duty. Most appeared to have elected to stay in their courtyards, bent over tasks Liberty could not quite make out. Jaes waited for them, though, along with his dogs, the rest of the company board, and Noel and Frank's families.

Noel cut the engines. "Lines!"

They tossed out the ropes. While those on the ground hauled the blimp down, Liberty noticed that many of the crates and cartons had vanished from the arena.

Vona and her children and Noel's sister and family rushed the gondola as everyone climbed out. Liberty edged around the hugging group with a twinge of envy. At least someone was glad to see them back.

She found herself face to face with Jaes.

"Welcome back," he said.

She grimaced. "I'm sorry we couldn't bring better news."

He glanced past her at Ishda. "Later. My lord, I believe there's a reception committee for you."

Ishda turned slowly.

The entrance to the military courts lay in their line of vision past the end of the gondola. In that broad archway stood two heest figures, Tsebe and the smaller form of a man in camp clothes. At a lift of the man's chin, Tsebe marched across the arena toward the blimp. Liberty heard Ishda draw a slow, deep breath.

Tsebe reached them and crossed her arms over her

chest, her eyes alight. "My lord Ishda and friend Ib-ih-tee, I rejoice in seeing you returned safely. There has been much grief at the news of Da-in's loss. My lord, His Imperial Highness your brother welcomes your return also, and invites you to walk in the hills with him."

"Thank you for bringing the message, Kxa-Tsebe." Back stiff, Ishda marched for the archway.

"Remember, it's the duty of the ruling house to know everything that touches the Empire," Liberty called after him.

He gave no sign whether he heard or not.

"Now let's talk," Jaes said. "In my quarters. Please excuse us, Tsebe."

Tsebe crossed her arms over her chest, but following Jaes, Liberty noticed that the heest girl watched humans and hees with troubled eyes.

Indra recrossed her legs on her cushion and looked up with a grin from the computer as they trooped into Jaes's quarters. "These mountains are fascinating. The only scenario I can find to account for them is a head-on collision between two fast-moving plates, and they have to be a light stone, not granite." She pulled a pale switch of hair across her shoulder and chewed on it. "And they won't last long, geologically speaking."

"I'm more interested in logistics than geography," Jaes said. "Do you have those figures?"

"Are you sure you want them?" A shadow crossed her eyes. "At a payload of fifteen hundred kilos a trip, moving everyone will take—"

"Moving everyone!" Frank exclaimed. "Jaes, there's nowhere to go!"

Jaes sat down on the cushion behind his desk table and signaled the dogs to lie. "We have to find someplace. I have people talking about using dynamite and the rifles to wipe out the troopers. They think we have time to put up fortifications around the estate before anyone outside becomes suspicious and sends an army to investigate. It wouldn't work forever, of course, and we'd lose people, but I'm beginning to wonder if that isn't our only way out. Liberty, Tsebe has told me the stories about the highlands. What do you know? What did you see there?''

She remembered her own thoughts about using the highlands for a sanctuary. "It isn't heavily populated. I remember just one village, a cluster of quonset-type lodges. Ishda called it a camp. The Bethxim are nomads." She told him the other things Ishda had said about Bethxim, and about the general's journal. "They don't sound very friendly."

Jaes smiled wryly. "At least there would be fewer of them to fight. What I really hope, of course, is that we'd be there just temporarily while we explore the north further. We might still find a place up there."

They might, or they might have to fight again. Liberty sucked in her lower lip. Fight the Hees, fight the Bethxim, fight the northerns . . . and every skirmish would take human lives. Had he given up the idea of negotiating their way out? "Won't Xa-hneem talk to you?"

The smile became a grimace. "We've talked several times, and he's always scrupulously polite and very charming, but somehow we never talk about what I want to." He ran his hand over a dog's head. "I suspect that means he's already made decisions about us."

But Xa-hneem had not acted yet, so it might not be too late to change his mind. When the meeting ended, Liberty went looking for Ishda.

She found Tsebe instead . . . standing with arms folded on top of the wall above the arena, staring outward. The object of her attention became obvious the moment Liberty joined her . . . two male figures sitting in the grass on the crest of the next hill.

"They're still talking?" Did Ishda have that much to

report? If only there were a way to know what was being said. "Would you like to go for a walk, too, Tsebe?"

A lime green eye ranged toward her. "We cannot." Tsebe's scalp twitched.

A chill slid down Liberty's spine. "Why can't we?"

A graceful ear flicked. "I heard His Highness give General Be-ed orders that no human may leave the compound any longer."

The cold became icy claws.

On the next hill, the hees stood and started back. Xahneem limped.

"Is he hurt?" Liberty asked.

Tsebe's chin tucked. "He is only stiff. He told me he had not ridden so long a time in years." She paused. "Why is everyone afraid?"

"Afraid?" Liberty did not take her eyes off the men. What had happened between them? Or perhaps she could guess. Ishda looked up at the compound, but away again when his gaze crossed hers. Her gut knotted.

"Please don't treat me as if I were half-souled. Only great urgency drives a man who does not ride to make a courier's ride, and I have interpreted as he talked to your people. I saw fear beneath his pleasantries. I see it also in your people, and anger."

Liberty strolled down the wall. "Excuse me, but I need to see Ishda."

"Humans are also forbidden in the military courts while the Emperor is in residence."

She stopped, staring at the burly trooper blocking the top of the steps down into the military side. The number of guards had doubled, she noticed now. She eyed them, counting, then turned back to Tsebe.

"It is very, very important that I speak with Lord Ishda. Tsebe, will you go see him and tell him that I ask to meet with him? I'll wait here for you."

The heest girl hesitated, her eyes searching Liberty's

face, then her chin lifted. "I will go." She trotted along the wall and down the steps into the military courts.

Liberty leaned out over the wall to watch the brothers climb the hill and vanish through the outer military gate. Sliding back down to the walkway, she turned to lean her back against the battlement and realized that human guards had increased, too, especially in the arena around the blimp. Tension hissed in the air. She bit her lip.

Tsebe came back at a run, but when she stopped in front of Liberty, the flare of her nostrils did not look due to exertion. That twitch in her scalp certainly was not. The claws in Liberty's spine dug deeper even before the girl spoke. "Lord Ishda regrets he cannot speak with the honorable stranger visitor Ib-ih-tee."

Such formality. Her own skin wanted to twitch. "How did he look when he said it?"

Tsebe's voice lowered. "He had eyes like a ha-gho-wu I once caught stalking an u-tse calf."

Her nerves jerked tight and breath stuck in her chest. A decision had been made, all right. Now the question was, when did Ishda plan to carry out his orders? "Did you happen to see the Emperor, too?"

"Only in passing. He was probably wanting to rest for the ride tomorrow."

Liberty's breath caught. "Ride tomorrow?"

"While we were watching the air boat land he said that now he could go back to Ku-wen."

The child was a positive sponge. Did she ever realize the significance of what she soaked up and regurgitated? No matter. Liberty gave fervent thanks for her. If the Emperor planned to leave before he had recovered from his first ride, then Ishda must be ordered to act very soon, perhaps even late tomorrow.

She had to find a way into the compound to see the Emperor!

"Please, Ib-ih-tee, what's wrong?" Tsebe pleaded.

Liberty looked up at her. "The Emperor wants to kill us."

"*Wants*—" The girl broke off and lowered her voice. "That can't be!"

"You yourself noted his fear of us, and he has good reason to be afraid. If our weapons and knowledge fell into the hands of a King like Nui-kopa, it could destroy the Empire."

"But . . . a host slaughtering his guests?" Tsebe's eyes splayed, taking in both trooper and human guards. Her hide rippled madly. "Even the children?"

Liberty touched the heest girl's arm. "I think I can stop it, but I have to talk to the Emperor to do so. Will you help me get into the military courts?"

Tsebe stiffened. "Shouldn't discussion be between Captain Zhes and the Emperor?"

"I don't think the Emperor will agree to talk. He has to be forced to it. Tsebe," she said urgently as the girl backed away, "I don't ask you to betray your people or your Emperor. I want to save lives. Some of our people want to fight our way to the highlands and that may kill many of the troopers and humans you've learned to know. Help me. Please."

An ear flicked. "You said *force* the Emperor to talk."

"I mean confront him. I don't intend to hurt him. I don't want *anyone* hurt."

Tsebe's scalp twitched. "This will save heest lives?"

"And heest honor. You don't want the name of your house associated with such a shameful deed, do you?"

Tsebe took a breath. "My house."

The magic word, Liberty reflected, hating herself for being so manipulative.

"What do you want me to do?" Tsebe asked.

Liberty made a trip to their room, ostensibly to change to dark clothing, but when Tsebe's back turned, she dug to the bottom of her carton for Dalyn's gun and shoved it down the back of her jeans. Then they returned to the arena, where they politely requested a guard at the archway to pass a message to Major Kus.

The major appeared shortly, eyes bright. "You wish to ride, Kxa-Tsebe?" He knew, of course, what house she came from.

Tsebe crossed her arms over her chest. "I wish to show our honored guest what a Kxa can do when ridden by an experienced rider."

Liberty winced. Tsebe sounded wooden.

"If it is no imposition on you, of course, major," Liberty said.

The major looked Tsebe over and lifted his chin. "It is an honor."

Fortunately Tsebe stopped being wooden the moment she climbed the girth loops. The girl could ride, Liberty had to admit. By some magic she made the ponderous u-tse fairly dance. Liberty almost regretted stopping the exhibition.

"Tsebe," she called. "Does he feel right in his left fore?"

Tsebe halted the u-tse. "Then I am not imagining a slight lameness?"

Kus stiffened. "Lame? With all respect, young Tsebe, that animal is perfectly sound."

"I don't think so," Liberty said. "Gait him, Tsebe."

While the hees watched with concern and the humans frowning—Liberty could almost hear them thinking: *what kind of person is she to be playing at a time like this?* —Tsebe walked and trotted the u-tse. Using her weight right, she did manage to throw its stride off.

A suddenly worried Kus called Tsebe over and began examining the leg in question, feeling and prodding. Liberty and Tsebe debated the cause. Several other troopers joined in, offering their opinions and suggestions on treatment. Eventually even the placid Kxa became tired of being messed with and began to fight its head. Spectators and kibbitzers scattered, all but those who urged the animal back toward the stables, still arguing the merits of various herbal bandages.

In the midst of it all, the guards at the archway overlooked one slim human among the heest bodies.

In the stable courts Liberty broke away from the group and ducked under the rope mesh of a stall holding another Kxa to huddle down in the straw at the rear.

Dark came with maddening slowness. It seemed to Liberty forever before shadows blackened the stall and the footsteps of troopers making the last watering faded from the court. Stiffly, she stood and stretched, and pushed away the big head that nosed her curiously. "Sorry, kid. No time to play, though I thank you for your hospitality."

She ducked out of the stall and quickly, before someone came through the court, shinnied up a post and dragged herself over the edge of the loggia roof. Pain sliced her breath short. Gritting her teeth against it, she crawled along the loggia and over the roof into the next court.

The visiting officers' court where Ishda, and presumably the Emperor, had their rooms lay on the far end of the compound. In the light of the near-half moon sliding down the western sky, the distance looked like a thousand kilometers of roof. It would have to be crawled on her belly, to blend into the tiles and avoid notice by the guards on the wall. Every step had to be tested for loose tiles, too, to avoid those that might break loose. She would be crossing over barracks and officers' courts along the way.

The trip began to feel like a thousand kilometers. The roofs had not been made for traffic, as she remembered from the palace the night of the fire. Being barefooted helped, but crawling, her knees made more contact than her feet and the jeans slipped on the tiles. And with every missed step, every slither, some stopped only at the expense of the skin on her toes and palms, her heart pounded, expecting an outcry as some trooper looked up at the sound and spotted her. Voices floated up from the courts, troopers singing and laughing and playing Fivedice. She passed mere meters from them. What if the Emperor were not in the visiting officers' court? she thought suddenly, and swore under her breath.

But two guards stood at the entrance of the court. One knot loosened. She looked down on them, then slipped over the roof onto the court loggia.

From what she could see, half a dozen rooms opened into the court. Except for the one she knew was Ishda's, any of them could be Xa-hneem's. She would have to check each.

The one farthest from Ishda seemed a good place to start.

Taking a slow breath, but not too deep, she eased over the edge of the loggia and dropped into the court. The shock of landing drove air out of her in an involuntary grunt. Clapping a hand over her mouth, she flattened where she landed. Shadows surrounded her. She could be another . . . dark, shapeless, inconspicuous.

But no one came to investigate the grunt. After several minutes, Liberty cautiously pulled her legs under her and crept across the loggia to the first room. She saw nothing through the vents and heard no sound. The second room seemed empty also. The third, around the corner, lay in full view of the court entrance. She flattened against the wall to approach it.

Oh, for the heest ability to look in two directions at once, but the best she could do was watch the court entrance and listen at the ventilation slits. That proved to be enough. The rumble of breathing reached her clearly from inside.

Easing past the slits, Liberty wrapped her hand around the door handle and pulled. The door did not move. Liberty pulled harder. The door still refused to budge. He must have it pegged.

She swore silently, fighting an urge to pound on the door with her fists and shout at him to open up. She would not be denied reaching him now, not even if she had to tear down the wall bare-handed to do it! Then she sighed bitterly. Tearing down the wall was obviously impossible. How *would* she reach him?

The ventilation slits caught her eye. No hees could fit through them, of course, but what about someone much narrower?

Liberty pulled the gun out of the back of her jeans and slid sideways into the central vent.

Narrow as she was, her ribs and hips still jammed halfway into the opening. She hooked her arm around the far side of the partition and pulled while she wiggled, trying to drag herself through. The stone scraped at her through the fabric of her clothes, pulling at her flesh, and her ribs screamed in agony. Sweat broke out across her forehead. She bit her lip to keep from crying out. But she still could not slip through.

She swore, panting, straining into the stone. Let it scrape off her skin and rebreak her ribs. She had to get through . . . had to! Knives stabbed her chest but still she forced herself into the vent, straining, pulling with her inside arm. Voices talked outside the court entrance. She stiffened, thinking for the first time of the guards. What if they saw her? She had to be gone before they could. She swore at her body, willing it to shrink, to *move*!

Then suddenly, it did. She popped through the vent with a suddeness that sent her to her hands and knees. The gun clunked against the floor.

The breathing of the man caught and stopped.

Liberty froze in place, holding her breath, too.

On the pallet, cloth rustled. The vague form moved almost soundlessly toward the desk table, where something

scraped. Liberty sat up, wrapping both hands around the
gun, so that when the sparks jumped from the striker set to
the lamp wick, kindling it into a warm glow, Xa-hneem
stared down the barrel of Dalyn's gun.

"God's good, Your Highness."

She did not need to tell him what she held. From the
way he sank slowly to a cushion, eyes never leaving the
barrel, he had been told already. The pearly green eyes
moved only once, one flicking beyond her toward the
door.

"It's still pegged," she assured him. "I came in my
own way."

Only the sudden dilation of his pupils betrayed fear in
him. "May I ask why?"

She met his gaze over the top of the gun. "I can't let
you destroy my people."

"Killing me won't stop it." Fear was fading, she saw.
He remained watchful, but his mind had resume working,
racing, she suspected.

"This is only to get your attention. Of course, I'll use it
if I have to, which will destroy the Empire. My people
will take command of this compound and use the blimp to
spread word of your death to the Kings before Ku-wen
learns. The power struggle may take years but we can wait
here until time to treat with the victor. I'd prefer to reach
an agreement with you, of course."

Rehearsing the story in the u-tse's stall, she had wondered if she could make it sound convincing, but from the
stillness of Xa-hneem's face, he believed her. "And just
what—"

Voices rose outside. Footsteps pounded down the loggia
to the door, and a hand slapped the wood. "My brother!"

Ishda! Liberty wiggled the gun. "Be very careful how
you answer," she whispered.

Xa-hneem watched the gun. "Calmly, my brother. What
do you need?"

"Ib-ih-tee is missing, along with her weapon! Knowing her nature, I sent someone to check on her and they could find her nowhere in the human courts. Kxa-Tsebe denies any knowledge of her whereabouts, but I fear she will try to come here. Let me change rooms with you tonight."

Xa-hneem lifted one eye to Liberty's face. "That will not be necessary."

Outside the door Ishda stood silent for a minute, then said, "Ib-ih-tee, let me come in and talk."

Liberty's mind raced. If she refused, he might call the guards, then she would be forced either to surrender or shoot Xa-hneem. Standing without moving the gun off Xa-hneem, she sidestepped to where she could unpeg the door. "Sit down with your brother, Ishda."

His gaze went to Xa-hneem first as he slipped into the room, but after closing the door behind him and taking a seat on the sleeping pallet, his attention focused on Liberty. "Do we have to talk with a weapon between us?"

"For the time being, I'm afraid so. Your Highness, there must be some solution to this problem."

The Emperor's chin tucked. "I wish there were. It does this house no honor to wipe out a people. Still, if you live, you will destroy the Empire."

"Have you thought of the knowledge you'll be losing that could benefit the Empire: agriculture, medicine, astronomy, chemistry?"

"My young brother mentioned something to that effect this afternoon." The green eyes glinted like ice in the lamplight. "Is that worth all else you bring, the weapons and the blasphemous ideas . . . war is immoral, slavery is evil, and women should choose the number and times of their pregnancies? What have you done on that far world you come from, dared to usurp the powers over life and death that belong to God alone?"

Her gut knotted. If he feared their ideas more than the weapons that might fall into the Kings' hands, what argument could she possibly offer for their lives? Despair welled up bitterly through her.

Ishda's pale eyes watched her. Slowly, he said, "You give my brother reasons for not destroying you. You don't say how we might benefit by keeping you alive."

Anger flared in her. The bastard. What was the difference?

Xa-hneem splayed an eye toward his younger brother. "I begin to wonder, my brother, whom you serve."

Ishda stiffened. "I serve our house and none other, as I always have."

The Emperor's nostrils flared. "I will be relieved to see that demonstrated."

Liberty caught one flash of misery before Ishda's face and eyes hardened into unreadable opacity. The anger redirected at Xa-hneem. That *toad*, using destroying the humans to make Ishda prove his loyalty! Or perhaps it was punishment for finagling the trip north. And of course Ishda would follow orders, despite any personal reluctance. House came first after all.

Then . . . why had Ishda's question stung Xa-hneem? she wondered, and replayed the sentence in her head. What had the Emperor heard in it that she had not? Her pulse leaped.

On repeat, the two statements no longer sounded alike. A subtle difference separated them. And what else lay buried in the words . . . a prompt, a hint that helped without putting him on her side? She thought fast, the cold and anger in her dissolving.

"We may offer new ideas, but we also offer service no one else can give you, Your Highness. Consider the north. What trade possibilities might be there? We could explore the north for you, and its markets. They might have metal to sell."

Xa-hneem stared silently at her. Liberty held her breath, crossing mental fingers.

"They might also be bloodthirsty barbarians, a land of

Tu-Nan-see's, and they would learn of our existence," he said.

She forced her voice to remain even. "In which case, we could patrol the highlands in the blimp to see that none of them ever find their way south."

For a moment she thought he might be wavering, but the hope flaring in her died in his sigh of regret. "I am being cruel to allow you to continue. You offer interesting arguments, but they are pointless. Before I left Ku-wen, my spies in Th'upeen sent word that Kaem is dispatching letters to all the other Kings asking them to ally with him in overthrowing me. I have selfishly withheld weapons and knowledge for my own benefit, he claims. He promises that if he sits on the imperial throne, he will divide the strangers among all the Kings, so that they may share in the knowledge."

Liberty sucked in her lower lip. If the Kings allied . . .

"I cannot see Kings like Po-xan, Andas, and Nui-kopa committing their armies for Kaem's benefit," Ishda said.

"Nor can I, my young brother, but his suggestion will stir their personal ambition. As long as there is anything to be gained, I will find myself facing the armies of every kingdom in the Empire."

"Perhaps the humans can be persuaded to help defend you," Ishda said.

Xa-hneem turned both eyes on him. "You do seem to forget why you live."

"Don't listen to him," Liberty snapped in English as Ishda shriveled. "He's just using your own guilt about being alive to manipulate you and there's nothing to feel guilty about. You have as much right to exist as anyone, no matter how you happened—" Lightning struck, leaving Liberty numb. That was it! The solution. Why had she not thought of it before? "No matter how you happened to be born," she finished in Akansh, and turned to Xa-hneem. "There's no question of his loyalty and you know it! Tell me honestly, are you in the least afraid of someone coming to him, either us or a King, and turning him against you?''

After a moment he replied, ''I am not. The Kings know better than to even try.''

She ignored his suggestion that humans might try. ''Even though he is adopted?''

His scalp furrowed. ''That makes no—'' He broke off, suddenly staring at her.

Beside him, Ishda straightened, eyes widening.

Liberty forced herself to sit silent while Xa-hneem's thoughts moved in the direction she had pointed them. Let him bring up the idea himself, not have it thrust on him by an alien.

''Adoption,'' he breathed.

She sighed inwardly in relief. Now she could speak. ''If we were members of your house, wouldn't that render us useless to anyone with interests against yours?''

His nostrils flared. ''More than that, it would commit you to supporting and defending this dynasty. In self-interest, you would be restrained from mentioning destructive ideas, though the useful ones would be seen as largesse flowing from the imperial throne.''

And no one knew more than he about self-interest, Liberty reflected. Like God, Ishda had called Xa-hneem. God was both good and evil. Well, she could probably live with that. A member of the ruling house was in a good position to carefully and subtly introduce new ideas.

''There would have to be education of your people, of course, so they would understand their duties and position.'' Xa-hneem paused. ''It is an interesting possibility. Let me think about it overnight. Then if I do decide it's feasible, I'll have to take the idea to Ku-wen. I may be Emperor, but I'm not house headman, and adoption is a choice of the headman and headwoman. Will you leave me to meditate and pray?''

Liberty and Ishda left the room.

As he slid the door closed, Ishda said, "When you die, may I have your hide?"

Liberty stepped out into the court and stared up at the alien constellations glittering overhead. Sometime she ought to learn their names. The gun dragged at her arm. She looked down, hefting it, thinking of its owner. *What do you think, Dal? You're supposed to be all-wise now. What are our chances?* She smiled thinly. Look at her, already taking up heest ways.

She repeated the question aloud.

Ishda rubbed an ear. "Wuku is a wise man and He-po ruthless in her dedication to the maintenance of the house. Adoption serves the house directly, and indirectly, if trade with the north adds prestige to the Thim Dynasty. I cannot see Xa-hneem or Wuku and He-po denying that to the house, no matter how bizarre your appearance and how difficult you may be to educate. I expect that within a week, you'll all be Thims, and how I would love to be in some royal courts when the news arrives there." His nostrils quivered. Then the nostrils flared. "It's right that you and I should become brother and sister."

"Do you suppose we can talk Xa-hneem into letting us be his eyes in the north? That way we can both serve from a comfortable distance."

"I will pray that my ancestors suggest that to him."

But that was for the future, when possibilities were certainties. Right now she had a more pressing duty. Liberty shoved the gun down the back of her jeans and glanced sideways at Ishda. "Well, brother-to-be, I think we'd better go back to the human courts and warn my people what I've let them in for."

DAW

JO CLAYTON

"Aleytys is a heroine as tough as, and more believable and engaging than, the general run of swords-and-sorcery barbarians."

—*Publishers Weekly*

The saga of Aleytys is recounted in these DAW books:

- ☐ **DIADEM FROM THE STARS** (#UE1977—$2.50)
- ☐ **LAMARCHOS** (#UE1627—$2.25)
- ☐ **IRSUD** (#UE1839—$2.50)
- ☐ **MAEVE** (#UE1760—$2.25)
- ☐ **STAR HUNTERS** (#UE1871—$2.50)
- ☐ **THE NOWHERE HUNT** (#UE1874—$2.50)
- ☐ **GHOSTHUNT** (#UE1823—$2.50)
- ☐ **THE SNARES OF IBEX** (#UE1974—$2.75)

The Duel of Sorcerers Series

- ☐ **MOONGATHER** (#UE1729—$2.95)
- ☐ **MOONSCATTER** (#UE1798—$2.95)
- ☐ **CHANGER'S MOON** (Forthcoming, 1985)

NEW AMERICAN LIBRARY,
P.O. Box 999, Bergenfield, New Jersey 07621

Please send me the DAW BOOKS I have checked above. I am enclosing
$_____ (check or money order—no currency or C.O.D.'s).
Please include the list price plus $1.00 per order to cover handling costs.

Name _____

Address _____

City _____ State _____ Zip Code _____

Please allow at least 4 weeks for delivery

DAW

**The really great fantasy books are
published by DAW:**

Andre Norton

☐ LORE OF THE WITCH WORLD   UE1750—$2.50
☐ HORN CROWN   UE1635—$2.95
☐ PERILOUS DREAMS   UE1749—$2.50

C.J. Cherryh

☐ THE DREAMSTONE   UE1808—$2.75
☐ THE TREE OF SWORDS AND JEWELS   UE1850—$2.95

Lin Carter

☐ KESRICK   UE1779—$2.25
☐ DRAGONROUGE   UE1982—$2.50

M.A.R. Barker

☐ THE MAN OF GOLD   UE1940—$3.95

Michael Shea

☐ NIFFT THE LEAN   UE1783—$2.95
☐ THE COLOR OUT OF TIME   UE1954—$2.50

B.W. Clough

☐ THE CRYSTAL CROWN   UE1922—$2.75

NEW AMERICAN LIBRARY
P.O. Box 999, Bergenfield, New Jersey 07621

Please send me the DAW Books I have checked above. I am enclosing
$_____ (check or money order—no currency or C.O.D.'s).
Please include the list price plus $1.00 per order to cover handling
costs.

Name _____

Address _____

City _____ State _____ Zip Code _____
Please allow at least 4 weeks for delivery